ADVANCED
CALCULUS
OF
MURDER

Erik Rosenthal is also the author of
Calculus of Murder

ADVANCED CALCULUS OF MURDER

Erik Rosenthal

St. Martin's Press
New York

Library of Congress Cataloging-in-Publication Data

Rosenthal, Erik.
    Advanced calculus of murder / by Erik Rosenthal.
        p.   cm.
    "A Thomas Dunne book."
    ISBN 0-312-01726-X
    I. Title.
    PS3568.08374A67   1988
    813'.54—dc 19   87-38249

First Edition

10 9 8 7 6 5 4 3 2 1

To Peter and Carol, Walter and Nancy:
special friends, special people

ADVANCED
CALCULUS
OF
MURDER

$\int$ 1

My name is Brodsky. If this were the story of my life, it would be about studying and teaching mathematics and about looking for academic jobs. It would be a boring story. In the narrative that follows, you will meet some mathematicians and learn something of what we do, but this is really a story about greed, jealousy, and murder. You see, I pay the rent as a private investigator.

It began innocently enough on a Thursday afternoon last March. I know it was Thursday because I was working in my Evans Hall office at the Berkeley campus of the University of California, and Thursday is the day I set aside for doing research. My objective is to obtain a job as a regular faculty member in a university, and the primary requirement for such a position is an impressive publication record. I get the office at Evans Hall because I hang around the math department and teach part-time.

Paul Hobart, who had been my mentor when I was a graduate student, walked in and said, "Dan, you know that COTCA will be in Oxford next summer?" By *COTCA*, he meant *Conference on Operator Theory and C*-Algebras*. He was five feet nine inches tall and had a slight build and gray-streaked brown hair. His childish face was adorned with horn-rimmed glasses, and he looked more like a clerk than a mathematician of international repute.

At that time, much to his chagrin, he was chairperson of the Department of Mathematics. Two years earlier the department had needed a new chair. Four faculty members actually wanted the job, but two of them were regarded as incompetent by their colleagues, and the other two represented differing political factions. The result was that none of the four was acceptable to the department. After some arm twisting, they found one man who consented to a short stint as chair, but the university administration would not seat him because of the extent of his involvement in left-wing campus activities dating back to the Vietnam War protests.

Paul was gregarious, articulate, and well liked; his arms and legs were twisted; he agreed to serve for one year. He was also something of a left-winger but was much less outspoken than his colleague, and the administration accepted him. Paul made one mistake during his tenure as chair: He did a good job. He was thus unable to avoid two more years of bureaucracy.

My answer to his question about COTCA was, "Sure. You're on the program committee, aren't you?"

He nodded. "I thought you'd like to know we decided to invite you to speak. You should get the letter in a day or two."

"Excellent. Are you speaking?"

"They want me to give the keynote address."

"Appropriate. Bill DeMarco's running it?"

"He's the program chairman. Terry Henkler's handling local arrangements."

"Should be fun if it's as good as the one last year in Santa Barbara."

He smiled. "You might like this one better—we also invited Eileen St. Cloud."

Eileen was a mathematician at Rice University; she and I had an on-and-off relationship going back fifteen years. Not too many people knew about it, which was fine since she was married. "Like I said, it should be a fun conference."

"Kathy's planning to go, too."

Kathy was Paul's sixteen-year-old daughter, justifiably his pride and joy. She was a junior in high school and remarkably bright. Earlier that year she had won a statewide mathematics competition open to all high school students. She was also the editor of her school newspaper and a member of both the tennis and swimming teams. Along with all that talent went the sweetest of personalities, not to mention that she was developing into quite a beautiful young woman. Paul had every reason to be proud. It would be unfair not to point out that Paul's son, Brian, then eleven, seemed to be cut from the same mold.

I first met Paul as a student, but over the years our relationship turned into one of colleagues and friends. As that friendship developed, I got to know his kids and watched them grow. They even adopted me as their uncle. (Kathy is now less inclined to call me "Uncle Danny" than she was when she was younger, especially in front of her friends.) My feelings for them are not too different from the ones I have for my niece and five nephews.

"Why does she want to go?" I said.

"To get back to London, I suppose. You know she spent last year there on that exchange program?"

"Yeah, sure."

"Well, Howard Williams' daughter was there, too,

and they became good friends. Somehow they tricked Howard and me into agreeing to take them both."

"Sounds like Kathy."

"Yes." The smile on his face and the tone in his voice made it clear that it hadn't taken all that much effort on Kathy's part to hoodwink Paul. Then he added, "There are pluses and minuses to everything."

"What, pray tell, does that mean?"

"Martin Kloss will also be invited."

Paul Hobart is an easygoing guy with few enemies; Martin Kloss was one of the few. While Paul did not like to talk about it, it was well known (in the community of mathematicians who studied bounded linear operators on Hilbert space) that he felt that Kloss had stolen some of his work. Kloss denied the charges. I personally believed Paul, and not simply because of our friendship. The only outstanding publication due to Kloss contained the presumed purloined ideas; Paul, on the other hand, was considered one of the best mathematicians at Berkeley, and it has one of the strongest math departments in the country. He was acknowledged to be a much deeper thinker than Kloss, and he was much more likely than Kloss to have produced work of the quality that appeared in the disputed paper. Moreover, as someone who has worked closely with him, I can tell you that Paul is a generous co-author and not the type to make wild accusations—I can't conceive of Paul making such charges if there was no merit to them.

I said, "Look, Paul, Kloss isn't one of my favorite people, either. But there'll be two hundred of us there. You can ignore him."

"I know. But he galls me."

The telephone interrupted us, and I picked up the receiver. "Dan Brodsky."

4

"Got a job for you, Danny." It was Greg Langley. A close friend and an attorney, he was a major source of income, usually in the form of process serving.

"Another subpoena?"

"No, though it does involve tracking someone down. Can you come by the office this afternoon?"

"Greg, it's Thursday."

"How'd I know you were gonna say that?"

"Because it's Thursday."

"That's probably why I set up an appointment for tomorrow morning at eleven."

"Your office?"

"Yeah."

"Do I get lunch out of it?"

"No way."

"Greg, this better not be one of your poverty-stricken, sob-story clients."

"Well, they're not rich. But don't worry, it's not a freebie."

"Good. What sort of case is it?"

"A woman trying to find her mother. Should be easy."

"Fat chance. See you tomorrow."

I hung up, and Paul said, "Got a job?"

"Looks like it. Something about a lost mother."

"Well, I've got a job, too. I better get back to it." He left, and I continued with my research.

I was teaching a linear algebra course that met Tuesday and Thursday mornings. My office hours were supposed to be ten-thirty to noon, but students tended to come by at whatever time they found convenient. One showed up at three o'clock. He was a tall, athletic-looking young man. I recognized him from class but could not remember his name.

"Professor Brodsky," he said, "do you have a few minutes?"

"Sure. Question about the exam?" I had returned their midterms the previous week, and a number of students wanted to ask me about it. Most of them had found it tough; only one student did really well.

"No. That was all right. I was looking ahead a little bit and wanted to ask you about the spectral theorem."

"The *spectral* theorem? That's more than a little bit ahead. Where did you get that from?"

"My physics professor said something about it. He made it sound very mysterious."

"It's not," I said. "Though it does have some important applications."

We discussed the spectral theorem awhile, and it quickly became clear that he was very bright. I said, "By the way, what's your name?"

"Steve Vadney."

"You're the one who got the ninety-eight on the midterm?"

"Yeah. It didn't seem so hard to me."

"I guess not. Do you have a major yet?"

"Computer science," he said.

"Why computers?"

"There're supposed to be lots of good jobs for computer people."

"So your idea is to go to work programming computers after you graduate?"

"Something like that."

"You haven't considered graduate school?"

"Not really."

"That may be a mistake," I said. "You're cutting off a number of options by not—"

"What kinds of options?"

"Well, for example, there are high-paying research jobs in industry—more interesting than anything you can get with only a B.A. There are also low-paying but much-more-fun academic jobs. Whatever your interests, you need a Ph.D. for those kinds of positions."

"You think I should go to graduate school?"

"Probably," I said. "I don't know you very well, but you seem to handle mathematics pretty well."

"You mean I should give up computers?"

"Not necessarily. But mathematics is an intrinsic part of computer science. In fact, the most interesting questions about computers are essentially questions in pure mathematics. Whatever your inclination, you should surely study a lot more mathematics, and most likely you should plan on graduate school."

"I'll think about it."

He did. He spent a large part of the rest of the semester in my office asking questions and talking about mathematics, sometimes about something he had read, sometimes even about my research. At first he was a bit shy, afraid he would take up too much of my time. That was in fact the case, but I encouraged him anyway: He was a rare student, enthusiastic and very smart, and it was a pleasure to watch him learn, which he did quickly and easily.

The next morning Herman, my '52 Studebaker, whisked me—well, given his age and the fact that he makes effective use of only four cylinders, *whisked* is not much of an exaggeration—to the offices of Halloran and Mackey, Attorneys at Law. Emily, the receptionist, ushered me directly into Greg Langley's office. Greg and I had known each other for twenty years since our freshman days at Brooklyn College. We had come to California together to study (law for Greg, mathematics for me).

Greg is one of those people who is never dressed quite properly, regardless of the cost of his wardrobe and regardless of how well tailored his duds are. It has a little to do with his pudgy waistline, but mostly it's his personality: His dress reflects the disorganization fundamental to his life-style. The suit and tie he was wearing indicated that clients were due shortly, but his appearance was not all that different from the anarchy that covered his desk. I often wondered whether it were all an act designed to obscure a penetrating mind with a penchant for observing the smallest detail. If so, he would never admit it, not even to me.

Greg and I chatted until Emily brought in a man and a woman, each in their forties, and a young woman, probably still in her teens. Greg greeted them warmly and introduced them to me as Gene Leopold, his wife Linda, and their daughter Joanne. Joanne was perhaps five feet six inches tall, slender and pretty; her mother was a very thin, bespectacled brunette; her father was a tall, overweight man whose bald spots were beginning to outdistance his brown locks.

Greg directed them to the sofa and picked up the telephone, dialing a single digit. He said into the mouthpiece, "Emily, could you bring some coffee? . . . Of course, Dan's here." He hung up and said, "Joanne, why don't you explain what you want Dan to do for you."

"It's simple," she said. "I'm adopted and want to find my biological mother."

I tend to be suspicious of first impressions, but the Leopolds appeared to be very together. Perhaps it was because Mr. and Mrs. Leopold were holding hands, or

8

perhaps it was the way they looked at their daughter when she spoke. Whatever it was, I had a strong sense of *family* from them, and I wondered if it was wise for Joanne to seek a mother she had never seen. I said, "Mr. and Mrs. Leopold, how do you feel about this?"

Gene Leopold spoke. "It was my idea. Joanne is our daughter in every sense of the word except biology. She is naturally curious about the woman who gave birth to her. But more than that, I know Joanne wants to know why that woman gave her up."

His wife added, "If you think we're afraid we'd lose her or some such thing, nothing could be further from the truth."

"That wasn't what I had in mind. Your daughter's mother. . . ." I paused, embarrassed.

"Mr. Brodsky, Joanne is adopted, but she is our daughter. We're not ashamed; you shouldn't be embarrassed."

I looked at Joanne. "You certainly have nothing to be ashamed of—I'm sure you're very proud."

"We are. If you'll be more comfortable using her mother's name, it's May Connors."

I smiled. "I will be. She did give Joanne up for adoption. There are any of a number of reasons why she might have done that. The point is, it's not unlikely that finding her could be very painful, perhaps for her as well as for you. I'd like to know that you've considered all the possibilities and are sure of what you want."

"We've been talking about it for over a year," Joanne said. "I want to find her, and my parents agree completely."

"All right." It still didn't seem to me to be the best of ideas, but I said, "What can you tell me about her?"

Joanne looked at her father, and he said, "Not much, other than her name. She—"

There was a brief rap on the door, and Emily came in with a pot of coffee and a plate of doughnuts. She put the tray on the desk, winked at me, and made her exit, saying, "Danny, you don't deserve the service you get around here."

Her meaning was obvious when I tasted the coffee: It was a rich, full-bodied, aromatic blend of Maracaibo and Kona coffees with a touch of dark-roast Colombian, surprisingly similar to my own.

With a Cheshire cat grin on his face, Greg said, "Do you approve?"

"Certainly. What'd you do, steal the stuff from my kitchen?"

"No. We got it from the House of Coffee." He turned to the Leopolds. "Dan's a bit of a coffee nut. This particular blend is known as *Danny's Choice*."

Joanne said that she didn't drink coffee, but her parents had some. Mrs. Leopold said, "This *is* good." It was obvious her husband wasn't so sure. He said, "Shall we get back to the business at hand?"

"Yes," I said. "Tell me whatever you can about May Connors."

"Joanne was born in Los Angeles eighteen years ago. May was a teenager at the time."

"A high school girl in trouble?"

"That's what we thought, but she wouldn't tell us much."

"I assume from what you're saying that you didn't go through an ordinary adoption agency."

Mrs. Leopold answered. "No. We were unable to have children of our own. At that time, we had debts from school, and, although Gene had a good job, we

10

were told that there were long waiting lists and we would have to settle down financially before there was much likelihood of their finding a child for us."

"That's right," he said. "A good friend of ours worked at Planned Parenthood in L.A.—we lived down there then. She told us that young girls frequently try to get abortions when it's too late to do it safely."

"May Connors fit that description?"

"Yes. She was seven months pregnant when we met her. My impression was that her parents had thrown her out. We never knew for sure. She lived with us until the baby was born."

Greg leaned forward and said, "You mean she lived with you for two months, and you didn't learn anything about her?"

"Very little," Mrs. Leopold said. "She had her own room and stayed there most of the time. She never told us anything about her parents. She didn't say much."

"And after Joanne was born?"

"I don't know. She and Joanne were in the hospital for three days. When we brought them back to our apartment, she packed her bags and left. She hardly said good-bye."

"Seems strange," I said.

"It did to us, too. She was pleasant enough, and we were fond of her. She must have been very frightened."

"Is there anything else you can tell me about her? Anything at all?"

They shook their heads, and Mrs. Leopold said, "We felt very bad. We wanted to do something for her. But she refused our help."

"You never saw her after that?"

"No."

"Do you remember what hospital Joanne was born in?"

"I even know that," Joanne said. "Lakeside Memorial in Pasadena."

"Have you tried to locate her yourselves?"

Mr. Leopold said, "Yes. We looked through phone books. There were lots of Connors, but no May Connors."

"Of course, she may have changed her name, say if she got married."

"We thought of that, but without the new name . . ."

"Did you check with the hospital?"

"They wouldn't give us any information."

"What about Planned Parenthood?"

"They didn't have anything to do with it after May moved in with us."

"Not much to go on. Do you have a picture of her?"

"Yes." He pulled a black-and-white photograph from a briefcase in his lap and handed it to me. "She was five four, maybe a hundred pounds. She had blue eyes and brown hair. Will that help?"

"Some. With the photograph and description, if I do find her, I can be sure I've located the right woman."

"You think you'll be able to?"

"Very likely. No guarantees, of course. She could be anywhere in the world. But probably I can. The place to start will be the hospital."

Mrs. Leopold said, "Do you think they'll give you any more help than they did us?"

I smiled. "That's what you're paying me for."

"As long as you've mentioned it," Mr. Leopold said, "how much is this going to cost?"

"Thirty dollars an hour plus expenses."

"If you spend a week in Los Angeles, that could be two or three thousand dollars."

"That's true," I said, "and I can understand your concerns. But I have to earn a living. I assure you I'm not a rich man. If you try one of the larger agencies, it'll cost a lot more than that."

"I'm sure you're right. And we trust Greg's judgment. But we're not that rich either."

"I understand," I said. "If you'd prefer to hire someone else . . ."

"No, I don't mean that."

"If you want to think about it for a few days, that's okay. I'm still not completely convinced that finding her is a good idea."

He looked at his wife and daughter and said, "We've thought about it a lot, and we want to find May Connors. When can you start?"

"I have a job on Sunday and a couple of things to do during the week. How does next Friday sound?"

"Fine."

∫ 2

The "job" I had referred to in the meeting with the Leopolds was insignificant but rather bizarre: a stolen dog. The mutt was being held for ransom; I was hired to be the intermediary. My role was to deliver the cash (would you believe fifty thousand bucks!) and to return the animal to its bereaved family.

There were no problems with the exchange itself; indeed, I had the impression that the villains were happy to be rid of the little pup. *Tiny* would be more accurate: She was a *Pomeranian* named Moomoo, not much larger than a kitten but looking more like a snapping turtle wearing a chinchilla coat—I learned quickly that she had a personality to match.

There were apparently two dognappers (they were never caught and we were never sure), and they turned the pooch over to me in a small cardboard carton with air holes. She was quiet—in the box. Keeping poor Moomoo caged up that way seemed cruel, and letting her run free in Herman's back seat appeared safe enough. That was my first mistake: When I reached into the carton to free Moomoo, she decided that my hand was dinner. I dropped the box and the mongrel along with it.

The exchange had been made along the Pacific Coast Highway on the western edge of San Francisco, and she scampered off toward the beach as fast as her tiny little legs could carry her. I gave chase, yelling, "Moomoo, stop! I'll take you home." I don't know why I said that; certainly the brain of the deformed rat was too small to understand.

She wasn't very fast and couldn't outrun me, but catching the thing was another matter. She stayed on the beach but away from the ocean. My first attempt was to dive on her; the result was a mouthful of sand.

There was an eight-foot cement wall separating the beach from the highway; every hundred yards or so concrete steps gave access to the sandy shores. I succeeded in cornering Moomoo between the wall and the steps. She barked and growled and hissed, and I slowly moved in. She made her move and I dove again, but all I caught was another mouthful of sand.

I lit out after her, cornering her in the same manner a second time. This time I removed my coat, and when she tried to run, I threw it over her, slowing her down enough so that my dive resulted in a handful of hind leg in addition to the usual mouthful of San Francisco's finest silicon granules. I used my free hand to lift myself onto my knees and then managed to get both hands on her.

I stood up and held her at arm's length, fearing her razor-sharp teeth. She began yelping in a high-pitched bark, closely approximating an acid rock band. I'm not usually concerned with my dignity, but running along the beach covered with sand, carrying a ball of fur yapping away as if it were getting the treatment it so richly deserved, is a bit ridiculous.

The next problem arose when I reached the car: How do I open Herman's door? I needed both hands to hold onto Little Dracula safely, and the keys were in my pocket. The solution was to get down on my knees and pin Moomoo against the pavement with one hand (very carefully) while reaching into my pocket with the other for the keys. Unlocking and opening the door while holding her down proved to be a surprisingly difficult maneuver, but I ultimately succeeded in throwing her in the backseat.

Herman's front seats were high enough to protect me, so try as she might, the werewolf was unable to strike. I did have a revolver in the trunk, but even if I knew how to use it, I didn't want blood on Herman's upholstery. Besides, I lacked the requisite silver bullets.

There were no additional difficulties bringing her home other than a remarkable barrage of barks, yelps, snarls, and growls, along with a continuous pounding on the back of the front seat as the bitch (fortunately unsuccessfully) tried to pounce on my neck and finish me off.

Mrs. Marnikovy, Moomoo's mommy, greeted me at the door (I had left the bloodsucker in the back seat). Astonishingly, when Mrs. Marnikovy picked her up, Moomoo was sedate. We went inside, where three-year-old Ronny was anxiously awaiting his playmate. Moomoo ran over to him and licked his face, impersonating a pet. The transformation was amazing; its behavior with me can only be attributed to poor breeding.

I was exhausted when I got home that afternoon, but there was a three-word message on my record-a-phone: "Jamaica Blue Mountain." That could mean only one thing, and I jumped into Herman and set him on a course for the House of Coffee. Jamaica Blue Mountain is probably the finest coffee available in the world—from the Blue Mountains of Jamaica, of course. It's a smooth, mellow, aromatic coffee of unequaled flavor. Annual production is limited, and it tends to be difficult to obtain, not to mention very expensive.

The House of Coffee is located in the northwestern part of Berkeley in a block that consists of a number of "gourmet" food stores. It's a small shop with a long glass bar on one side and shelves and a dairy case on the other. Under the bar are bins with a large variety of coffees. They also sell tea, spices, and cheese.

There was a teen-age girl serving customers when I arrived. The bin containing the prized objective was at the end of the bar, and I greedily went straight for it. I picked up a bag and began filling it with the treasure, when the girl caught sight of me and ran over, saying, "Sir, customers are not permitted behind the bar."

"You're new here, aren't you?"

"Yes, but . . ."

I aimed a finger and said, "Do you see that bin? What's it say on it?"

"Danny's Choice, but . . ."

"I'm Danny."

"Yes, but . . ." She was very flustered.

"Perhaps you should get Herb." Not knowing what to do, she ran through a door in the back to find Herbert Radzinski, the owner.

Several years earlier Herb had had a problem with a supplier. At a time when wholesale prices were rising sharply, the supplier offered him a deal that amounted to his paying for a year's worth of coffee at the then current prices. The beans were never delivered, and Herb was close to bankruptcy.

He knew me pretty well (we had already created Danny's Choice, and it had become one of his most popular blends), and he hired Greg and me. I did the legwork; Greg did the legal work.

I was able to ascertain that the supplier, himself faced with bankruptcy, had signed similar contracts with a number of retailers in order to get his hands on some cash. The deals he had put together were insufficient to save his business, and he was unable to deliver the coffee.

The information I gathered was all Greg needed. He convinced the supplier that if he didn't make restitution, he would serve at least a year in jail. Herb ended up with expenses plus punitive damages on top of his original investment. Needless to say, he was pleased. He owed me five hundred dollars and offered me the choice of my fee or free coffee for life. It was an easy decision.

By the time the salesgirl returned with Herb, I had served two customers in addition to helping myself to two pounds of the brown gold from Jamaica.

Herb had a big smile on his face and said, "Dan, this is Tina. You didn't have to frighten her half to death."

"Sorry. I didn't realize she was so young."

"She's a high schooler and will be working here three afternoons a week."

"You can use the help."

He nodded. "I see you found the Jamaican."

"Of course."

"What took you so long to get here? I called this morning."

"I just got your message."

We chatted awhile, but I didn't stay long: The coffee was shouting, "Get me home and drink me."

The reason for relating these events goes beyond the pleasure I get from contemplating that savory Jamaican brew. As we shall see, those delicate beans affected the outcome of what I now refer to as *The Oxford Murders*.

∫ 3

I picked up a rent-a-car when I landed at Los Angeles International Airport on Friday and drove to Lakeside Memorial Hospital in Pasadena, where Joanne Leopold had been born. That fact was the only clue I had to the whereabouts of May Connors, and it seemed likely that cooperation at a large, municipal house of quacks would be hard to come by—a somewhat devious approach was in order.

It was eleven A.M. when I entered that venerable institution and discovered that afternoon visiting hours were from one to three. I settled in a motel and retured to the hospital a little before one, wearing a three-piece suit. There were perhaps thirty visitors in the waiting room; most of them possessed plastic cards entitling them to enter those hallowed halls and call upon the incarcerated inmates.

At one o'clock sharp a security guard came in and told us that visiting hours were commencing, reminding us to keep our passes visible at all times. Nevertheless, he did not look all that closely when thirty people simultaneously pushed past him.

There were three elevators waiting to deliver visitors to loved ones sojourning on the upper levels. Among the ten people sharing the ride with me were a middle-aged couple and a man in his late twenties. The woman, bubbling with excitement, said, "I'm so anxious to see the baby," and the young man responded, "It'll only be a few more minutes now." I left the elevator with them on the fifth floor, assuming that the turmoil created by new fathers and grandparents in the maternity ward would ensure that security would be sufficiently lax for my purposes.

I wandered the halls and was noticed by a nurse, who said, "May I help you?"

Acting the bewildered new father, I said, nervously, "I'm looking for Dr. Heller."

"I don't know him. What's your wife's name?"

"I need to speak with Dr. Heller. He's not my wife."

Seeing that I was less than rational, she smiled and patted me on the shoulder. "Wait right here. I'll see if I can find him."

I ignored her advice and eventually found a door labeled DOCTOR'S LOUNGE. There was a rectangular table with a pot of coffee against the wall opposite the door, and several round tables in the center of the room. Three young men, probably interns or medical students, occupied one table, and a fourth man, in his forties, sat alone, sipping from a styrofoam cup.

I poured myself some coffee and walked to the table wtih the single occupant. Extending my hand, I said, "Mark Heller," and took a chair, in the process hiding a white smock that was draped over the chairback.

He smiled and shook my hand. "Hal Cortland. You on staff? I've never seen you here before."

"No. One of my patients delivered this morning."

"Cesarean or vaginal?"

"Vaginal. Short labor. No problems."

"Sounds like an easy one."

"Yes. Say, maybe you can help me with something. I

need to check on the family history. The girl's mother was a patient here eighteen years ago. Where can I find the records?"

"That would've been before we were computerized," he said. "The old records are stored in the basement next to the computer room. You can't miss it."

"Thanks. I should . . ."

A voice through a loudspeaker said, "Dr. Cortland, please report to the fifth floor nurses' station. Dr. Cortland, please report to the fifth floor nurses' station."

"That's me," he said. "Nice to meet ya." He left, leaving the hidden smock behind. I waited a minute or two, made my exit with the smock slung over my arm, and put it on in the hallway. A badge pinned to the lapel read, Dr. HAROLD CORTLAND, CHIEF OF OB-STETRICS. Since he was undoubtedly well known in the maternity ward, I pocketed the badge and made my way to the elevators. After a ten-minute wait an elevator arrived and took me to the basement.

Finding the computer room was easy, and a door next to it was marked RECORDS. It was locked.

In my student days at Berkeley I'd been busted a couple of times during anti-Vietnam War demonstrations. On one such occasion I met a professional thief who'd been caught breaking while entering. We became friendly, and he gave me a set of lock picks. I never mastered their use.

I wandered the halls again and located the staff cafeteria, also in the basement. It was after two by then, and only a few people were present. I pinned Cortland's badge on the smock—admittedly something of a gamble—and took a seat at a table occupied by a young woman. "Mind if I join you?"

She looked at the badge and said, "Dr. Cortland. I'm so pleased to meet you. I've heard so much about you."

"Intern?"

"Yes."

"What's your name?"

"Corey Blumfeld."

"When did you join our staff?"

"September."

We discussed the hospital and careers in medicine. I was careful to answer her questions with questions, and my complete ignorance of the subject was never revealed; she was pleased that the great Dr. Cortland was taking such an interest in her.

After a while I said, "Corey, how would you like to do me a favor?"

"Sure."

"Been here long enough to figure out where records are kept?"

"Umm. No."

"When you leave the cafeteria, go down the hall to the end. Make a left and you'll see the computer room. Records is the door after that."

She stood up and started to leave. "Oh, what am I looking for?"

"A file on a woman named May Connors. She gave birth to a child on March 11, 1970."

She set out on her mission but was back in five minutes. "It was locked. No one was there."

"This really doesn't seem like such a difficult task to me."

"But—"

"No buts. You're supposed to be a doctor. Use your imagination." Back to the Great Quest (though somewhat perplexed and no longer so sure about the renowned Dr. Cortland).

She was gone for thirty minutes this time. She returned with a smile on her face and the prized file under her arm. "I had to see Dr. Alabastor," she said, handing it me. "He gave me the key as soon as I told him it was for you."

"Thanks. You've been a big help. Do you still have the key?"

"Yes."

"Perhaps you should take it back to Dr. Alabastor?"

"Won't you need it to return the file?"

"Don't worry. I'll take care of it. Thank you, you've been very helpful." I opened the file and began reading, effectively dismissing her.

As soon as she was out the door, I left the cafeteria and ducked into a men's room. Fortunately, it was unoccupied. I put the smock on a hook in one of the stalls, stuffed the contents of the file into my pocket, shoved the folder behind the toilet, mussed my hair, removed my tie, put on sunglasses, and hung my coat and vest over my arm.

These precautions proved to be justified: When I reached the elevators, Corey Blumfeld, followed by two security guards, was saying, "He was reading the file and must still be in the cafeteria." Evidently Drs. Cortland and Alabastor had met up and concluded that something was amiss. I felt sorry for poor Corey, but it seemed unlikely that anyone would blame her. Besides, what did they need an eighteen-year-old file for, anyway?

I successfully exited Lakeside Memorial without further incident and drove back to the motel to study the file. There was a lot of medical stuff, some of which I understood, most of which appeared to be nonsense. The only useful information was the name and address of her parents. They had lived in Pomona, a town thirty miles southeast of Pasadena. That was in 1970. Would they still be there? Very likely not, but it was the only thing I had to go on.

At five o'clock I pulled up in front of what I hoped was still the Connors house; a middle-aged woman answered my knock.

"Hello. My name is Dan Brodsky. I'm trying to locate a woman named May Connors. She lived in this house twenty years ago."

"I'm afraid I can't help you. We've only been here for three years."

"Do you remember who you bought it from?"

"Yes, and they weren't Connors."

"Did they buy it from the Connors?"

"I don't know."

"Is there anyone in the neighborhood who might remember them?"

"You might try the Beekmans across the street. Number Six. They got the house from their parents and have been there a long time."

A man about my age answered when I knocked at Number Six. My introduction was pretty much the same: "My name is Dan Brodsky. I'm trying to locate a woman named May Connors, who lived across the street twenty years ago. One of your neighbors thought you might remember her."

"What do you want her for?"

"She has an eighteen-year-old daughter who wants to meet her."

"Is this for real?"

"Yes. The daughter was adopted and never knew May."

He stared at me, apparently trying to determine whether I was telling the truth. Perhaps he thought I was the police, or maybe a bill collector. After a while he said, "I don't remember May, but I did know the Connors family when I was a kid. They moved away fifteen, twenty years ago. When I was in high school."

"Do you know where they went?"

"No. I didn't know them very well."

"Isn't there anything you can tell me?"

He sighed. "Yeah. Maybe. Wait a sec." He closed the door, leaving me standing on the front steps. The door reopened a few minutes later, and he said, "My sister remembers May." He handed me a sheet of paper with his sister's name and address. "She lives in Anaheim. She expects you in half an hour. Don't be late." He closed the door.

I had a street map with me but still had some difficulty finding the place, and it was forty-five minutes before I got there. An attractive brunette in her mid thirties opened the door before I rang the bell. "Linda Arcann?" I said.

"Mr. Brodsky?"

"Yes."

"I expected you fifteen minutes ago."

"Sorry. I got lost. May I come in?"

"No. Not now. It will have to be tomorrow. Call me at one-fifteen. Be nearby when you call." She closed the door before I could say anything. Strange.

I left plenty of time the next morning and called from a phone booth three blocks from Linda Arcann's home. She answered on the first ring and told me to come right over. I rang the doorbell two minutes later; my hand was still on the button when the door opened.

"Mr. Brodsky, let's take a walk." After walking in silence for two blocks, she said, "You must be wondering why I'm being so secretive. It's simple: I don't want my husband to know about this."

"Why should he care about someone you knew twenty years ago?"

"Before I answer that, how can I be sure you won't speak with him later?"

"You can't. I can promise not to talk to him, but would that satisfy you? I'm not sure I'd trust the word of a stranger."

"If you're really representing May's daughter, you'd have no reason to talk to him."

"I don't know any way I can prove that to you."

"What's the name of the people that adopted May's daughter?"

"Leopold," I said. "Gene and Linda Leopold. The daughter's name is Joanne. She's eighteen. Born on March 11, 1970."

"Knowing that doesn't really prove anything, does it? I have to be sure before I betray the confidence of a friend."

"You and May are friends?"

"We were. Yes."

"Look at it this way. You apparently already knew that May had a child. Don't you think she'd want to see her daughter now?"

She took a deep breath and exhaled. "I guess so. But how can I be sure?"

"I don't know. Maybe you should ask her?"

"Not very easily."

"Mrs. Arcann, from what you've said so far, I assume May is or has been in some trouble. The only thing I can say is, I have nothing to do with that part of her life. I don't even know what that trouble is. Sometimes you have to take a chance. And maybe hearing from her daughter can help her."

She said nothing for several minutes. Then she stopped and turned to me. "Mr. Brodsky, I'm going to trust you. But you must promise never to talk to anyone in my family about this. Never to me again. And if you find May, don't tell her how to find me."

"Agreed."

"We were in high school in the sixties. It was a tough time for us. The so-called sexual revolution. We were too young to handle it, too old not to be part of it. I'm not sure it was any easier for boys in those days, but at least they didn't have to worry about getting pregnant."

"Which May did." I said.

"Yes. But it was more than that. Our parents couldn't handle it either, and it meant endless fights. When May got pregnant, she didn't know what to do. She was afraid to tell anyone. By the time she'd gone six months, it was too late for an abortion, and she couldn't hide it anymore."

"Did she confide in you?"

"Not at first. She talked to me before anyone else, but what could I do? I was only seventeen and just as scared as she was."

"I'm sure it was difficult."

"Believe me, it was. When her father found out, he went crazy and beat her. I'll never forget. It must've been three o'clock in the morning."

"You were there when he beat her?"

"No. No. She came over to my house. My bedroom was on the ground floor, and May crawled through the window. She was all bruised. She looked terrible."

"What about the father?" I said. "I mean the father of the child."

"They had broken up by then. I don't think he even knew she was pregnant."

"So what'd you do?"

"She was afraid to go home. She stayed with me that night. My parents didn't know she was there. We snuck out early in the morning."

"From what the Leopolds told me, you must have taken her to Planned Parenthood."

"That's right. We met a woman there, a doctor, who was very helpful. She introduced May to the Leopolds."

"I know that May lived with them until the baby was born," I said. "What I need to know is what happened afterward."

"She was still afraid to go home. Apparently the Leopolds were willing to help even after they had the baby, but she needed to get away."

"So she came to you."

"Yes. I helped her run away. Maybe I shouldn't have, but we were scared kids."

"I can imagine. Where did you take her?"

She hesitated and then said, "To the wrong people. She became a prostitute and made some porno movies."

"Do you know where she is now?"

"No. I haven't seen or heard from her in ten years."

"But you do know where she went then."

"I think so. She hooked up with a producer who was going to make her a star. A porno star."

"You know his name?"

"Clemenceau. Big Bad Bob Clemenceau."

"You're kidding."

"No. That's what he called himself. They went to San Francisco. That was the last I heard of her."

"Anything else you can tell me?"

"No."

"One thing I don't understand. Why the secrecy? Why are you so afraid to let your husband know about any of this?"

She stared at me and then said, "You don't need to know that part of it. It won't help you find May."

I wasn't at all sure that it wouldn't help, but it was obvious that she had no intention of revealing her own secrets. I conjectured that she had joined May Connors in some sordid activities, and that her husband was ignorant of them, but all I said was, "Okay. Thank you. You've been very helpful."

She stopped and looked at me. "I hope so, Mr. Brodsky. And I do hope you can find her and let her meet her daughter. But don't contact me again. Ever." She turned and walked off. I never did discover her secrets, but my fears that finding May Connors might do more harm than good were beginning to appear well founded.

I flew home that evening and was greeted with bad news. Hypatia, my pet guinea pig, had died. I had left her with a veterinarian because of a respiratory infection. It had developed into pneumonia, and the vet had been unable to save her. She was six years old, and I had become very attached to her. Six years is a long life for a guinea pig, so I suppose it was her time. But that was small solace: I would miss her.

$\int 4$

I called the Leopolds the next morning. They sounded pleased with my progress even though the only clue I had, Big Bad Bob Clemenceau, was ten years old. The next step in the search for May Connors was not at all clear, but I didn't tell them that. I also didn't tell them that she had become a prostitute and had gotten involved with pornography. I would have to discuss that with them eventually, but not yet. My misgivings about the case began to gnaw at me: It appeared that finding May Connors would break Joanne's heart. For the moment I would continue; if I did find May, I would always have the option of not telling the Leopolds.

The obvious approach was to peruse the sex shops common to San Francisco's North Beach, but I didn't relish the idea of wandering through topless bars and porno bookstores. A woman I had met during my student days provided an alternative.

I had been a teaching assistant (TA) at Berkeley several times to help defray the expenses of graduate school. (Teaching assistants are graduate students who lead recitation sections of about thirty students. The lectures, which may have anywhere from two to five hundred students, are handled by a professor.) In one such course, a student tried to seduce me in exchange for a grade. I'm not especially prudish, but that wasn't my idea of the way to win the heart of a charming young damsel. (My reaction to the student's overtures may have been influenced by the fact that I was seriously dating Anne Howe, a graduate student in the math department. Anne finished her Ph.D. that spring and is now a member of the mathematics faculty at Mills College in Oakland.) The student was a long-legged, slender brunette named Peggy Brown, and I had a long talk with her.

Most professors care a lot about their students, but at a large institution such as Berkeley it is difficult for students to get to know faculty, and it may appear to them that their professors are aloof. Peggy was surprised to find that I took a genuine interest in her, and she responded by working hard and did quite well on the final, earning a B for the semester even though she had failed the midterm. The following year she decided to be a mathematics major, and she came to me regularly for advice. We became quite friendly, and she eventually opened up to me. Her story was not an unusual one: divorced parents, running away from home, prostitution. Summoning up the strength to leave that world, she went to a community college and then to Berkeley. She graduated two years after the class with me and is now teaching mathematics in an Oakland high school. She and I remain friends.

I knew that Peggy's career as a hooker had ended fifteen years earlier, but I called her hoping that she might still know someone who could help me locate Big Bad Bob Clemenceau; we agreed to have lunch at my place that afternoon.

The luncheon conversation was a rehash of old times. I served the Jamaica Blue Mountain after the meal since Peggy was one of the few friends able to appreciate that superb brew. She sipped and smiled. "Danny, you never cease to amaze me. Where did you get the stuff?"

"Herb got it in and of course called me right away. You can take some home if you like."

"I'll do that. Now, tell me, what do you need to know?"

"I'm trying to find a woman named May Connors. She apparently made some porno flicks eight, ten years ago."

"Never heard of her. That wasn't my scene."

"I know, but you must've known something about it."

She smiled. "Yeah. Maybe a little."

"You know what I like best about you, Peggy? You're never embarrassed or ashamed of your past."

"I'm not proud of it, either."

"As a matter of fact, you have a lot to be proud of. But that's not why I invited you to lunch."

"Danny, I really don't know much about pornography."

"But surely more than I do. Have you ever heard the name Big Bad Bob Clemenceau?"

She laughed. "Yeah. He was a jerk."

"Tell me about him."

"He was a photographer. He got into doing nude photography, probably because he wanted to watch the girls. He started selling pictures to girlie magazines. Then he tried to be a pimp and got himself beat up. You heard his name in connection with this May What's-her-name?"

"Connors. Yeah. The story I heard was that she met him in L.A., and he brought her to San Francisco."

"To make dirty movies?"

"Something like that."

"He might've gone down there after his short-lived career as a pimp. If he came back to Frisco, I never knew about it."

"Do you know anyone who might?"

"Maybe. I still have some contacts. I'll try." She went into the kitchen and picked up the phone. I heard only her end of the conversation: "Hello, Ginger? It's Peggy. . . . I know, I've been busy. . . . I'll try. . . . Listen. I wanna ask you something. Do you remember Big Bad Bob Clemenceau? . . . Have you heard of him recently? . . . Is that right? . . . That's hard to believe. . . . A friend of mine is trying to find a sister. He says Big Bad Bob was using her in some skin flicks." She covered the mouthpiece and said to me, "Danny, what'd you say her name was?"

"May Connors."

"'May Connors.' . . . What about Clemenceau? . . . Yes, sure. When? . . . I imagine so. . . . Good. . . . I'll call you soon." She hung up.

"Got something?" I said.

"I think so, yeah. That was a friend from the old days. We were roommates for a time."

"And she knows Clemenceau?"

"She knows of him. She said he's made it pretty big making dirty movies. She thinks you can find him in a place near Market Street. I'll tell you where to go."

I parked Herman in a garage in the financial district the next afternoon and had no difficulty locating the address Peggy had directed me to. It was an old nondescript, dirty building in an alley off Market. Peggy had told me to walk in and go up two flights, and I found myself in a kind of alcove with a door and a window. A woman appeared behind the window and said, "You're a little old for this sort of thing, aren't you?"

"I didn't know that I was that old."

"We need the young studs, if you know what I mean."

"I suppose. But I think you may have the wrong idea. I'm looking for Bob Clemenceau."

"You a cop?"

"No."

"You're not a friend."

"What makes you so sure?"

"His friends call him Big Bad Bob."

I smiled. "So I understand. Is he here?"

"Hold on. I'll see."

She disappeared. Five minutes later a curly-haired man with a large scar on his cheek put his head through the door and beckoned me to follow him. He was tall and muscular, wearing tight jeans and a black T-shirt cut off above the navel. He did not look like the sort of man I would want to meet in a dark alley—I wasn't sure I wanted to meet him at all.

I followed him down a long, drab hallway. He brought me to a small, dingy office that contained a metal desk and a couple of chairs; the walls were bare save for a couple of centerfolds and peeling paint. An obese man with a round, puffy face sat behind the desk. He was bald to his ears; the hair he did have was gray and hung down to his shoulders. The first man left without having spoken; the man behind the desk said nothing.

"Are you Big Bad Bob?" I said.

"Who wants to know?"

"Brodsky. Dan Brodsky."

"What's a Brodsky?"

"I'm looking for May Connors."

Something flickered in his eyes. "Cop?"

"Private."

"Who's May Connors?"

"You met her in Los Angeles ten years ago. You brought her to San Francisco to be a movie star."

He moved his hand under the desk, though I could not detect what he did with it. He said, "You've been checking up on me. I don't think I like that."

He was trying to sound tough, but his high-pitched voice and churlish appearance belied his threatening tone. I refrained from laughing and said, "No. I'm trying to locate . . ."

The first man returned. He held a pistol at his side, his index finger massaging the barrel—it was a surprisingly menacing gesture.

Clemenceau smiled. "I've got nothing to say. Any objections?"

"Yes. I need to find May Connors." I heard a clicking sound behind me. I suppose I should have been frightened, but the incongruity of the two men was too ludicrous for fear. "What's he going to do, shoot me?"

"Whatever it takes."

"Don't be ridiculous," I said. "Cops frown on that sort of thing. I mean, not in your own office."

"If that's what it takes . . ."

"I'm just looking for a missing woman."

"What makes you so sure I know anything?"

"Because you brought her here from L.A."

"Even if I did, why should I tell you anything?"

"Why not?" I said. "Unless you have something to hide."

He sat back and stared at me. His face broke into a

smile and he waved his arm, dismissing the other man. "All right, you're not a threat and I have nothing to hide. So why should I talk to you?"

"For May Connors' sake. She has a daughter who wants to find her."

"This daughter hired you?"

"Yes."

"And you're not a cop?"

"No."

"Well, I haven't seen May in five years."

"But you did know her."

"Yeah. I met her in L.A. She came up here and made a couple of flicks for me. She was doin' all right. Then she got involved with one of the actors. They ran off together."

"What was his name?"

"He acted under the name Billy Bang. His real name was William Lancaster. He was a limey."

"And May," I said, "what name did she use?"

"Heavenly Box." I broke into a laugh, and he said, "You think that's funny?"

"Mildly amusing. Do you know what happened to them?"

"He wanted to go home. They went to England. But I dunno. That was five years ago."

"Anything else you can tell me?"

"Nah. I didn't keep tabs on 'em once they left. Think you can find her?"

I shrugged. "I'm a lot closer than I was a few days ago. Got any messages if I do?"

"Yeah. Say I'm not mad anymore. She'll understand."

I thanked him and left; I was glad to be out of there.

$\int$ 5

The time had come to discuss what I had learned about May Connors with the Leopolds: I couldn't take the search to England without their approval, and I couldn't ask that without their being made aware of all I knew. I called Gene Leopold and asked to meet with him and his wife but without Joanne. He suggested dinner that evening, and they met me at a French restaurant on Lake Merritt in Oakland. It was an inexpensive, family-style place, but the food was good, the coffee acceptable.

"Let me begin by explaining why I thought it necessary to talk without Joanne," I said. "I've been able to trace May Connors to five years ago, when she went to England with a man she'd met in San Francisco."

Gene Leopold said, "So you thought we might not want it to get too expensive, and . . ."

"No. Don't worry about the expenses. That's not the problem."

"Then what is?" Mrs. Leopold asked.

"I told you that May came to San Francisco ten years ago with a man she'd met in L.A. That wasn't the whole story."

"So?" She sounded suspicious.

"What I held back was that May had become a prostitute shortly after Joanne was born. The man who brought her to the Bay Area made pornographic movies, and he used May in several. She went to England with a man she'd met making one of those films. The question is, knowing that, do you still want me to find her?"

"You mean you want to know if we're willing to pay for a trip to England?"

"No. The expenses won't be a problem. The—"

"Why not?"

"We can talk about that if you want me to pursue the case. But I'd like to separate the question of expenses from the real question: Are you sure that Joanne wouldn't be better off not finding her mother?"

"We're sure, Mr. Brodsky," Mrs. Leopold said. "When we first talked about finding May, we considered all the possibilities. Gene and I know that Joanne is mature enough to accept her, regardless."

I wasn't completely convinced, but it wasn't my place to make decisions for clients. I said, "All right, then. I'll do my best to find her."

"And the expenses?"

"I'm going to a conference at Oxford University in July, so the only expenses you'll be charged will be to cover the few extra days I spend looking for May. You won't be billed for the airfare, and it may even be possible to do some investigating during the conference. Of course, you will have to wait until July."

"That's no problem," he said. "After all, Joanne's already waited eighteen years."

You may be wondering why I didn't ask the Leopolds to foot the bill for the sojourn to England. I may not be the most honest person in the world, but it did seem less than ethical to have them shell out for a trip I had already planned. Besides, I wasn't going to pay for it: You were. To be precise, your tax dollars were. Paul Hobart was the project director of a large National Science Foundation grant, and the grant gave me some support in my research efforts. Since I was scheduled to deliver a paper at the conference, it would pay for the trip.

There has been some controversy surrounding such grants. Some questions have been raised about expenditures for travel—for example, for trips to Europe. While there has undoubtedly been some out-and-out fraud, on the whole the travel is important: Researchers must meet and talk with each other.

Another source of controversy has been the nature of the research itself. I remember one senator complaining about the amount of money being spent to study the mating habits of bumble bees. Such an investigation may contribute to our knowledge of evolution or improve honey production, and the criticism reflects a complete misunderstanding of the nature of basic research.

There has also been controversy surrounding individual researchers. My favorite example concerns Stephen Smale, a professor of mathematics at Berkeley. There is no Nobel Prize in mathematics. It is not entirely clear why, though there are several theories.[*] In mathematics the closest thing to a Nobel Prize is the Fields Medal. It lacks the financial benefits associated with the Nobel Prize, but it is equally prestigious—at least to mathematicians. It is awarded every four years at the International Congress of Mathematics. In 1966

[*] For a discussion of one such theory, see Chapter 24 of *The Calculus of Murder*. Ed.

the Congress met in Moscow, and Smale was to be a recipient of the Fields Medal.

Smale was also active in the anti-Vietnam War movement, including helping to organize troop train sit-ins and the "International Days of Protest" in 1965 and 1966. As a result, he was subpoenaed by the House Un-American Activities Committee. He was unable to appear at their hearings because he was in Moscow receiving the Fields Medal. The San Francisco *Examiner* ran the headline: "UC Prof Dodges Subpoena, Skips U.S. for Moscow." If I remember correctly, Smale had that headline taped to his office door for more than a year.

Half a dozen congressmen attacked the National Science Foundation and the funding of research grants when the story broke—none had the integrity to apologize when the truth emerged.

The next couple of months were occupied with finishing up the course I was teaching and with preparing for the conference. I did get some work, enough to keep bread on the table, but nothing very exciting (though there was one case in which I was decked by an irate wife for serving her husband with a subpoena—you wouldn't believe her left hook).

Steve Vadney continued his regular visits to my office, and I mentioned COTCA on one such occasion. He said he'd already been planning to spend the summer hitchhiking around Europe, and that I could expect to see him in Oxford.

From the sublime to the ridiculous: Shortly after Steve left my office, another student in the class came by and asked if she could take the final during the summer. Having a student take the exam late creates two nontrivial problems. First, the student has to be given a grade of I (incomplete), and when she does take the exam, a new grade must be submitted. A fair amount of paperwork is involved. Secondly, an extra exam has to made up and graded, and it's hard to be sure that the make-up exam is equivalent to the original. She did, however, have a good excuse: Her father had died. Naturally I said okay.

A few days later I was talking with Hal Brachman, a professor in the math department at Berkeley, and happened to mention the need to give an extra final at the end of the summer. When he heard the student's name, Hal said that she had not taken the final in his class a year earlier because her father had died. A little research revealed that her father's much reported death had conveniently occurred on three prior occasions just before finals. I suspected that she was in for a bit of a shock when she discovered that she'd received an F in my course instead of the I she'd been expecting.

The conference was set for the last week in July. It was scheduled to start with registration and an informal dinner on Sunday, and then to run through the following Friday. Paul and I made reservations for Saturday flights. Traveling with us were his daughter, Kathy; Howard Williams, a mathematician at the Santa Barbara campus of the University of California; and Howard's daughter, Amy. Kathy and Amy had been together on a high school exchange program in England a year earlier and had become close friends. I had met Amy a couple of times but didn't know her very well.

My original supply of Jamaica Blue Mountain was

long gone, but, fortunately, Herb had set aside sufficient quantities to satisfy my needs. I was thus able to
take a pound with me to Oxford. I had to leave my
heavy-duty coffee grinder behind—it was simply too
large to carry on a plane—but the little one would be
adequate for a week.

The flight was uneventful, although getting through
security was worse that usual because of recent hijack-
ings and plane bombings. I can't remember the movie,
probably because they had a nineteen-inch screen and
we were fifteen rows from it. My only recollection of
the flight was that Kathy and Amy seemed to be giggling nonstop for seven hours; I'm glad they enjoyed
themselves.

There's an eight-hour time difference between England and the West Coast, so the plane landed at
London's Heathrow Airport at seven Sunday morning.
Paul is the type that's uncomfortable unless he has a
car available, so he had made arrangements to rent
one, a cute little Ford Fiesta. Howard had no intention
of learning how to drive on the wrong side of the road,
and he took the train to Oxford with the girls. (They
were planning to take the train with or without adult
supervision.) I accompanied Paul.

The technique Paul and I used to deal with left-
handed driving was based on the assumption that it
was unlikely that both of us would forget where the car
was supposed to be at the same time. We thus made it
the responsibility of the passenger to navigate and con-
tinually remind the driver to keep left. It worked reasonably well. (At least for an entire week we managed
to avoid hitting anything substantial, like pedestrians
or other vehicles competing for highway space.)

The navigation, on the other hand, frequently left

something to be desired. When we exited from the airport, Paul was driving and I was navigating. We were supposed to take the M4 north to the M40. It was about three miles, so after driving for five minutes, I told Paul that it seemed that maybe we should have found the M40 already; after another five minutes, I was sure that maybe we should have found the M40 already.

"Wanna know something?" Paul said. "The sun rises in the east. We're going south."

"Good point." What had happened was simple: As anyone in his right mind knows, if you get off a plane and the sun is shining, it must be the middle of the afternoon; ergo, the sun is to the west. "It might be a good idea to exit," I suggested as Paul zipped by an off-ramp at seventy-five. (The British are relatively slow drivers for Europe but much faster than Americans—many cars passed us at that speed. We were led to believe that they do give speeding tickets in England but never saw any direct evidence.) Five miles later Paul did figure out how to exit to the left and successfully made a U-turn.

We had no further difficulties until we got lost in the city of Oxford. I was driving by then. Staying on the left side of the road turned out not to be all that difficult, but there were a number of little things that did cause discomfort. The worst was the rear- and side-view mirrors: They were in the wrong place. When you're driving on the right, the rearview mirror is to your right and the side view is to your left. You automatically glance at them and generally know if there are cars behind you or if one is coming up to pass. In England everything is backward, so those little automatic glances give you no information, and you're left

43

with this uneasy feeling that something is missing (like important information about surrounding vehicles).

Another problem was making right turns. Lefts were easy since all you had to do was hug the curb. But rights were another matter. To make one, you had to swing wide, cutting across traffic. Since the cars you were trying to avoid were coming from the wrong direction, you always had this peculiar sensation that there was a large lorry lurking somewhere, waiting for the opportunity to squash your tiny Fiesta like a bug.

We reached the Oxford Moat House at nine-thirty. We had written to the hotel to explain that we would arrive early, and they had rooms ready for us when we checked in. After dropping our bags in our rooms, we went to the hotel restaurant and found Howard and the girls finishing up a traditional English breakfast.

A complete English breakfast is substantial. It begins with cold or hot cereal and a bowl of fruit. Next come bacon, sausage, and eggs accompanied by toast and fried tomatoes. The Moat House also served sautéed mushrooms and baked beans. Beverages were selected from several (canned and rather tasteless) juices. And of course tea or coffee.

The effects of the jet lag upon me were obvious: The coffee seemed fine. (The following morning, with my brain and taste buds functioning again, it became clear that the hotel did not know what a coffee bean was. After that, I made my morning coffee in my room with the Jamaica Blue Mountain.) The girls appeared unaffected by the flight. I was awake enough to observe that the English accent that Kathy had brought home with her the previous year had manifested itself again.

Howard, Paul, and I had singles, and the girls shared a room. We agreed to nap until three and then to register at the conference. At three-twenty I found Howard sipping the Moat House's tasteless brew; a bleary-eyed Paul followed shortly. He said Kathy had left him a note saying that she and Amy would be in their rooms by midnight and that we shouldn't worry. Howard was, nevertheless, worried; Paul expressed a degree of confidence in the girls that I was not at all sure he felt.

The conference was held at St. Catherine's College, one of the many that constitute Oxford University. St. Cat's, as it was referred to by the locals, was quite modern, having been erected in the sixties. Given that several of Oxford's colleges date back to the thirteenth century, we were disappointed with the site. The reasons for that choice became clear when we had a chance to explore Balliol College (1263) and Trinity College (relatively new, 1555). Teaching in the old colleges was done primarily through tutorials, and there were no lecture halls; St. Catherine's had a two-hundred-seat auditorium, perfect for the conference.

There were three sessions scheduled each day, one in the morning and two in the afternoon, and two types of talks: long (forty-five minutes) and short (twenty minutes). In the morning there were two long talks separated by a coffee break. After lunch each session consisted of a long talk and three short ones; afternoon tea was served between the two sessions. Wednesday's schedule was different: The afternoon was left open with an optional tour of Oxford available. Larger conferences often have parallel sessions, but that was not the case here.

My talk was of the full-length variety and was slated to be the opener Monday morning. I had wanted to get it over with early and enjoy the conference, and Paul, being on the program committee, had been able to get my presentation, as well as Eileen St. Cloud's, scheduled for the first day.

We had little difficulty finding St. Catherine's with Paul driving, Howard navigating, and me cautioning Paul to keep left. When we pulled in, we found another advantage of St. Cat's over the older colleges: a parking lot. For some reason they didn't have the foresight to build adequate parking facilities in the thirteenth century.

The college was made up of several modern buildings that more or less formed a rectangle with a grass-covered quadrangle in the center. We entered through a lobby that was called the Lodge, and we registered there. We were in time for afternoon tea, which was in the college dining hall.

Afternoon tea at the conference meant coffee or tea and cookies. I tried St. Cat's "coffee" exactly once: It was without doubt the most unpeasant warmed-over mouthwash that has ever insulted my taste buds.

It was not a large conference, attracting only those mathematicians interested in operator theory and in C*-algebras. There were close to two hundred participants. Almost half came from the United States; Britain was well represented because of the location; sixty or so came from Europe; the remainder came from various parts of the globe. I knew perhaps a hundred and knew of another thirty. If that surprises you, you should understand that the number of mathematicians interested in this particular branch is limited. We read each other's papers and attend the same conferences. As a result, a small community exists, and we know each other well.

One member of that community I was anxious to see was Eileen St. Cloud. She was a mathematician at Rice University and a very attractive brunette; at least I found her so. We'd first met at a conference at UCLA fifteen years earlier. We were both graduate students then, and something of a relationship developed during the conference. She was studying at the University of Texas at Austin, so we were separated by two thousand miles, and the relationship became a whenever-I-see-you kind of thing. It continued even after her marriage to Bob St. Cloud, an algebraist she had met when she took the position at Rice.

I spotted her standing with a cup of tea in one hand and a cookie in the other. She was talking with several men, three of whom I knew. One was Barry Donardy, a thin, balding man in his late thirties. He had been a student of Eileen's father, Arthur Rothenberg. Rothenberg died in an automobile accident, after which Donardy began studying with Martin Kloss. He was the classic perennial student: He was still studying with Kloss after fifteen years.

I first met Donardy at the Summer Meetings of the American Mathematical Society at the University of Oregon in Eugene. (Most people think of California when they think of the West Coast, but with a coastline of unequaled beauty to the west, majestic mountains to the east, and towering green forests in between, Oregon is the land of the gods.) We were both students and somewhat intimidated by the experienced mathematicians, so we spent some time together in Eugene. I would not have classified him as a friend, but I had gotten to know him that summer. He was shy and insecure and probably couldn't function very well away from the academic world.

I had the opportunity to speak with Donardy at dinner later that evening, and he claimed that he was close to finally finishing his Ph.D. He had proved a theorem about the class of subnormal operators that satisfied Kloss's condition (so named because it was first defined in a paper written by Martin Kloss). He said that he was sure that if he could generalize the result by eliminating Kloss's condition from the hypothesis, he would have enough for a Ph.D. dissertation.

Martin Kloss was also in the group chatting with Eileen. He was a smug little man whose personality grated on me. He was five feet—any way you measured him. He had unkempt jet-black hair and a small moustache. When he got upset, which was fairly often, his left eye and the left side of his upper lip twitched. I'm sure he disliked me, if for no other reason than that I had been Paul's student, and he hated Paul.

Kloss was the most arrogant man I had ever met. Most mathematicians tend to lose even their colleagues when explaining their own work. It's been said that there are three parts to a mathematician's lecture: The first is understood by most of the audience, the second is understood by a few experts, and the last is understood by no one. The usual explanation is that the third part shows that the work is nontrivial. It's more accurate to say that the lecturer has been investigating the ideas intensively for several years, and he understands it very well and thinks it's easy (which it rarely is). With Kloss it was different: In his lectures, he would jump directly to the third part because he wanted to be sure that no one understood anything. It is an understatement to say that he always did his best to make anyone he was talking to feel inferior.

I didn't know Kloss that well, and I'm certainly not

qualified in psychology, but it was my opinion that he was a classic paranoid schizophrenic. For example, rumor had it that he thought that students made jokes about him when he was writing on the blackboard with his back to the class. I could almost have felt sorry for him if he weren't so disagreeable.

There was another man talking with Eileen whom I knew: Calvin Barnett. A charming, good-looking man, always meticulously dressed and always smiling, I imagine he thought of himself as a ladies' man. My first impression of him had been that he was a bit of a con man, but over the years I'd learned to respect him more. He was involved with the Hobart-Kloss dispute, having co-authored the paper that was based on ideas purloined from Paul, but Paul never considered him to be responsible. Since Eileen was indirectly involved with that controversy, and since it had started at the UCLA conference at which she and I had met, this is an appropriate point to describe it in detail.

Paul had attended the UCLA meeting to deliver a paper. He was a young, untenured assistant professor at Berkeley, although he had already demonstrated his abilities, and there was little doubt that it would not be long before he was tenured. Nonetheless, he was surely concerned about getting tenure, and it must have been important to him to receive proper recognition for his contributions to mathematics. (In case you're unfamiliar with the academic life, the only real measure of performance in the major universities is research. That applies to hiring as well as to tenure and promotion. Tenure, which is awarded after several years of satisfactory research, is a kind of job security that makes it difficult to fire a professor except for serious cause, although in recent years so-called financial ex-

49

igency has sometimes been used to terminate tenured professors.)

Eileen's father, Arthur Rothenberg, was also at that conference. He was one of the leading mathematicians at the University of Texas, and he heard Paul's talk. Very impressed with the young man, he took Paul to dinner that evening. They talked mathematics, and Paul described his current research interests, including some recent results. He outlined the proof of a theorem that had several interesting consequences. The proof was surprising simple and very elegant. Martin Kloss, an assistant professor concerned about tenure at Texas, was also at the dinner.

A few weeks after the UCLA conference, Rothenberg was killed in an automobile accident, and a month after that, Kloss and Barnett submitted a paper containing Paul's research to a journal. The editor of the journal had no knowledge of the situation, and, purely by coincidence, asked Paul to referee the paper! (Journals contain articles that describe accomplished research; the referees verify that a paper is sound and of sufficient significance to be worthy of publication.)

Paul was furious when he read the paper. He had three options: He could refuse to referee the paper, he could accuse the authors of plagiarism, or he could referee it and recommend to the editor that the paper not be published. The last alternative did not make sense because it was good work, and he saw nothing to be gained by creating a public controversy. As a result, he simply declined to referee it. He also wrote a one-line letter to Kloss; it read, "You're a thief."

Paul believed that Barnett was unaware that Kloss had stolen the work since Barnett had not been at the dinner and since he was already tenured and thus not as "hungry" as Kloss. Paul also liked Barnett and didn't see him as a thief. On the other hand, that paper was far superior to any research ever accomplished by Barnett (or by Kloss). I myself never fully trusted either one of them, though I must say that I especially disliked Kloss. In all fairness to Barnett, I should also point out that he had written a very good paper with Arthur Rothenberg, and that many people, including Eileen and Paul, respected him both personally and professionally.

That fifteen-year-old dispute was destined to have a major impact on the conference.

I ambled over to the group and said, "I see the great state of Texas is well represented."

Donardy and Barnett said hello, and we shook hands; Kloss nodded in recognition; Eileen spoke only with her eyes. There was a fourth man with them, Ross White from Rice. I had seen some of his work and knew his name, but we had never met before. Eileen introduced him to me, although I could identify him from his name tag since he had already registered. He was well dressed, wearing a suit and tie, unusual for an academic. He was in his mid forties with hair graying at the temples.

I chatted with them awhile, being sure to mention the hotel at which I was staying; Eileen duly took note. During the conversation I discovered that Eileen and Barnett were staying at the Randolf Hotel, probably the best in Oxford and within walking distance of the conference while White, Donardy, and Kloss had opted for the much less expensive accommodations at St. Catherine's. I also learned that Kloss, who was probably too lazy to walk, and Barnett, who had been traveling in England for two weeks, were the only ones to rent cars; in particular, Eileen had not.

I pulled out my camera and took pictures, individually and collectively. It was not merely an excuse to get a photograph of Eileen; over the years I had developed a fair collection of mathematicians, mostly at conferences.

The keynote address was set for six o'clock and was delivered by Paul. He welcomed us and talked about the recent spurt of interest in operator theory and in C*-algebras. He discussed several important questions that had arisen in the last couple of years and raised a couple of new ones. It was a good talk and set an appropriate tone for the rest of the conference.

The food at the buffet supper that followed Paul's talk left something to be desired, but I did have the opportunity to say hello to a number of friends. One of the nice side effects of this type of conference is that one develops and maintains friendships with mathematicians from around the world.

I got back to my hotel room at ten and spent an hour looking over the notes for my talk. Eileen had no difficulty finding my room, and the remainder of the evening was not concerned with mathematics.

$\int 6$

Nick Zorn, a friend of mine from the University of Kansas, chaired the Monday morning session, and he introduced me. Without getting too technical, my talk concerned a famous open problem in mathematics known as the Invariant Subspace Question. There have been a number of partial answers; far and away the best of these was proved in 1973 by a Russian mathematician named Lomonosov. His result amazed a lot of people. In fact, it was so good that it appeared that he might have solved the entire problem, though few of us thought that likely. In my talk I presented an example of an operator that showed that Lomonosov had *not* solved the entire problem.

Based on the number of questions, it appeared that my talk had been well received. After the last comment from the audience, Nick said to me, "The important question is, when and where's the game?"

"Tonight," I said. "My room. Eight o'clock." The "game" he was referring to was poker. At the Santa Barbara conference the previous year, Paul and I had gotten a few of the conferees together for poker, using the regular Monday night game at my Berkeley apartment as a model, and Nick had been one of the players. It was more of a social affair than serious gambling: dime ante, three raises, fifty-cent maximum.

It was possible to win or lose as much as thirty dollars, but that wasn't very likely, and even that wasn't that expensive for an evening's entertainment.

The other speaker scheduled that morning was Martin Kloss. After the coffee break Howard and I followed Paul to seats in the first row. When Nick introduced Kloss, Paul whispered to me, "See you at lunch." Then he stood up, put on his coat, gathered up his things, and walked out, all very deliberately and ostentatiously. It was an impressive performance. I wanted to applaud but thought better of it; Howard was covering his mouth with his hand in a not entirely successful attempt to refrain from laughing; I could hear a number of snickers behind me. Kloss was not the most popular man at the conference, and Paul was well liked and well respected; I'm sure that most people in the audience appreciated his melodramatic departure.

Kloss was furious; his teeth were clenched, and his eye and lip started twitching; he was unable to control himself. While he had never been a very good speaker, this talk was particularly bad.

As I was exiting from the lecture hall, I heard a voice say, "Professor Brodsky." It was Steve Vadney.

"I see you made it."

"Yes. I liked your talk."

"Thank you. We're on our way to lunch. Why don't you join us?"

"I don't think so."

He was an eighteen-year-old freshman, undoubtedly intimidated by the presence of so many professors. "Ah, c'mon," I said, "there's always room for one more."

"But . . . well . . . You see, I haven't registered."

I smiled and thought of my own student days, remembering the conferences I had attended without registering and in particular the one at which Paul had snuck me into the banquet, an expensive lobster and steak dinner. "Don't worry about it," I said. "We were all poor students once."

He shrugged. "Okay."

We joined Paul and Terrance Henkler, who were already seated in the dining hall. Henkler was an Englishman attached to Trinity College, though he'd been trained at Cornell. He was a fine mathematician, and, though I didn't know him very well, I'd always found him pleasant. He had been responsible for local arrangements (a thankless job) because of his association with Oxford University.

I described Kloss's talk (or, rather, his inability to talk) to Paul. He was certainly pleased but acted the innocent. "I had to go to the bathroom," he said.

The Texas contingent—Kloss, Eileen, Cal Barnett, Ross White, and Barry Donardy—were sitting a couple of tables away. When Kloss caught sight of Paul, he came over and said, "You piece of shit."

Paul remained calm. "You got a problem, Martin?"

"I could kill you."

"Don't you think that's a little extreme?"

Kloss trembled but said nothing; he returned to his table.

I said, "Paul, you're pushing him too hard."

"Dan's right," Howard said. "You made your point." He smiled. "Very well, I might add. But it's time to ease off."

"Okay. Okay. I'll leave him alone."

"One question," I said. "Why now? I mean, why did it take fifteen years for you to do something?"

A self-satisfied grin crossed his face. "It was pretty much spur of the moment. It felt like the right thing to do."

Henkler said nothing but was obviously amused. I imagined that most people would look back and regard Paul's little farce as the highlight of the conference. As it turned out, I was utterly mistaken.

The afternoon sessions were mixed. Eileen spoke, and I'm pleased to report that her presentation was excellent, but the other long talk, given by Henkler, was lousy. On more than one occasion I could see Kloss staring at Paul; there was murder in his eyes.

Eileen and I had agreed to meet before the Big Game for a quiet dinner. The day's proceedings were concluded by five, leaving me time to stop at the Moat House for a shower. Kathy Hobart had slid a note under my door asking me to come to her room *as soon as possible.*

I had to knock several times before she opened the door. Her eyes were red, and her pillow was scrunched up on the bed; she'd obviously been crying into it. Before I closed the door, she put her arms around me and said, "Oh, Uncle Danny, what'm I gonna do?"

I kicked the door shut behind me and hugged her. "What's wrong?"

"It's Amy. She's so mean. I'll never forgive her."

"What'd she do?"

"It was . . . we were . . . I hate her."

I sat her down on the bed and caressed her back. "Do you want to tell me about it?"

"We went out yesterday. Wandering about. We found a disco and hopped in."

"Something happened there?"

"Yes." A tear slid down the side of her nose. "It was horrible."

She rambled on, but I was eventually able to piece together what had happened. It seems that Kathy had spotted this "really cute boy" named Colin, and she had succeeded in getting him to ask her to dance. She introduced him to Amy, who accepted an invitation to dance. Amy and Colin kept dancing, and Kathy came back to the hotel and locked herself in their room, not letting Amy in when she got back a couple of hours later.

"Where did Amy sleep?" I said.

"I don't know. And I don't care!"

"Probably in Howard's room."

"I hope she had to sleep in the street!"

"Don't you think that's a little extreme? A few days ago you said she was your best friend."

"That was before I found out what a bitch she is."

"Kathy. It doesn't sound like she did anything that terrible. After all, it was apparently Colin's choice."

"She could have said no."

"Maybe she should have. But you'd only danced with him once. It wasn't as if you'd been dating him a long time."

"But I saw him first."

"Kathy, it's not that easy to find good friends. I think Amy's pretty nice."

"I don't care. I hate her!"

"It seems to me that Colin's the one you should be mad at."

"I hate him, too."

"Have you spoken to your father about this?"

"Daddy? About boys? He . . . he wouldn't understand."

I put my hand under her chin and held her face up. "Let me ask you one question. And I want you to tell me the truth. Are you sure that you're not mad because you're a little jealous? Because Colin chose Amy over you?"

"How can you take her side?" She pulled away from me, threw herself down on the bed, and cried into the pillow.

I put my hand on her shoulder, but she pushed me away. "Kathy, I'm not taking anyone's side. I'd just like to help you patch things up with Amy." She didn't move. "How would you feel if I could introduce you to an eighteen-year-old boy who's good looking, really nice, and very smart?"

"Who?" She spoke brusquely and into the pillow.

"His name's Steve Vadney. He was in my class this spring, and he's in Oxford now."

"He won't like me, anyway," She cried into the pillow again.

"Kathy, look at me." She turned over, and I said, "You're developing into a beautiful young woman. You're charming and bright, and any boy would be crazy not to fall for you."

"Yeah? Then why did Colin choose Amy?"

"I guess he must be crazy." She didn't respond, so I added, "Kathy, different men like different kinds of women. If that weren't the case, we'd all fall in love with the same one. Some men are afraid of intelligent women. Maybe Colin was afraid of you."

"You think so?"

"I don't know, but I'll bet anything Steve'll like you. Want to meet him?"

"Maybe."

"Should I try to find Amy and see if we can't patch things up?"

She shrugged a begrudging okay, and I dialed Howard's room. He answered, but the sound of Amy crying came through. Howard and I did some negotiating, and the girls agreed to meet in their room and talk things out.

I closed the door behind me after Amy came in, but I could hear that their discussion began with shouting recriminations. I don't know what happened during the next fifteen minutes, but they came to Howard's room holding hands and giggling.

Eileen had already been seated when I arrived at the Italian restaurant that she had suggested. I expected her to ask about my tardiness, but, even before I sat down, she said, "What the hell was Paul Hobart trying to do this morning?"

"You don't know?"

"No."

"I'm surprised. Your father was involved."

"My father?"

"Yes. When Paul was a kid, he met with your father and Martin Kloss during a conference at UCLA. The one when you and I met. Paul described some ideas he had, and Kloss published a paper based on Paul's work."

"You mean he thought *my father* stole his work?" She sounded incredulous.

"Certainly not. Your father's car accident was a few weeks later. Kloss and Cal Barnett co-authored the paper."

"I can't believe Cal would ever do anything like that."

"Why not?"

"When Dad died, Cal was really nice to us. To Mom, to Tommy, and to me." Tommy was her younger brother.

"He could still be a thief."

"I don't think so. He took me on as a student and was always very helpful. There are a couple of things in my thesis that were largely due to him, and he insisted that I take full credit for them."

I shrugged. "You're probably right. Paul never thought Cal had anything to do with it."

"I'm glad. Cal helped me a lot. It was very tough when Dad died."

"It must have been."

"Yes. Dad was only forty-eight. He was so full of life. And the way he died."

"I suppose it was very sudden."

"It wasn't just that," she said. "Dad had a hundred-thousand-dollar insurance policy with a double-indemnity clause, so the insurance company made sure there was a police investigation."

"You mean they thought there was foul play?"

"No. It was routine, and of course the investigation didn't lead anywhere. But it was very upsetting at a very difficult time."

I held her hand and squeezed gently.

The waiter came, and we discussed her talk after placing our orders. Since I was hosting the poker game, I made sure we finished our dinner in time to get back to the hotel by eight.

Five players showed up by eight-thirty: Cal Barnett, Nick Zorn, a colleague of his from Kansas named John Grabowski, Bill DeMarco, one of the conference organizers, and Donald Edelson, a Berkeley mathematician. Howard had no interest in poker, and he took the girls out to dinner and spent the evening with them. We were sure Paul would eventually show up, but we started without him.

I did well almost from the beginning. Cal won the first two hands, but I learned quickly that he was a bluffer when he tried to beat my straight with a pair of deuces. I was surprised by his large bets with poor hands. After forty-five minutes he lost a big pot to Nick and must have been down by at least ten pounds—a lot for this kind of game. He took a short break and then played more conservatively, although he continued to lose.

I was ahead by fifteen pounds when Paul finally put in an appearance at ten-thirty. He was a mess: His face was dirty, his shirt was torn, and there was grease on his sleeves.

"Car broke down," he said, breathless. "Let me clean up, and I'll join you in twenty minutes."

I was still doing well when we dealt him in half an hour later. The first hand was seven-card stud. (It's a dealer's choice game, and seven-card stud is the game most frequently called.) I was dealt a seven and a ten in the hole and a second seven up; Paul had a deuce showing, which he bet. Don and John dropped immediately. I got the third seven and Paul the second deuce on the next card. He bet again and I raised—it was going to be a big hand. By the sixth card Nick was out, and Paul had a pair of jacks to go with the deuces. Bill and Cal appeared to be looking for flushes, which was fine with me since I had filled my full house with a second ten. It seemed likely that Paul also had a full house, but he'd bet his deuces from the beginning, so mine looked bigger than his.

My last card was a jack, increasing the likelihood that Paul's full house was deuces and jacks (and not the other way around). Bill folded, but Cal braved it with his flush. When Paul called after the last bet, there was close to twenty quid in the pot. Cal was disgusted when

I showed my hand; I was disgusted when Paul tabled the third jack. Cal had enough at that point and had the sense to quit; for me it was all downhill from there. When we quit at two A.M., Paul must have won forty bucks, half of which was mine.

Eileen was expecting me at her hotel after the game, so it was after four before I nodded off in her arms. The poker game forgotten, I slept soundly.

∫ 7

Since I was holding the receiver, I must have picked it up, but I remember neither the phone ringing nor answering it; I only remember Howard saying, "Dan, wake up. This is important."

"Hmmh?"

"WAKE UP!"

I shook my head and opened my eyes. "I'm awake. What time is it?"

"Nine. Paul's been arrested."

"That's nice. Is Paul there with you?"

"Goddamn it, Dan! Wake up and listen! Paul's been arrested!"

I sat up with a start. "What?"

"Paul's been arrested."

"What's the charge?"

"I don't know. I was called by someone named William Norman. He's the custody sergeant on duty, or something like that."

"He didn't tell you the charge?"

"No. I didn't think to ask. I guess I was flustered."

"I'll find out," I said. "Do you know where Paul is?"

"Yes. They're holding him at the police station on St. Aldate's. He told me it's down near the river."

"I'll go right over." I climbed out of bed and realized that I was still in Eileen's room. She had evidently left for the conference without waking me (thank god!). She was staying at the Randolf, and their coffee was almost tolerable, good enough at least to get me going.

The Randolf is located in downtown Oxford, and I was able to walk to the police station in ten minutes. While much of Oxford is quite old, the police station is a twentieth-century brick building. I walked in and found a small lobby with two windows; neither was manned. I pressed a buzzer, and several minutes later a uniformed constable appeared behind one of the windows.

"May I 'elp you, sir?"

"Yes. A friend of mine was arrested this morning, and I'd like to see him."

"A Yank, are ya?"

"Yes."

"Must be that 'obart fellow you're lookin' for?"

"That's right."

"Detective Chief Inspector Bailey's in charge." He picked up the phone. "Inspector Bailey, there's a man 'ere says 'e's a friend of the American arrested this morning. . . ." He looked at me. "What's your name?"

"Dan Brodsky."

"Dan Brodsky, sir . . . yessir." He hung up and said, "Says 'e's been expecting you and 'e'll see you in 'is office in a few minutes. You can wait there. He pointed to a bench in the lobby across from the window.

Twenty minutes later a man wearing a shirt and tie came over to me and said, "Mr. Brodsky?" He was a tall, thin man in his late thirties.

"Yes?"

"I'm Detective Sergeant Smythe. Inspector Bailey will see you now."

I followed him up two flights of stairs, and we en-

64

tered a pleasant office with a large window; the words DETECTIVE CHIEF INSPECTOR EDMUND P. BAILEY were etched on a plaque riveted to the door. The occupant, a balding, middle-aged man wearing a gray suit, was sitting behind a steel desk writing when we entered. Without saying anything, he motioned us to sit; Smythe and I took chairs in front of his desk. In a minute or two Bailey put the pen down, removed his glasses, and looked up.

"You're Mr. Brodsky?" He had a deep, resonant voice.

"Yes. Dan Brodsky. Paul Hobart's a friend of mine."

"You're the one he asked us to call?"

"Yes."

"We had to make two calls to find you."

"We didn't find him, sir," Smythe put in. "We spoke to a Howard Williams."

"Howard found me," I said.

Bailey leaned back and said, "Well, what can I do for you?"

"To begin with, what are the charges?"

"Homicide."

"What!"

"You needn't shout, Mr. Brodsky. The charge is murder. We have evidence indicating he killed a man named Martin Kloss."

I could not believe what I was hearing. Kloss murdered? Paul accused? We were in Oxford for an academic meeting to discuss abstract mathematical concepts and to present new ideas about them. Violent crime is simply not part of that world. I stammered something like, "Paul Hobart's not capable of murder."

"I'm sorry, Mr. Brodsky, but we believe he is. The evidence is substantial."

This could not be happening. And yet it was. I recognized that I had to get control of myself, but my mind was racing wildly. He was accusing Paul Hobart, a man I'd known and admired for twenty years.

It suddenly dawned on me that the responsibility of discovering the identity of the real criminal would fall on my shoulders. I took a deep breath and said, "What makes you think Paul's guilty?"

"I really shouldn't say anything, but I realize he's a foreigner in a strange country. . . ."

"Not that strange. We do speak the same language."

"Almost the same language." I grinned slightly, and he continued, "I suppose it won't hurt to explain what happened."

"Please do."

He opened the file in which he'd been writing and picked up a sheet of paper. "We received a telephone call last evening at 9:17. The caller said he'd seen a man dumping a body from a car out along route A40." He looked up at me. "The caller couldn't identify the man, but he'd got the index number of the car. It . . ."

" 'Index number'?"

"I believe it's called *license* number in America," he said. "We determined that the car had been hired."

"Paul's car."

"Yes. We traced it to Hertz, and they said it had been hired by an American named Paul Hobart."

"Didn't you look for the body first?"

"Sergeant Smythe—he's the SOCO on the—"

" 'SOCO'?"

He smiled. "Scenes of crime officer. He does the on-site investigations."

I looked at Smythe. "You were at the scene?"

"Yes," he said. "Two constables joined me to search the area. D.C.I. Bailey . . ."

"'D.C.I'?" I said. "Oh, Detective Chief Inspector."

"Very good, Mr. Brodsky." Bailey said. "He had the index number checked at the same time." Reading from the file, he continued, "At 9:57, Sergeant Smythe called in to say they'd found the body. The man was dead. He'd been shot in the head. We're still looking for the weapon."

"Why did you arrest Paul? You must've had more to go on than a rented car."

"We did. The Hertz people gave us the name of the hotel at which Mr. Hobart was staying. We had no difficulty locating the vehicle."

"You searched the car?"

"Yes." He looked at the file again. "At 12:15 this morning two constables found the vehicle parked on the hotel grounds. They found bloodstains in the boot."

"Did they have a search warrant?"

"It wasn't required under the circumstances."

"It's a little different in the U.S.," I said. "How did you get in?"

"We're experienced at that sort of thing."

"I see. Was the blood Kloss's?"

"We'll know that after the P.M."

"'P.M.'?"

"Postmortem."

"Oh," I said. "Still doesn't seem to me you had enough to make an arrest."

"We did. We spoke to the people at Hertz. They said it was unlikely there'd been bloodstains when the car was taken by Mr. Hobart. They say they're very careful about that sort of thing."

"Maybe Paul cut himself."

"Possibly. We'll know more after the P.M."

"It's still not clear to me why you arrested him."

"The phone call, the body, and the bloodstains made us suspicious. We immediately impounded the vehicle. We checked with the hotel and found Mr. Hobart's room. He wasn't there, so two detectives waited inside."

"He was arrested when he came back to his room?"

"That's correct. At 2:08 this morning."

"Inspector Bailey," I said, "I've had some experience with this sort of thing. You don't have much of a case."

"The investigation has just begun. But we have enough to hold him."

"Let me ask you something, Inspector. I know Paul Hobart very well, and I know he could not have murdered Martin Kloss. It happens that I have a private investigator's license in the States. I realize it has no validity here, but I'd like to try my hand at clearing up this matter."

"I don't think an imitation Sam Spade is likely to clear up anything. Having one American murder another is already a lot more trouble than I'd like to deal with."

"I'm not the Sam Spade type, and I think I can stay out of trouble."

He stared at me, shaking his head. "You Yanks."

"Look at it this way, Inspector. Cooperation is a two-way street. For example, there's an obvious direction for your investigation to take, but you're not likely to know what that direction is. At least not yet."

"And what is that direction, Mr. Brodsky?"

"Like I said, cooperation works both ways."

"I could arrest you for interfering with an official investigation."

"What would you gain by that?"

"It would make me happy."

"But it wouldn't further your investigation."

"No. It wouldn't." He looked at me, then at Smythe. "All right, Mr. Brodsky. But if you turn up any evidence, you tell me what it is. Now, what are you holding back? Let me warn you, this better not be a trick, or I *will* hold you."

"Paul and Kloss, and me for that matter, are all here for the same reason. We're attending a conference at St. Catherine's College."

"A conference?"

"Yes. About two hundred mathematicians are here. The conference runs through Friday."

"And how will this help the investigation?"

"It's virtually certain that whoever did kill Kloss is attending the conference."

"We believe we already know who that is."

"Yeah, sure," I said. "But you're not that certain, and you need a lot more evidence. The place to find it is at the conference. Besides, even if you're right, you need to determine motive."

"Anything else you can tell me?"

"Yes. Kloss came from Texas. There are a number of Texans at the conference. I would concentrate on them."

"I see. I presume that Mr. Hobart is not from Texas."

"I'm glad we're beginning to understand each other."

"Do you know if any of these Texans were at odds with Mr. Kloss?"

"I don't know them that well, but most people didn't like him very much." Realizing that the police would soon learn about the purloined paper, I added, "There was some animosity between Paul and Kloss, and it's my guess that someone used that to frame Paul."

"Unless Mr. Hobart committed the crime, and this animosity was his motive."

"Not likely, Inspector. Their dispute is fifteen years old."

He looked at me awhile and said, "Mr. Brodsky, I expect you to share any evidence you uncover."

"No problem. May I see Paul?"

He sat back. "Why not?" He picked up the phone. "Burke. Mr. Brodsky would like to speak with Mr. Hobart. . . . That's right." He hung up and said to me, "You can see him in an interrogation room. Sergeant Burke will be present during your discussion."

"Inspector, I've been cooperative and will continue to be so. But Paul Hobart is my client. I need to speak with him alone."

"You're very persuasive, Mr. Brodsky," he said, smiling. "Sergeant Smythe will show you where to go."

I thanked him and followed Smythe. He led me downstairs to a small, windowless room with a table and several chairs; there was a single overhead light. A police sergeant entered shortly with Paul in tow.

Paul smiled weakly when he saw me. He looked haggard, not surprising under the circumstances, and appeared to have been up all night, which was probably the case.

"You okay?" I said.

"I'm fine. Have you seen Kathy?"

"No. I came straight here."

"Tell her I'm okay and not to worry."

"I will." I looked at Smythe, who nodded and whispered to Burke; they left together. I said to Paul, "How the hell did you get into this mess?"

"I have no idea. They were waiting for me when I got back to my room last night."

I sat back and sighed. "This is unbelievable."

"You don't have to tell me. What do we do?"

"First we see if we can get you out of here. Did you ask about bail?"

"Didn't think about it."

"What, you like it here?"

He put his head in his hands and rubbed them along his forehead and over his eyes. "I've been sort of stunned . . . not thinking . . . about anything."

"Paul, I know it's difficult, but try to pull yourself together."

He closed his eyes, took a deep breath, and exhaled slowly. "I'll be okay. How do I prove I'm innocent?"

"I guess that's my job."

"Your . . . Oh, of course. How do you get started?"

"With whatever facts we have. Kloss must have been killed when you were having car trouble, so tell me everything that happened last night from the time you left the conference to the time you got to the game."

"Cal Barnett asked me to meet him for dinner. He said he didn't want things to get out of hand between me and Kloss, so he wanted to talk to me. I mentioned that I was playing in the game. He said that he was going to play, too, and that he'd make reservations for six o'clock. That'd give us plenty of time to talk and to get to the game. So I said okay."

"Where did you eat?"

"Le Tricolor. A French place, maybe ten miles west of Oxford."

"Out the A40?" He nodded, and I said, "When did you arrive?"

"At six. Cal showed up five minutes later."

"You didn't go together?"

"No. We met there."

"What'd you talk about?"

"He said he understood how I felt and apologized for his part in it, saying he hadn't known they'd used my ideas."

"What'd you say to that?"

"I never thought Cal was responsible."

"Why not? That was Barnett's best paper. By a lot."

"Maybe, but he wasn't there when I talked to Rothenberg about it. And he never struck me as the sort to steal someone else's work. Besides, he did okay on his own. He didn't need it."

"Still, it was his best paper. But yeah, everyone seems to like him. What else did you talk about?"

"He asked me to let it go. He said that Kloss had gotten the message, and enough was enough. Something like that. I said fine."

"Doesn't sound like you discussed it very much."

"No. He seemed satisfied. We mostly talked about cars."

"Cars?"

"Yeah. Cal's a car buff. He owns four of 'em."

"Never knew that," I said. "Did you discuss Kloss any more?"

"Not much. Cal said he'd already talked to him, and Kloss had agreed to be civil during the conference if I'd be."

"Did he happen to mention what Kloss did for dinner?"

"I think he went out with Barry Donardy."

"Maybe Barry knows something," I said. "What time did you leave the restaurant?"

"Around seven-thirty."

"That's when the car broke down?"

"Yeah. After driving for five or ten minutes, I

smelled gas. I stopped and looked under the hood. There was a leak in the fuel line."

"So what'd you do?"

"There were no tools in the car. I walked until I found a gas station. They had the right tubing and lent me some wrenches and a screwdriver. I was able to replace the line. Then I returned the tools and drove to the hotel."

"What did you do with the broken tubing?"

"Threw it away. Does it make any difference?"

"It would help to prove that your car had broken down."

"The guy who sold me the tubing will probably remember me."

"That's not enough. You could have been trying to set up an alibi."

"Would it be that different with the broken tubing?"

I sighed and shook my head. "No, I guess not. I don't know what to say, Paul. You know they found bloodstains in the back of our car?"

"They didn't tell me. Was it Kloss's?"

"They don't know yet. If it is, we've got problems."

"Not necessarily, Dan."

"What do you mean?"

"Kloss has never been near the car. If it's his blood, we know someone's trying to frame me."

"That's true, isn't it? That might help, too. But it still gives the police a strong case."

He smiled. "But nothing Dan Brodsky can't handle. Where do we go from here?"

"Socratic dialogue. If the bloodstain is not from Kloss, they have no case. If it is . . ."

"We're in deep shit."

"How can you make jokes at a time like this?"

"False bravado. If you want to know the truth, I've never been so scared in my life."

"I can imagine. But we'll get you off. I do believe that."

"I wish I had your confidence, Dan. What do we do if the bloodstains are Kloss's?"

"We ask the question: Why make you the patsy?"

"I don't know."

"There are essentially two possibilities; convenience or grudge. If it's a grudge, the killer is someone who didn't like either you or Kloss."

"Nobody liked Kloss."

"Maybe. But someone killed him. And since we're assuming that you were intentionally framed, it had to be carefully planned. Kloss wasn't murdered simply because he offended someone."

"So who wanted to get rid of me and Kloss?"

"That, my friend, is the sixty-four-dollar question. But there is one obvious answer."

"Yes?"

"Cal Barnett."

"That doesn't make sense, Dan. He got along with Kloss. And I don't think he has anything against me."

"Maybe. But how's this sound? Kloss showed your result to Cal fifteen years ago. Arthur Rothenberg would never have let them get away with publishing it, but he died. So Barnett and Kloss publish it. Maybe stealing your stuff was even Barnett's idea."

"But how does that lead to murder?"

"Suppose Kloss didn't really want to do it, but Barnett talked him into it. Then your little drama yesterday set him off. He tells Barnett that he's going to tell you everything. So Barnett decides to kill him. He takes you out to dinner to set you up. It all fits."

74

"Maybe, but I don't think so. Did you find out when the murder took place?"

"No, but the body was apparently dumped around nine."

"Then Cal couldn't have done it: You're his alibi."

"The poker game."

"Yes. What other suspects do we have?"

"No matter who did it, Paul, you were a convenient patsy. The killer was most likely someone who knew Kloss well enough to want to get rid of him. That makes it likely that he—"

"Or she."

"What does that mean?"

"Nothing special except that it could have been a woman."

"Paul, I know you well enough to know when you've got something on your mind."

"The events of fifteen years ago may well play a role in all this. That includes Arthur Rothenberg."

"So?" I wasn't at all sure I liked what he was leading up to.

"Suppose Kloss killed Rothenberg. That paper did get him tenure, after all. If so, the motive for killing Kloss could have been revenge."

"You mean Eileen."

He shrugged. "Anything's possible."

"But not Eileen," I said. "For one thing, Rothenberg's death was investigated by the police and turned out to be an accident. And even if she did kill Kloss, she would never have framed you."

"You're probably right. But you can never be that sure of anyone."

"Does that include you?"

He smiled. "I guess I'd better not say, 'You know me better than that.'"

"I guess not. Am I a suspect, too?"

"No. You have an alibi."

"Maybe I sneaked out in the middle of the game."

"Not enough time. You'd need at least an hour, probably a lot more. In fact, the only conferees who aren't suspects are the poker players."

"At least those who were there on time."

"Yes," he said. "But that still leaves close to two hundred suspects."

"True, but I think we can concentrate on the Texans. Especially anyone who was in Austin fifteen years ago."

"I hate to say this, Dan, but that does include Eileen."

Sergeant Smythe reappeared and said, "Mr. Brodsky. D.C.I. Bailey would like to speak with you."

I stood up and said to Paul, "I'll look after Kathy."

"If she lets you."

I followed Smythe upstairs. When I entered his office, Detective Chief Inspector Bailey said, "Mr. Brodsky, we have a preliminary autopsy report. The blood in Mr. Hobart's car was Mr. Kloss's."

"How can you be sure?"

"The blood type was A negative. Not that rare, but less than ten percent of the population has that type. Mr. Hobart is O positive."

"I see. That's useful to know. It means the killer intended to frame Paul."

"Perhaps. But that's not our interpretation of the evidence."

"I understand. Did you learn anything about the weapon?"

"Yes," he said. "It was a nine-millimeter revolver.

The bullet was in reasonable condition, which means that if we do find the weapon, we will be able to perform ballistics tests."

"Do you know the time of death?"

"We believe it to be approximately nine o'clock last night."

"What about bail?"

"A foreigner accused of murder? Not likely. There will be a bail hearing at ten tomorrow morning."

"Do you object to his daughter coming to visit him?"

"He has a daughter here in Oxford?"

"She came with us."

"I see. I'm sure we can arrange something."

"Thank you. Paul'll appreciate that."

"One other thing, Mr. Brodsky. We will want to interview each person at this conference. What we'd like to do is address the entire group."

"I'm sure that can be arranged." I looked at my watch; it was almost twelve-thirty. "If we go over there now, they'll all be together eating lunch."

∫ 8

Detective Chief Inspector Bailey drove me to St. Catherine's while Sergeant Smythe assembled the team that would interview the conferees. It was before one when we arrived. That meant that lunch would last for another thirty minutes, giving us sufficient time to stop at the conference office, which was in the Bernard Sunley Building, and pick up a list of participants before proceeding to the dining hall.

The dining hall had several lounge areas, one of which contained a bar, and a large dining room that was sparsely furnished with twenty long, rectangular tables. I spotted Kathy and Amy eating with Howard when we entered.

I said to Bailey, "I see Paul's daughter. Let me talk to her privately before you address the group."

He nodded and waited by the entranceway. I walked over to Kathy's table, and, before I could speak, she said in her charming English accent, "Daniel, have you seen my father?"

"Yes. He gave me a message for you. Let's get out of here so we can talk. Howard, you and Amy might as well come along, too."

Amy smiled and said, "So mysterious-sounding." She had also perfected her British accent.

I looked around the room as we walked out. A

number of people watched us, but I was unable to ascertain anything from facial expressions.

After we had taken seats in one of the lounges, Kathy said, "What is this mysterious message, Daniel?"

"He asked me to tell you not to worry. I've just seen him and . . ."

"Not to worry about what?"

"He . . . he's been arrested."

"What happened? Is he . . ." She was speaking American.

"Don't worry. He's perfectly okay. I'm sure we'll be able to get him released within a few days."

"Why was he arrested? What's the charge?"

"There's no easy way to say it." I put my hands on her shoulders. "A man was murdered."

"Murder? Oh, Uncle Danny." A tear trickled down her face, and she threw her arms around me.

"Don't worry. We'll get it straightened out. I promise." I squeezed her and patted her back.

Amy was shocked, sitting motionless with her mouth open. Bewildered, Howard simply said, "Who?"

"Kloss."

"Who's that?" Kathy said.

"A mathematician. He and your dad never liked each other."

"Daddy couldn't have done it?"

"Certainly not. But whoever did do it knew they were enemies."

"You mean Daddy was framed?"

"Yes. But it's very difficult to frame someone that perfectly. That's why we can be sure of getting him off." I wished I were as confident as I sounded.

She sat up abruptly. "What can we do?"

I couldn't help smiling. "We'll talk about that later.

Right now I've got to talk to a cop waiting in the dining room."

"You mean the man you came in with?"

"Yes." I turned to Howard. "Stay with the girls. I'll catch you later."

Inspector Bailey was waiting for me and said, "Are we ready?"

"Yes." I went into the dining hall and said in a loud voice, "Could I have your attention please." Some people looked up, others didn't, so I repeated myself, louder, and this time everyone quieted down. It was evident that Kloss's demise had not become general knowledge.

"Most of you know me. For those who don't, my name is Dan Brodsky. I'm sometimes associated with the University of California. With me is Detective Chief Inspector Edmund Bailey of the Serious Crime Squad. He's here because Martin Kloss has been killed."

There was a mixed reaction: Some froze in their seats; some dropped utensils; others asked questions.

"Please, let me finish." I waited until they quieted down again. "Kloss was murdered. Paul Hobart is being held, although the investigation is in its early stages. Inspector Bailey would like to interview each of you. He's got a team coming over here shortly. But it will take a lot of time. I hope you'll all cooperate."

There were a few comments, such as, "What about the conference?" and "How long will it take?"

"It'll take a couple of days to interview everyone. I'd like to suggest that we postpone everything for forty-eight hours."

Several people asked questions that amounted to, "What does that mean?"

"Inspector Bailey has a list of all participants. He'll set up a schedule to interview each of you between now and Thursday morning. Then we can pick up where we left off and go through Sunday."

A number spoke at once, saying, in effect, "We've got to get home," and, "What about airline reservations?"

"Inspector Bailey has assured me that he'll deal with the airlines. He will guarantee that you'll get plane reservations as required. He'll also make arrangements with the hotels."

There were many objections. I held up my hands and said, "Look, I understand your problems. But Martin Kloss was one of us. I think we owe it to him, not to mention to Paul, to do everything we can to help the police determine the killer's identity."

The objections continued. The crime had to be solved while we were still in Oxford, and I wanted as much time as possible. I had suggested the two-day postponement more to get extra time than to save the conference. In order to maximize the pressure to accept my proposal, I said, "Anyone who's unwilling to stay the two extra days is apt to be looked upon suspiciously. Let's put it to a vote."

There was more discussion, but after a few minutes we did vote. Many people felt either an obligation to Paul or a responsibility to Kloss; perhaps others knuckled under the pressure of the threat. Whatever the case, the overwhelming majority voted for the proposal. I took careful note of the dozen or so who voted against it, my assumption being that they were innocent: The guilty party was unlikely to risk drawing attention to himself.

I returned to the lounge after introducing Inspector Bailey to the group. Howard looked up, his expression saying, "What's the story?"

"Kathy, will you be okay?"

"Of course. Dan Brodsky's on the job." Her bravado was unmasked by her language: She was still speaking American.

I smiled and said, "We've agreed to postpone the conference for two days. That should give us enough time to get to the bottom of things." I continued to express a degree of confidence that I hardly felt.

"Amy and I have decided that we want to help with the investigation. We'll do whatever you tell us to."

"I'm sure you'll be a lot of help." (What else could I say?) "But let me talk to Howard first."

"Alone?"

"Yes."

"Why?"

"Kathy, I know you're sixteen—"

"Almost seventeen."

"Almost seventeen," I said. "I know you feel grown up. And you are very mature. But there are certain things—"

"All right. All right. We'll wait outside."

After they left I said, "I don't know Amy that well, but if she's at all like Kathy, there's no way to stop them from snooping around."

He nodded. "Definitely no way. So?"

"Let's at least try to control what they do."

"How?"

"By letting them work for me."

"You're planning to investigate?"

"I have to. We certainly can't count on the police—they think Paul did it."

"Have any ideas?"

"Not realy. My geuss is that someone from Texas is the killer."

"Why? Lots of people didn't like Kloss."

"Two reasons. First, all that's happened apparently

stems from the events of fifteen years ago. Even if there's no relation between Kloss's demise and the theft of Paul's work, the Texans are the ones who dealt with Kloss on a daily basis and are most likely to have hated him enough to want to kill him."

"Do you include the Rice group?"

"I think so."

"Eileen, too?"

I smiled. "No more than you or Paul."

"You know I was in Austin fifteen years ago?"

"Oh, that's right. You got your degree under Arthur Rothenberg. But hadn't you left by then?"

"I was a post doc for three years after finishing."

"So you were still there when Rothenberg died?"

"Yes."

"Well, you've got an alibi. Kathy and Amy. You did spend the evening with them?"

"Yes. I . . . uh . . . took them to dinner. Then to a movie."

"Then back to the hotel?"

"Yeah. We got back about eleven and went straight to bed."

"Did you see anyone else?"

"No. Not even at dinner."

"You're a big help."

"What did you expect us to do? Follow the killer?"

"That would've been useful."

He ignored me and said, "Any suspects besides the Texans?"

"Just about everybody."

"Maybe we should look at it the other way around. Who *isn't* a suspect?"

"I imagine a lot of people have solid alibis, but at this point the poker players are the only ones who—"

"Wait a second, Dan. Didn't Paul play last night?"

"Yes. But he didn't show up until after ten. Car trouble."

"Great timing. And convenient for the murderer."

"A little too convenient. That's why I'm convinced Paul was framed."

"Where do we go from here?"

"We get to work," I said. "You should go inside. The police want to interview everyone. I'll talk to Kathy and Amy."

The girls were outside, talking. They stopped as soon as they saw me, as if they didn't want me to hear what they were saying. I wondered if Kathy wanted me to "catch them" whispering to prove that she and Amy could have secrets, too.

I said, "Got any ideas?"

"No. Just girl talk. We were waiting for you."

"Kathy, are you sure it wouldn't be a good idea to leave the investigating to me? That is supposed to be my job."

"I know. But we want to help. He *is* my father."

"And my friend," I said, "I assure you, I'm going to do everything I can—"

"And so will I."

"Me, too," Amy said.

I wasn't terribly thrilled with the idea of two sixteen-year-old girls poking their noses where they didn't belong, but what could I do? I said, "All right, maybe you can do something."

"What?"

"It's my guess that the real culprit is one of the Texans. They all know me, but none of them know you. I'd like you to follow Ross White. If you're careful, you can find him from his name tag. But don't let him see you. Take notes on everywhere he goes and everyone he meets. But be careful. Make sure he doesn't spot you."

"Maybe he saw us today?" Amy said.

"Even if he did, he probably won't remember you. Why're you here, anyway?"

"When we got back last night," Kathy said, "I stopped at Daddy's room. He wasn't there. Still playing cards, I figured. Then he didn't come down for breakfast, and I didn't want to wake him, so Howard suggested we come to the conference."

"What time did you get back last night?"

"The movie got out at eleven. We went straight to the hotel."

"Did you have a good time?"

"Uh-huh. Supper was good, and so was the movie."

"It was one of those British farces," Amy said. "Very funny. Daddy should have come with us. He'd've liked it."

"Howard didn't go to the movie with you?"

"No. He said he didn't feel like seeing it and would wander around Oxford."

A voice behind me said, "Professor Brodsky." It was Steve Vadney. I turned, and he added, "This wasn't quite what I was expecting from the conference."

"No."

"Do they really think Professor Hobart did it?"

"Yes."

"But you don't."

"No chance," I said.

"I heard someone say you were a private investigator. Is that true?"

"Yes. Paul's innocent, but I'm not at all sure the police will do anything. That seems to leave me."

"Is there anything I can do to help?"

I looked at him and thought, Not another one. Of course, it was possible that Kathy and Amy would turn up something useful, and I had promised to introduce Kathy to Steve. I said, "Maybe there is. There's a man at the conference named Barry Donardy. He probably hasn't noticed you. What you can do is follow him. Take note of everywhere he goes and everyone he meets."

"Is he a suspect?"

"Only to the extent that he comes from Texas. But that's all we've got to go on at the moment."

"How will I recognize him?"

"Look for his name tag. But be discreet."

I introduced Steve to the girls and told him to be sure to maintain contact with Kathy. My explanation was that she was Paul's daughter and would stay in touch with me; my motives, however, were somewhat different.

I went back to the dining room; conferees were still making appointments to be interviewed by the local constabulary. I looked for Terry Henkler, hoping that, as an Oxford mathematician, he would be able to suggest an attorney for Paul.

"I know just the man," he said after I'd found him and made my request. "Sir Reginald Wellingham, Q.C."

"'Q.C.'?"

"Queen's Counsel. He's retired now and lives in Oxford. He's a wonderful old man and a brilliant barrister."

"Paul's bail hearing's in the morning. Do you think—"

"I'll call him this evening."

∫ 9

There were two hundred possible suspects. My intuition was that Paul's little melodrama during Kloss's talk precipitated the sequence of events that led to the murder, whatever that sequence was; that the purloined paper was intimately tied up with the whole affair; and therefore that the best suspects were currently from Texas or had been there fifteen years ago. If my assumption that the killer was a Texan were erroneous, there was little chance of my discovering his or her identity. But I saw no alternative: Given the time constraints (after all, there wasn't much hope of solving the crime after the conferees left Oxford), it was necessary to limit the number of suspects as much as possible.

For many reasons, not the least of which was to satisfy myself of her innocence, I elected to begin the investigation with Eileen. After she made an appointment to be interviewed by Detective Chief Inspector Bailey and his men, we walked to a coffee shop on Banbury, a mile north of St. Cats.

Eileen was in a state of shock. Her hands were clenched, her face was white, and she did not speak during the twenty-minute walk to the café. After we were sitting in a booth and sipping surprisingly good cups of espresso, the color slowly returned to her face.

She looked at me, bewildered, and said, "I can't believe all this has happened."

"It has."

We lapsed into silence again. After a while I said, "Paul's in trouble."

She managed a smile, which widened when she said, "Not with Dan Brodsky on his side."

"I wish it were that easy."

"C'mon. You're the super dick."

"My being a detective isn't that funny."

"Did I hurt poor Danny's feelings?"

"Eileen, Paul happens to be a good friend. I wish you'd take this seriously."

"I do. But you must realize that your being a private eye is ridiculous. You're supposed to be a mathematician."

"Find me a job, and I'll be a mathematician."

"You love that line, don't you? But I know it's hogwash even if you don't."

"What's that supposed to mean?"

"It means that you could get a job if you wanted one. We'd hire you."

"We've talked about that, and you don't really want me to come to Rice."

"I never said that."

"But you meant it. You're not about to break up with Bob. At best, my being down there would be awkward."

"Even if that's true, there are lots of jobs for mathematicians these days. Maybe ten years ago it was hard to find the kind of position you want, but not now."

"It's not that easy if you consider location."

"Of course it's tough if you refuse to move out of the Bay Area. What do you expect if you limit yourself to

Berkeley and Stanford? If you want to know the truth, I think you like being a gumshoe."

"Are we through psychoanalyzing me?"

"Almost. Why do you object to my understanding you?"

"I don't. You happen to be wrong, that's all. I do like my life. And the life-style I've become accustomed to. But I still want an academic job."

"Danny, if you were honest with yourself, you'd realize that's exactly what I've been saying."

"As you wish. Not to change the subject, but as long as I am a detective, let me do some detecting."

"As you wish."

"Eileen, my dear, you're pushing your luck."

"Not with you. Never. But go ahead, detect."

"My assumption is that the culprit is either currently from Texas or was there when your father died. I want to find out as much as I can about anyone in that category. Let's start with Kloss."

"What do you want to know?"

"Everything."

"Okay. First and foremost, he was not the ogre everyone made him out to be."

"No?"

"No. He wasn't. Yes, he was arrogant. Yes, he could be very unpleasant. But there was more to him than that."

"Such as?"

"Oh, Danny, come on. You sound as if you thought he was a devil."

"Tell me about his good points."

"You can't measure a person that way. You can't give him good marks and bad marks and add them up."

"Sure, and I didn't know Kloss that well. But I've

met him often enough to be happy I didn't know him any better."

"Most people felt that way. I didn't particularly enjoy his company, either. But there was a tender side to him, too. A real sensitivity."

"In all honesty, I find that hard to believe."

"Because you didn't know him. A couple of weeks after my father died, they held a memorial on campus. The Arthur Rothenberg Chair in Mathematics was established. A lot of people spoke. Colleagues, former students, administrators. They talked about how much he had contributed to mathematics and to the university. His students extolled him."

"Kloss was one of the speakers?"

"No. But after the memorial, he came up to me and said, 'I know you never liked me very much, but I understand how much Arthur meant to you. They said a lot of nice things about him in there, and they were all true. But they left out how important his family was to him. Especially you. I know how much you'll miss him.'

"It wasn't simply what he said. There was real feeling. He touched me more than anything said during the memorial." Her words and tone of voice completely belied my impressions of Martin Kloss. She continued, "What nobody understood was how much he hurt inside, how lonely he was."

"In what way?"

"He wasn't the most pleasant-looking man, and he had lots of emotional problems. He never had friends when he was a kid. He was always the butt of jokes, always lonely."

"He told you that?"

"No. On top of all his obvious problems, he was gay. It was a lot harder to be a homosexual twenty years ago than it is now. The one friend he did have was his roommate."

"Sexual partner or friend?"

"Both. They'd met in college. Keith—Martin's roommate—was gay, too. Keith wasn't as screwed up as Martin was, but he'd also had it tough."

"Keith told you about Kloss?"

"Yes. There was a department Christmas party before I left Austin, and I met Keith there. Then I ran into him once when I was having lunch, and we spent the afternoon talking."

"That's when he opened up to you?"

"Yes. In fact, I had the feeling that he'd been looking for me."

"Why?"

"He knew that I was the only one in the department who tolerated Martin."

"But why did he seek you out?"

She shrugged. "I'm not sure. Martin was depressed. Keith seemed to think that he needed a friend in the department."

"You?"

She nodded. "Me. He said that Martin trusted me."

I reached out and squeezed her hand. "I can understand why."

She gazed at me with the smile that had broken a thousand hearts. She said, "I sometimes wonder if I should have married Bob."

"Would you have left Texas?"

"Would you have left Berkeley?"

"Who knows?"

"That's not what you said six years ago."

"Maybe," I said. "But you weren't all that sure of what you wanted. Or if you wanted me."

"I was sure, Dan."

"You certainly didn't make that clear to me."

"Would it have made any difference?"

"I don't know. Possibly . . . I wasn't that sure, either."

"That was the real problem," she said. "You wanted me to make a commitment that you weren't willing to make yourself."

"It wasn't that simple. You told me that Bob had proposed, and you'd marry him if I didn't do something. I couldn't just drop everything."

"Danny, I was in love with you. You knew that. How long was I supposed to wait? Until you found a job?"

"What do you want me to say? I'm me."

"Yes. You always will be. . . . That's why I'm still in love with you."

I looked at her, wondering if I hadn't made the biggest mistake of my life six years earlier.

She said, "Nothing to say? A moment to remember: Dan Brodsky speechless."

"Eileen, there's nothing to say. We all make choices, frequently by default. I made a default decision; you made an active one."

"You made a choice; I made a decision."

"That's not fair."

"Maybe not, but it's accurate. You loved Jennifer, not me."

"I did love you, Eileen."

"And Jennifer?"

"She wasn't an issue."

"She was for me."

"It was nothing more than an affair. You were dating Bob. Was that so different?"

"Yes, it was. I wouldn't have dated anyone if you'd asked me not to."

I leaned back and sighed. "We've been over this a hundred times. It never changes; it never does any good."

"No, I guess not. Besides, we have to save Paul, don't we?"

I was ruminating about those choices and didn't hear her words; I merely said, "Yes."

"How?"

"What?"

"How do we save Paul?"

"Oh. Yes." I shook my head. "I wish I knew."

"You're the detective."

"Then let's get back to the problem at hand. Tell me about Cal Barnett."

"You don't really suspect him, do you?"

"I would, but he's got an airtight alibi: me."

"He was in the poker game?"

"Yes. He couldn't have done it."

"Why don't you trust him?"

"I don't know. He always seemed like a con man to me. But I know you like him. Paul trusts him. Everyone does. Except me."

"But he couldn't have done it."

"No. He couldn't."

"Dan, I think you want him to be guilty."

"Maybe. But someone did do it. What about Barry Donardy?"

"You probably know him as well as I do. He's very quiet. He's been hanging on in Austin for almost twenty years. I don't know if he ever expects to finish his degree."

"How does he support himself?"

"He teaches part-time. They always need somebody. The way Berkeley hires you."

"I don't live on what Berkeley pays me."

"He teaches two courses a semester and during the summer. He ekes out a living."

"What kind of relationship did he have with Kloss?"

"I don't know. They seemed to get along well enough when I was in Austin."

"Do you think he blamed Kloss for not letting him finish his Ph.D.?"

"You thinking of Karel de Leeuw?" Karel de Leeuw was a mathematician at Stanford University who was murdered by a student who considered de Leeuw responsible for his not finishing his Ph.D. after seventeen years.

"It had crossed my mind," I said.

"Not Barry. He's too much of a wimp to murder anyone."

"Eileen, you don't think anyone did it."

"I'd like to think that I don't know too many killers."

"I hate to say this, but you do know at least one."

"Does it have to be somebody I know?"

"Most likely. Even if it wasn't someone from Rice or Austin, you do know most of the people at the conference."

"But you think it was somebody from Texas."

"Yes. That's my assumption. In particular, my guess is that the murder is somehow related to the paper Kloss wrote with Cal Barnett."

"So your best suspects are people who were in Austin when my father died?"

"Yes. Do you remember who was there besides Barry and Cal?"

"I was. Am I a suspect?"

I smiled and said, "Do you know you have the cutest Texas accent?"

"You're avoiding the question."

94

"No, you're not a suspect. You could be except for one thing: You would never have framed Paul."

"I'm glad to know I'm innocent."

"So am I. Who else was in Austin?"

"The only other people I can think of are Ross White, Howard Williams, and Terrance Henkler. They were all. . . ."

"I thought Henkler had studied at Cornell?"

"He did. He came to Austin as a post doc to work with my father. Ross and Howard had been his students and stayed around for a couple of years."

"They were also post docs on your father's grant?" She nodded, and I said, "Anyone else?"

"I don't think so. For what it's worth, I doubt that Ross could be a killer. That leaves Howard and Terrance Henkler. I guess you'll vouch for Howard."

"I wish it were so easy: Neither of us are friends with Henkler, so he must be the killer. What can you tell me about Ross White?"

"You wouldn't like him very much. He's very straight, not to mention right-wing. I don't really know him that well."

"You've been in the same department a long time."

"Sure, but it's a big department. I've never been very friendly with him. Not that I have anything against him. I simply never got to know him very well."

"How long's he been at Rice?"

"He got there before I did. I think he spent a couple of years in Chapel Hill after he left Austin. He must have come to Rice ten years ago. . . . You know, Danny, I don't think we're getting very far."

"I didn't really expect to solve it chatting over coffee."

"So what are we doing here?"

"Mostly getting background. Besides, I like having you around."

"Meanwhile, Paul's rotting away in jail."

"Yeah." It was more of a sigh than a response. I was worried about Paul, and it wasn't all that clear how to proceed. None of the Texans was turning into a likely suspect. Ross White was the only one I had never met before the conference, and I didn't know Terrance Henkler very well, but my not knowing them hardly made them good murder suspects. With no better idea than to interview as many people as possible, I suggested that we return to St. Catherine's.

∫ 10

Eileen was emotionally exhausted and returned to her hotel. I gave her a note for Cal Barnett, who was also staying at the Randolf. I wanted to meet with him, and the note asked him to call the Moat House to make an appointment with me. I was physically exhausted and emotionally drained but went back to the dining hall at St. Catherine's. It was surprisingly quiet. Perhaps it was the combination of fatigue and concern for a close friend, but a ghostly silence seemed to have pervaded the place. Detective Chief Inspector Bailey was sitting near the bar with Sergeant Smythe; each was nursing a pint of bitters. Several conferees were milling about the lounges; others were being interviewed by pairs of police officers.

I went to the bar, ordered a half pint of lager, and took a seat with Bailey and Smythe. "Getting anywhere, Inspector?"

"Moving along. Moving along."

"I don't suppose you've found the weapon?"

"No. He probably got rid of it after he committed the crime."

"Whoever 'he' is."

"We think we know the answer to that question, Mr. Brodsky."

"Yes. Have you learned anything from these interviews?"

"We've been able to establish motive."

"You have?"

"Come now, Mr. Brodsky. You must be aware of the dispute between Mr. Hobart and Mr. Kloss."

"Inspector, I mentioned it to you this morning. But Kloss had fights with almost everyone here."

"Open battles? We also know there were death threats made at lunch yesterday."

"That's true, Inspector, but it was Kloss who threatened Paul, not the other way around."

"Perhaps. But we are fully aware that some years ago Mr. Kloss had plagiarized some research done by Mr. Hobart. While I admit to being unfamiliar with procedures at American universities, we do know that this research was of some importance to Mr. Hobart."

"That was fifteen years ago. Paul is now a world-famous mathematician—he's no longer concerned about that kind of recognition."

"That sort of argument may be appropriate in court, Mr. Brodsky, but—"

"I intend to prove you wrong," I said. "Did you learn anything else from the interviews?"

"Not much. You may be interested to know that several people refused to put off leaving England."

"Can't you hold them?"

"Two hundred foreigners? Not very easily."

"Did they tell you why they're leaving?"

"Prior commitments, mostly."

"I suppose it was inevitable there'd be a few. Do you mind giving me their names?"

He looked at me and then at the sergeant. "Smythe, do you have that list?"

"Yes, sir." Smythe shuffled through some papers and handed me one sheet. There were eleven names on the list; Ross White was the only Texan.

"Have you interviewed any of these?"

"Some," Smythe said. "More are being interviewed now."

"What about Ross White?"

"We finished with him at three o'clock."

"Did he have anything useful to say?"

"Mr. Brodsky," Bailey said, "we're happy to cooperate with you. But you're not a member of the Oxford Police Force."

"I understand. And I appreciate the cooperation you've given me." I stood and said, "I guess that means it's time for me to do some legwork."

I called the Moat House to check for messages—there were none. I tried to find Ross White, who was staying at St. Catherine's. He was not in his room, so I slipped a note under his door asking him to meet me that evening.

I arranged to hire a car, since the police were still holding the one that Paul had rented. I also called Howard, who had gone back to the hotel; we agreed to meet there for dinner.

The food at the Moat House was typically British, which is to say, totally uninteresting, but the conversation with Howard was another matter.

"Howard, there's something that needs . . . clarification."

"Yes?"

"You told me that you'd gone to dinner and a movie with the girls last night. They don't remember seeing you at the movie."

"You can't think I killed Kloss?"

"No. But I do want an explanation."

"There's nothing to explain," he said. "You must've

misunderstood me. I didn't mean to give you the impression I'd gone to the movie."

I looked at him, sure that he was lying but unwilling to believe he could be a murderer; I decided to leave it for the moment. "Tell me about Texas."

"What?"

"Texas. You were a post doc when Kloss stole Paul's work."

"So? I don't remember anything. What do you think I can tell you?"

"If I knew, I wouldn't have to ask."

"Well, it's not that obvious to me that what happened back then has anything to do with the murder."

"I can't be sure, but it looks to me as though Paul set things in motion when he walked out on Kloss. If that is what happened, then the events of fifteen years ago must be related."

"Even so, I don't know anything."

"You certainly can tell me about the people who were in Austin then."

"You mean the ones who are at the conference?"

"Certainly. They're my best suspects."

"Let's see if I can remember. Kloss, of course. And Cal. Eileen must have been there, too. She might've still been an undergraduate. I can't think of anyone . . . Oh, Barry Donardy was one of Arthur Rothenberg's students."

"Did Rothenberg have any other students?"

"Oh, sure. He always had a bunch around. Between his students and the post docs on his grant there must've been seven or eight people in the group." He looked off into space. "Those were good years. Arthur was an inspiration." He looked back at me with a wistful smile on his face. "We had a weekly luncheon.

It usually lasted for three hours. If you didn't have something intelligent to say, you felt guilty. Not that he put pressure on you. You just felt a responsibility to him."

"That's consistent with everything I've heard about him. I was impressed the one time I met him, but I was just a kid at the time."

"I was in Austin for six years and got to know him pretty well. God, I felt awful when he died."

"I didn't know you were that close to him."

"He was a very special man. He changed my life. I didn't know what it meant to be committed to mathematics until I met him. I was in the Ph.D. program because I couldn't think of anything better to do. Arthur taught me to love mathematics."

"He died your last year there?"

"Yeah. That was why I left Austin. Shortly before his accident, he asked me if I'd like a regular position there. I jumped at the chance."

"Had you stayed there, you never would have met Anita, and Amy, Ben, and Tom would never have—"

"I met Anita in Austin. In fact, Amy was born there."

"Is that right?"

"Where I was married," he said, "*that* I can remember."

"In any case . . ."

"I didn't mean to sound so sentimental. Santa Barbara's been good to me. But I still miss Arthur."

"You said there was a group of seven or eight hanging around Rothenberg. You mentioned Kloss, Barnett, and . . ."

"I wasn't counting Kloss and Barnett. They were

regular faculty. Still assistant professors, but regular faculty."

"Wasn't Barnett already tenured?"

"Could be. He's older than I am. Does it matter?"

"Possibly. The best work he did, or at least got credit for, was the paper he wrote with Kloss using material stolen from Paul. If he wasn't . . ."

"Dan, there's no chance that Cal knew it was Paul's work. I knew him pretty well when I was in Texas, and he—"

"That's what everyone says."

"You don't like him?"

"It's not that. I don't know him well enough to dislike him. But I don't trust him."

"You're probably jealous."

"Why should I be jealous?"

He leaned back and said, "I hate the taste of leather."

"What?"

"That's my foot you see in my mouth."

I stared at him and then realized what he was saying. "You mean Cal and Eileen had an affair?"

He nodded. "I assumed you knew."

"Was Barnett married?"

"As far as I know, he never has been. That's why I thought you knew. They weren't particularly secretive."

"Except with me, but that's beside the point. Who else was in Rothenberg's group?"

"Let's see. Duane Haber was there, but I think he left before Arthur died."

"Duane's not here anyway, so it doesn't matter. Who else?"

"Terry Henkler. He was a shy kid in those days. We wrote one paper together."

"What kind of relationship did Henkler have with Kloss?"

"I'm not sure, but I don't think they interacted very much. As you well know, Kloss was not an easy man to get along with. Arthur was the only one who tolerated him. Of course, Arthur was special."

"What about Cal? Their now infamous paper was not the only one they wrote together."

"Right. I think they were pretty good friends, even then. But I've never been the gossipy type and didn't know who hated who or who—"

"I get the idea, Howard. You did have some friends?"

"One or two. Cal and I got along. I was friendly with some of the younger faculty and with a couple of graduate students. One was a Danish kid. Hans Nystrom."

"Never heard of him. Is he here?"

"No. He never finished his degree. He was hurt in an accident and went home. Copenhagen. He became some kind of physical therapist."

"Howard, it feels like I'm pulling teeth. Without straining your brain too much, is there anyone else you can remember from those days?"

"I don't think . . ." He snapped his fingers. "Ross White was one of the post docs. We weren't especially friendly. He was kind of cold." He looked at me and quickly added, "Not that I think he's a killer. And no, I don't know what kind of relationship he had with Kloss."

"You've mentioned four post docs. Did Rothenberg have a big enough grant to support that many?"

"Big enough to support three, but we weren't all there at the same time. Duane went to Ann Arbor the year before Henkler arrived."

"So you, White, and Henkler were the post docs when Rothenberg died?"

He nodded. "There're a lot of people who owe Arthur a big debt. He always had students, post docs, and junior faculty around him."

"So the three of you worked closely with him?"

"Yes."

"Then you must have some idea of what he thought of White and Henkler."

"Terry was quiet and easygoing—everybody got along with him. I don't think Arthur liked Ross very much."

"Interesting. I don't know Ross White at all, but nobody seems to like him. Maybe he is a good suspect."

"I doubt it."

"Howard, somebody killed Martin Kloss. That somebody was almost surely a mathematician. One you know. One you're certain can't be a killer. Maybe even one of your friends."

He shook his head in dismay. "Have you ever been told you're a real party pooper?"

"Once or twice."

He leaned forward, staring at me with a big smile on his face. "I can think of one friend that might have done it."

"Wouldn't be a bad guess except I happen to have an airtight alibi: I was playing poker when Kloss got done in."

"What a shame. I guess we'll have to look elsewhere."

"Like Texas."

"Ann Laskey."

"Who?"

"She was one of Arthur's students. She finished her Ph.D. at Oregon."

"I think I know who she is," I said. "She's at Oregon State now?"

He nodded. "I think she was born in Oregon and went home when Arthur died."

"A lot of people left after his death."

"Oh, yeah. He was why we went to Austin in the first place, so there was no reason to stay. The operator theory group pretty much died with Arthur. Within two years Kloss and Barnett were the only ones left."

I looked at my watch; it was after nine. "I gotta go—I'm supposed to meet White. That means you pick up the check." I stood to leave. "By the way, what happened to the girls?"

"You don't want to know." He looked disgusted.

"What now?"

"You remember they went off on their own Sunday night?"

"So?"

"They went to a disco and met someone. They hooked up again with him today and went off somewhere to find the *big clue*. That kid you brought from Berkeley went with them."

"Steve Vadney?"

"He's the one."

"Where did they go?"

"I'm not sure, but they said they wouldn't be back until tomorrow."

"Why didn't you stop them?"

"Believe me, I would've if I could've."

"Howard, that was less than smart. But don't worry. Steve's a sensible kid. They'll be all right."

$\displaystyle\int$ 11

The hotel had taken one message for me. It was from Ross White, saying that I could meet him at ten in the bar in the dining hall. I reached St. Cat's by nine-thirty and went to his room. He was apparently waiting for me—at least he wasn't in his room—so I put my skills with lock picks to the test. I wish I could say that I had finally mastered their use, but, alas, that was not the case. After ten minutes I gave up in disgust. Getting in, however, turned out to be easy: When I tried the handle, I discovered that his door had been open all the time.

It was a small dormitory-style room with a single window, barely furnished with a cot, a desk and chair, a minuscule closet, and a tiny chest of drawers. He had carefully emptied his suitcase into the closet and the chest. He had not brought much with him, so I was able to search the place thoroughly, presumably leaving no trace of my presence, in less than fifteen minutes. I did not find the revolver that would have brought the investigation to a quick and happy conclusion, but there was a letter from Kloss that I discovered in a folder labeled COTCA. The letter was short, the interesting part being, "We can discuss it further at COTCA." It was not at all clear what "it" referred to: perhaps a mathematical question they had been discussing, perhaps something personal, perhaps a motive for murder.

I left the room, hopefully unobserved, and found White in the bar drinking beer with Terrance Henkler.

As soon as he saw me, Henkler said, "I've spoken with Wellingham, and he's on his way to see Paul now."

"Wellingham's the lawyer you know?"

"Barrister. Yes."

"That's good. I'm sure Paul'll feel a lot better after seeing him." I turned to White and said, "Ross, thanks for meeting me."

"My pleasure. Your note sounded urgent."

"The word I used was 'important,' not 'urgent.'" I turned to the bartender and ordered a half pint of lager.

"You were saying, Dan?"

"Why don't we go into one of the lounges. It's quieter."

"And more private?"

"Yes."

"Sounds like I'm not invited," Henkler said.

"No." I was served my beer, and I added, "I wouldn't mind speaking with you later."

"I shall be here."

White and I got comfortable on a sofa in one of the lounges, and he said, "What's up, Dan?"

"I'd like to get as much background on Martin Kloss as possible."

"Someone said you were a private eye. I thought it was a joke."

"No. I . . ."

"You working for Hobart?"

"He's a good friend. And he's innocent."

"The police don't seem to think so."

"What do you think?"

"Me? How should I know?"

"I have no idea," I said. "That's the problem. I have no idea about anything."

"So why ask me?"

"You knew Kloss when you were in Austin."

"Not very well. I was one of Arthur Rothenberg's post doctoral fellows, and I was only there for two years."

"You've never worked with him?"

"Not as such. We've talked about mathematics sometimes, but we've never . . . Do you suspect me?"

"I don't suspect anyone. Not yet. But I do want to talk to everyone from Texas."

"I wouldn't count on getting very far that way."

"Why not?"

"Because I know the people from Texas," he said, "and I can't believe any of them—us—are capable of murder."

"That may be true, but I still think the Texans are the people to start with."

He eyed me suspiciously, very likely assuming that I did consider him to be a suspect, which, of course, I did. He said, "Well, I don't think there's much I can tell you."

"Maybe, but you did know Kloss when you were in Austin."

"I left thirteen years ago."

"I understand. But you must have had contact with him when you were there. And Houston isn't that far from Austin."

"A hundred sixty miles. Texas is a big state."

"Look, Ross, everyone's nervous because of the murder. Even Howard Williams, who's a good friend of mine, was uncomfortable talking to me. But you're no more a suspect than anyone else and have nothing to worry about unless you're guilty."

"Paul Hobart might think differently."

"He was set up."

He raised his eyebrows and his head shot back in surprise. "He was framed?"

"That's right. It was carefully planned."

"It's not possible he's guilty?"

"No. I don't know how well you know Paul, but..."

"Not very well."

"Do you want him to be convicted if he's innocent?"

"Of course not."

"Then ease up and tell me whatever you can."

He gazed at me and then appeared to relax. "Okay. But I doubt if I can help."

"Do your best. Just talk about Kloss."

"There's not much to say. I never liked him very much. I went to Austin to study with Arthur Rothenberg. Not that I knew who he was. One of my professors in college recommended I do my graduate work at Texas because of Arthur."

"If I've got my dates straight, you got there before Kloss did."

He nodded. "Kloss arrived the year I was finishing up. He took the fun out of graduate school."

"You had trouble with him?"

"A lot. He always went out of his way to make it clear that I was a lowly student while he was faculty."

"Anything specific?"

"I got into a fight with him once. It was shortly after he got to Austin."

"What happened?"

"I was in the department commons. I was a TA in a calculus class and met a few of my students there before an exam."

"Didn't you have an office?"

"Yeah, but I shared it with other TAs. I was meeting the kids at noon, and the commons was usually empty then. It wasn't this time. Kloss was there. He insisted that the students were not members of the math department and had no business being there. He stood between me and the blackboard, making it impossible for me to work with them."

"What'd you do?"

"I swore at him. He threatened to throw me out the window." He shook his head, smiling. "It was a fourth-floor window."

"What'd he have against you?"

"I used to wonder. Then I realized he hated everybody. Even Arthur didn't like him."

"When you got your degree you stayed on as a post doc?"

"Right. Though that didn't change my relationship with Kloss. I was still inferior since I wasn't regular faculty."

"I guess you can't win," I said. "Sounds as if you hated him."

"I wouldn't say hate. Dislike, yes." Then he quickly added, "But not enough to kill him."

"Good. That eliminates one possible suspect." I found myself liking White, which surprised me in view of the things that Eileen and Howard had told me. I said, "I understand you're leaving on Friday."

"Saturday morning. My daughter's having a birthday party on Sunday. I want to be there."

"Your presence could make a difference in the investigation."

"Only if I'm guilty." He grinned. "I'm not."

"It could still make a difference."

"How?"

"Because you're a Texan."

He eyed me and said, "You do suspect me." Leaning back and smiling, he added, "I don't mind. I suppose you have to suspect everyone."

"You're no more a suspect than anyone else. I still think it'd be better if you could stay."

He shrugged. "I'll call my wife and we'll see."

"Good. What'd you do for dinner last night?"

"An Indian place downtown. With Terry Henkler. He and I were pretty good friends in Austin."

"Did you see anyone else?"

"No. Not at the restaurant."

"But you did later?"

"I came back here after dinner. There were fifteen or twenty people around."

"What time was that?"

"Oh, maybe nine. I'm not really sure."

We talked awhile longer, but I didn't learn anything useful. He said that since leaving Austin his contact with Kloss had been minimal. In fact, he left me with the impression that he had avoided Kloss over the years. He almost convinced me that he was not a serious suspect until I remembered the letter he had received from Kloss. Before looking for Henkler, I gave White a note for Barry Donardy, who also had a room at St. Cat's, asking for a meeting the next day.

Henkler was in the bar waiting for me. He was the proper Englishman and spoke British English, though the years he had spent in the United States did show up in some of the colloquialisms he used. I was surprised to learn that during his time there he had become interested in American football; I was dismayed to learn that he had become a fan of the Dallas Cowboys. Even worse, he had not learned the pleasures of a well-brewed cup of coffee. Such is life.

He had been unaware that I was investigating Kloss's demise, but he said that he could not believe Paul to be guilty and was prepared to offer whatever assistance he could.

"What makes you think he's innocent?" I said.

"Don't you?"

"Of course. He's a good friend, and I know him well enough to be sure he didn't do it."

"I can't say I know Paul that well, but I don't see him as the type to—"

"What is the type?"

He smiled. "That is the question, isn't it?"

"Yes."

"Why did you want to talk to me?"

"You were in Texas fifteen years ago."

"What does that have to do with it?"

"Not necessarily anything. But you knew Kloss then, and I want to get as much background as possible."

"I see," he said. "I didn't like him very much. Nobody did. He was an unpleasant man."

"I already knew that. Do you remember any of his friends?"

"I didn't know he had any."

"Terry, even Martin Kloss . . ."

"Yes, of course. I never saw him socially except at department parties. But that was fifteen years ago."

"Sure. What about—"

"Now that I think about it, he did get along with Cal Barnett. I don't know if they were friends or not, but Kloss used to hang out in Barnett's office a lot. As you know, they wrote some papers together."

"But you don't know anything about Kloss's personal relationship with Barnett?"

"No."

"What about with Barry Donardy?"

"He was Arthur Rothenberg's student when I was in Austin. He didn't study with Kloss until after Arthur's death."

"So you were both working with Rothenberg at the same time?"

"Yes. Arthur set up a weekly luncheon/seminar for his students and the post docs."

"After every week for a couple of years," I said, "you must've gotten to know everybody in the group pretty well."

"Some. But we mostly talked mathematics. Ross White and Bill Toomey were the ones I was friendliest with." He smiled and added, "Ann Kimberly for a time, too."

"I don't think I know her."

"She's Ann Laskey now."

"Oh, yeah. You were dating her?"

"For a year and a half. Until Arthur died."

"It ended because of his death?"

"Well, not really. It was ending anyway, and we were very upset by the accident. Ann said she couldn't stay any longer and went back to Oregon."

"Have you seen her much over the years?"

"We kept in touch for a while. We're still friends, but our contact now is primarily professional."

We discussed his years in Texas and the people he knew there, but he pretty much repeated the testimony of other witnesses. Some interesting facts did emerge when I asked about the evening of the murder.

"I went to dinner with Ross," he said. "We've been friends over the years, and it was the first opportunity we had to get together."

"What time did you go?"

"We left here on the early side. Five o'clock, I'd say. I was home by eight, so we must've finished dinner around seven-thirty."

The time was striking because White had told me that he had returned to St. Cat's at nine. One of them might have been mistaken, or White might simply have wandered around Oxford, or. . . . I said, "You didn't come back here with Ross?"

"No. I'd told my wife I wouldn't be too late."

"You live here. Of course."

He said with understatement so typically British, "It is convenient." I had momentarily forgotten that he was a member of the Oxford faculty.

I thought there was nothing further to learn from Henkler when he said, "You know Dan, something curious did happen yesterday."

"Yes?"

"I had gone into the lounge to meet Ross. Kloss and Donardy were there. I didn't hear much of what they were saying, but they were obviously arguing. Kloss did say something like, 'Forget it, Barry. Not yet.' He then left and Donardy came up to me."

"What'd he want?"

"He said that he thought he had enough for a dissertation and wanted me to look at his results."

"What'd you say?"

"I had no intention of being caught in the middle," he said. "I told him that Kloss was his advisor and it wasn't my place to evaluate his work."

"That was it?"

"Yes. Ross showed up. Barry asked Ross to meet him later. Then we went to dinner."

"Barry wanted Ross to look at his work?"

"Yes," he said. "But Ross told him the same thing I did."

"They didn't agree to meet later?"

"No. Not then, anyway."

It was after midnight when the desk clerk at the Moat House handed me a message—Barnett had called and would meet me the next morning.

I felt that I was beginning to make some progress; at least there appeared to be some genuine suspects. But I was depressed and emotionally wiped out. Paul was not only a good friend. He had trained me and taught me to be a mathematician. He wasn't that much older than I, and he certainly wasn't the father figure that Arthur Rothenberg appeared to have been to so many of his disciples, but I admired Paul in much the same way that they had admired Rothenberg. I owed him a great deal, and I feared that I would let him down. It didn't make sense—I had been investigating for only one day—but that fear was a constant pressure. Perhaps it was simply exhaustion.

I returned to my room wanting nothing more than a good night's sleep when I discovered a supine figure in my bed: Eileen. She opened her eyes when I turned on the lights and greeted me with the smile I needed so much.

"How'd you get in here?" I said.

"I have my methods."

I undressed, crawled into bed, and hugged her. "You can't know how glad I am to see you."

She ran her fingers through my hair. "What's wrong?"

"Everything."

"Having a problem with the investigation?"

"No. Yes. I don't know."

"Danny, you've just started." She kissed me. "You'll do it. I know you will."

"I wish I had your confidence."

"You're tired. That's all."

"You know, you're very special. You should've married me."

"Probably."

I held her close to me. Then I looked at her and said, "Why didn't you tell me about Barnett?"

"What d'you mean?"

"My investigations have revealed your little fling."

"Where'd you hear that?"

"From Howard."

"I didn't know he was such a gossip."

"He's not," I said. "He made it sound like common knowledge. I assumed you were just hiding it from me."

"No. It's not true. Cal was my advisor. And a friend. But that was it."

"Strange. I'll have to talk to Howard. Maybe you can clarify something else. Was Barnett tenured when your father died?"

"Yes."

"You're certain?"

"Yes. My father told me when Cal was awarded tenure. Anything else you want to know?"

"Lots. But nothing you can tell me."

I reached up and turned off the lights; I was asleep in seconds. I dreamed that I was in a castle, looking for Paul. I was carrying a torch down dark, eerie stone steps. An ethereal Eileen suddenly appeared, floating above me. She said in a monotone, "Proceed to the dungeon if you dare," and disappeared in a puff of smoke.

I reached a landing and came upon a thick, heavy wooden door with a window made of iron bars. I could see Paul inside, tied to a stake. He was guarded by four men, who were wearing black hoods and were piling logs at his feet; he was looking at me, smiling confidently.

I tried to open the door, but it was locked. I grabbed the bars and pulled, but the door wouldn't budge. The men stood and removed their hoods, allowing me to identify them: Cal Barnett, Barry Donardy, Terrance Henkler, and Ross White. Barnett reached through the bars with a hideous grin on his face. He took my torch and slowly moved toward Paul, all the while staring at me with that hideous grin. The others were laughing. When he reached Paul, he put the torch to the wood at Paul's feet, and the flames instantly engulfed him. The men danced around him as I watched helplessly.

I woke up in a cold sweat. Eileen was sleeping quietly beside me. I kissed the back of her head and calmed down a bit. I washed up in the bathroom and watched droplets of water drip down my face in the mirror above the sink. The agony of the nightmare slowly dissipated, but when I climbed back into bed, the sleep I so desperately needed eluded me.

Analyzing Paul's dilemma, I began to understand the source of my depression. I had previously investigated exactly one murder. In that case, I hadn't cared about my client, and the victim had been an evil man. Solving that one was a game whose outcome had no real impact on me (except possibly on my ego). This was different: Paul's life was at stake. The frame was tight, and it appeared that he had little chance unless I could unravel the mystery. I drifted off to an uneasy sleep, the burden of that responsibility weighing heavily upon me.

$\int$ 12

With the possible exception of a jackhammer, a ringing telephone is the most unpleasant sound known to man. I was awakened by its blast again the next morning, the caller a very excited Kathy Hobart.

"Uncle Danny, Uncle Danny—"

"Kathy, take it easy. What's the problem?"

"Colin had this idea and we went to a pub and there was a fight and—"

"Kathy, slow down. Are you all right?"

"I'm okay but there was a fight and Steve tried to help and the police came and—"

"Kathy! Get control of yourself! Where are you?"

"Oh, Uncle Danny. We're in jail."

Please let this be a dream. "In jail!?"

"Yes. We—"

It wasn't. "Was anyone hurt?"

Eileen, who had been lying in bed, sat up abruptly and said, "What's wrong?" At the same time, Kathy said, "No. I mean, not really. Steve has a black eye, and Colin has a bloody nose, and—"

I held my hand up to Eileen and said into the receiver, "Are you and Amy okay?"

"Yes, but—"

"You were arrested?"

"Yes, we—" She was crying.

"Try not to worry, Kathy. I'll take care of it. What're the charges?"

"Disturbing the peace or something. I don't know. I—"

"Doesn't sound too serious. Try to stay calm. I'll come to get you. Are you in the police station on St. Aldate's?"

"No. We're in Liverpool."

"Liverpool? What in god's name are you doing there?"

"I started to tell you. Colin had this idea—"

"Who's Colin?"

"I told you about him. He's the boy with Amy . . ."

"Oh, right," I said. "How did you get to Liverpool? No, don't tell me now. Wait till I get there. And don't worry. I'll take care of everything. Will you be okay until then?"

"I think so."

"Good. Stay as calm as you can, and I'll be there as soon as possible. You can explain what happened then."

"We'll be waiting."

"Who's 'we'? You, Amy, Steve, and this Colin?"

"Yes."

"Which police station?"

"Oh, they told me," she said. "It's the main one. I—"

"All right, don't worry, I'll figure it out. And I'll talk to Howard. He'll want to come with me."

"Will you talk to Daddy?"

"Not until later," I said. "He has enough on his mind already. Try to stay calm, and we'll get there as quickly as we can."

I described the conversation to Eileen as I was dressing. I said, "Do you know where Liverpool is?"

"It's on the west coast of England. It's at least a hundred miles."

"Oh, great. What the hell are they doing there?"

"Dan, maybe I should go. It'll take you the whole day."

"It'll also take you the whole day."

"Yes," she said, "but I'm not investigating a murder."

"Good point. Maybe there's a better way." I called the Oxford police and was put through to Detective Chief Inspector Bailey.

"What can I do for you, Mr. Brodsky?"

"I'm almost embarrassed to ask, Inspector."

"Have you uncovered some evidence that will strengthen our case against Mr. Hobart?"

"No, nothing like that. In fact, I'm beginning to develop a theory. But I'm calling about Paul's daughter."

"Oh, yes. You mentioned her yesterday. Didn't you say she would be by to see her father?"

"I did, but she had her own ideas. She decided to play detective and—"

"Mr. Brodsky, I thought we had an understanding. This is—"

"Believe me, Inspector, I'd've stopped her if I could."

"That doesn't wash. You—"

"Inspector, do you have any children?"

"Yes. They're both grown."

"Do you remember what they were like when they were sixteen?"

He paused. "I see what you mean." I could hear the smile in his voice. He said, "What's she done?"

"I'm not sure, exactly. She has a friend with her."

"From the States?"

"Yes. The daughter of Howard Williams. They apparently met a local kid and got some wild idea. They ended up in Liverpool."

"Liverpool?"

"Yes. Kathy called me. There was a second boy with them. A student of mine, I'm sorry to say. It seems there was some kind of fight in a pub. They all got arrested."

"What a mess! Mr. Brodsky, when I write my memoirs, you're going to be quite prominent." He was obviously amused, which was fortunate: His reaction might have been quite different.

"I hope your account won't be too harsh on me." I was surprised to find myself liking Detective Chief Inspector Edmund Bailey, since my prior experiences with officers of the law, both as a student at Berkeley and as a private investigator in California, had been less than pleasant.

He said, "You'd like me to get her out, I suppose?"

"If you could. It doesn't sound too serious, and she's a good kid. Actually, quite special. I suspect the night in jail has taught her a lesson."

"I imagine so. I'll call Liverpool and find out what happened. But I'm sure it wasn't too serious. Otherwise, they would not have permitted her to make the call herself."

"I'm not sure I understand," I said.

"Normally, the custody sergeant makes all phone calls for prisoners. They probably let her make the call because of her age and because she was an American. But they never would have permitted it had they regarded the charges as serious."

"I'm relieved to hear that."

"Are you in your hotel?"

"Yes."

"I'll get back to you shortly."

"I'll try to find Howard Williams." I glanced at my watch. "If I'm not in my room, try Howard's or ask them to look for us in the dining room. He's probably eating breakfast now."

"All right. Mr. Hobart's daughter's name is Kathy?"

"Right. The others arrested were Amy Williams, Steve Vadney, and Colin Somebody-or-other."

"We'll do our best."

"Thank you, Inspector."

Howard was eating breakfast. He was even more upset than I expected when I described the girls' escapades. He wanted to go straight to Liverpool but agreed to wait until Inspector Bailey called.

Bailey didn't take long, returning my call fifteen minutes later. A hotel clerk found me in the dining room, and I spoke to the Inspector on the phone at the front desk.

"I've learned something of what happened," Bailey began. "I believe we've got things straightened out."

"Very good. What's the story?"

"I didn't get all the details, but the Liverpool police are willing to drop the charges. The children will be arraigned this afternoon. They'll be released at one o'clock."

"Thank you, Inspector. I can't tell you how much I appreciate your efforts."

"All in the line of work, Mr. Brodsky. International relations and all that."

"It's appreciated anyway. Howard Williams wants to go to Liverpool. He'll pick them up."

"That's fine. Make sure he tells them to stay out of trouble."

"I will. Thanks again."

"One more thing, Mr. Brodsky. You may be interested to know that we've found Mr. Kloss's car."

"Where was it?"

"In the parking area at St. Cat's."

"Was it there since Monday or did someone move it?"

"I'm afraid I'm the embarrassed one now. We don't know. Yesterday evening, Sergeant Smythe learned that Mr. Kloss had hired a car. We didn't look for it until this morning. We tried to determine how long it had been there but were unsuccessful."

"I see. Have you checked it for fingerprints?"

"We're doing that now. You may call later if you like."

"Thanks, I will."

Howard, who had been standing next to me during the conversation, said, "They're free?"

"They will be this afternoon."

"Why don't we leave now?"

"You go, Howard. I've got the investigation to worry about. But there's no hurry. They won't be released until one. And I have another question for you."

He stiffened perceptibly. "Yes?"

"Yesterday you told me that Eileen had an affair with Cal Barnett. She denied it."

"You sure she's not . . . uh . . . fibbing?"

"I'm sure. The question is, who did you hear it from?"

"I thought it was general knowledge."

"Even so, Howard, you heard it from someone. Who?"

He frowned and said, "Come to think of it, it was from Cal himself. I had gone to Austin for a couple of

123

days—oh, maybe five years after I went to Santa Barbara. Eileen was Cal's student at the time. I don't remember the exact conversation, but he invited me to play bridge, and I made some stupid comment about bridge being a game for fairies. He got defensive and let it slip that he was involved with Eileen. The way he said it, I didn't think they were trying to hide anything."

"Strange. Well, I know you're anxious to see Amy, so you'd better rent a car. Make sure it's big enough to hold five people."

I checked for messages after Howard left. There was one from Donardy saying that he would be at St. Cat's all morning. Before heading there to meet him, I called Barnett at the Randolf; he agreed to join me for lunch.

Eileen had come down by then, and I finished my breakfast with her; I needed a dose of her presence to prepare for the task ahead of me.

"That's an interesting question."

Paul was speaking. I had wanted to clarify a couple of points with him before meeting Donardy and Barnett. I had telephoned Detective Chief Inspector Bailey from the Moat House, and he continued to be cooperative, saying that Paul would be in an interrogation room by the time I reached the police station. The question I had put to Paul was, "Who knew you were having dinner with Barnett?"

My response to his answer was, "Yes. Whoever framed you had to know you were meeting him."

"He also had to know where we were eating," Paul said.

"True."

"Unfortunately, most of the Texans knew. During afternoon tea on Monday Cal suggested we have dinner. He said he'd found a great French restaurant, which sounded good to me."

"Who heard the conversation?"

"Howard and Terry Henkler for sure—I was talking with them when Cal came up to me. Eileen and Barry Donardy were certainly within earshot." He looked up, frowning.

"Anyone else?"

"I'm trying to remember. There were a couple of women talking near me. One had been a student of Howard's, but I can't think of her name. The other was Ann Laskey. She's at Oregon."

"Oregon State."

"Yeah, somewhere up north."

"Can you think of anyone else?"

"We were standing near the rear door. Bill DeMarco was outside talking with Guy Thompson and somebody I didn't know."

"I'll assume he's innocent."

"I hope you never do mathematics that way."

"Don't worry," I said. "I wouldn't make an assumption like that with anything important."

"Good. I . . . Oh, wait. Kloss was giving me the evil eye. Ross White was talking with him and could've heard Cal." He paused and shrugged. "If there was anyone else, I can't remember or didn't notice."

"You're sure Barnett mentioned the name of the restaurant?"

"Yes. He gave me directions."

"Unfortunately," I said, "he also gave them to the murderer. By the way, why did you go in separate cars?"

"I suggested we go together since we were both playing cards. But he said he first wanted to stop back at his hotel and shower."

"You could've gone with him to his hotel."

"Sure. That's what I said. But he said parking there was a real problem and thought it would be easier if we met at the restaurant."

"What's he been doing with his car if he couldn't park it at the hotel?"

"St. Cat's. The Randolf's walking distance."

"Sounds like the car's more trouble than it's worth."

"Maybe," he said. "In any case, unless I'm missing somebody, it looks like you're right to concentrate on the Texans."

"Looks like. One last question. I want to be sure I have the timing right. When exactly did you leave the restaurant?"

"I think about seven-thirty. We wanted to get back in time for . . . You know, it might've been a little earlier. Cal wanted to go via his hotel. He needed to get some cash."

"How much did he think he needed for the game?"

"I don't think that was his main concern. He only had American money left and wanted to have some pounds with him."

"Did he stick you with the check?"

"No. In fact, he picked it up. They accept plastic money in this part of the world."

I shrugged, leaned back, and sighed. "Have you met your attorney yet?"

"He came by last night. He said he'd come to the bail hearing, which is supposed to take place this morning."

"Is there any chance you can get out of here?"

"He thought so."

126

"I'll be surprised, but let's hope so." I stood to leave. "I have appointments with Donardy and Barnett. You gonna be okay?"

"There's not a whole lot we can do about it for the moment, is there?"

"I'm working on it."

"I know." He smiled. "It's good to know who your friends are. Is Kathy all right?"

"Fine. She'll come by to see you later." I saw no point in telling him about her adventure in Liverpool before she was back in Oxford.

$\int$ 13

Donardy was in the lounge when I arrived at St. Cat's. When he saw me, he said, "I understand you're investigating Martin's murder."

"That's why I'm here."

"You think I did it?" He sounded nervous.

"No. But you studied with Kloss for fifteen years and knew him better than most people."

"So you think I can help?"

As with the other Texans, I asked about the operator theory group in Austin under Arthur Rothenberg's leadership. While he did fill in some minor details, he said nothing that would further the investigation. The discussion about his relationship with Kloss was more revealing.

"What made you choose Kloss as an advisor after Rothenberg died?"

"It wasn't my choice. He asked me if I wanted to work with him."

"He asked you?" I was surprised, since it's unusual and considered unprofessional for a professor to invite a student to study under him. The reason is simple: It's difficult and awkward for the student to say no. Professors sit on committees and judge the student, and such a request puts unfair pressure on him.

"Yes. I hadn't done anything about getting another

advisor, and Martin asked me what my plans were. When I said I didn't know yet, he suggested I work with him."

"How far along were you then?"

"I'd been working with Rothenberg for a couple of years and had some results."

"But not enough for a thesis?"

"I guess not. Martin didn't think so."

"You make it sound as if Rothenberg's opinion had been different."

"He'd said I was close. I'd added a couple of results before his death but never had a chance to show him."

"So you thought you were essentially done when you began working with Kloss?"

"I wasn't that sure of myself. But I thought so. Of course, Martin wanted me to do some work under his guidance, so I was willing to try to get more results. I wasn't in any hurry then."

"What's been holding you up? You must've gotten something in the last fifteen years."

"My support was running out, and I got a job offer from a community college. I didn't think I'd have any trouble finishing while I was working, so I took it."

"But you did have trouble."

"Yes. They had a fifteen-hour teaching load, and I didn't—"

"Fifteen hours?" That means five courses a semester; in most universities the load is at most two courses.

"That's typical of the community colleges."

"Tough if you're trying to do research."

"Yes," he said. "So I quit after three years. I had saved some money and thought I'd finish pretty quickly."

"But things didn't work out the way you planned."

"No. Someone published one of my best results. It was stupid. I could've written a paper but didn't because it was supposed to be part of my thesis."

"So it was back to the old drawing board."

"Yup. I thought about giving it all up," he said, "but I wanted to get my Ph.D."

I couldn't help feeling sorry for him, having almost achieved what he wanted with Arthur Rothenberg and then having to deal with Martin Kloss. "Barry, I don't mean to speak ill of the dead, and I know you must have been friendly with him, but—"

"We weren't friends." There was anger in his voice. "He never helped me. I should've changed advisors a long time ago."

"Why didn't you?"

"It wasn't that easy. I knew he'd be on my committee. I was sure he'd do everything he could to stop me from finishing if I switched."

"He seems to have prevented you from getting your degree anyway."

He nodded. "Before coming here, I had decided that if he didn't accept the results I've got now, I was going to get a new advisor."

"Did you talk about it with him?"

"On the plane. Not about changing. But we looked at what my thesis would be like."

"What'd he say?"

"Nothing. Not on the plane. He said he'd think about it."

"You must've been very frustrated," I said. "Did you talk with him here?"

"Yeah. After Paul Hobart pulled his stunt, it seemed like a good time to do something. I said to him, 'Look, I want to know if you'll approve my thesis.'"

"He said no?"

"Very emphatically. He said we could discuss it more at dinner."

"Which you did?"

"For over an hour. He did say one thing positive. Do you remember that result I was telling you about on Sunday?"

"Sure."

"Martin said that if I could get rid of the extra hypothesis, he might approve my thesis."

"'Might'?"

"Yeah. Might."

"*Might if you got the result.* You must've been mad."

"Boy, was I!" He looked at me sharply. "But that doesn't mean I killed him. I didn't need to. All I had to do was get a new advisor."

"Did you have anyone specific in mind?"

"Cal Barnett. He's the only other person in Austin I could work with without changing fields. I was also thinking of goin' somewhere else. I'm pretty sick of Texas anyway."

"Have you asked Barnett yet?"

"I spoke to him in Austin before we got here, but nothing definite." He smiled. "You interested in taking on a student?"

"Sorry. I'm not really in a position to. Barnett will probably be happy to do it. At least you don't have to worry about Kloss anymore."

I expected some kind of reaction, but he simply said, "No." If he felt anything, it was undetectable to me.

"When do you plan to talk to Barnett?"

"I tried him yesterday. In Austin he said he thought I was pretty close and that getting rid of that hypothesis would do it."

"Have you been getting anywhere?"

He shook his head and stared at me. Then he said, "Ah, you're not gonna try to steal my stuff."

"No."

He smiled. "I've got it! I worked hard on it after dinner with Martin." His smile broadened and he raised his eyebrows. "I've eliminated the hypothesis and generalized the theorem!"

"Sounds great," I said, though I wondered if he really had it, and if he did, whether he had found the proof himself. "Have you discussed it with anyone yet?"

"I tried to find Martin yesterday morning. Before I knew about the murder. I sent Cal a note when I couldn't find him yesterday. But he hasn't said anything to me."

"Maybe things'll still work out for you," I said. "Let me ask you about something else. I'd like to clarify the timing Monday evening. When did you leave for dinner?"

"Oh, about five-thirty."

"Where did you go?"

"I don't remember. I was kinda flustered." He frowned. "It was someplace downtown. On High Street."

"What time did you leave the restaurant?"

"Must've been around seven. He said he had to meet Barnett at seven-thirty."

"Do you know where?"

"No. But he came back here with me and took his car, so it had to be driving distance."

"Anything else you can remember from Monday?"

He shrugged. "No."

A constable was waiting for me outside the dining hall. He told me that Sergeant Smythe was in the parking lot and wanted to speak with me. He was in a police car; a door was open, and I got in.

Smythe began by saying, "Inspector Bailey's asked me to talk to you. He expected you to stop by his office after your meeting with Hobart."

"Sorry, I was in a hurry to meet some people."

"He wants to know what you've uncovered. We did have an agreement, you'll recall."

"Yes. I'm afraid I have nothing to report. All I've got so far is a skeleton of a theory."

"Would you like to fill me in?"

"There's nothing to fill in, Sergeant. I have no evidence that you don't have, and it's premature to accuse anyone."

He gazed at me and said, "Mr. Brodsky, Inspector Bailey will be very upset if you're keeping anything from us."

"I assure you, Sergeant, I'm not. If I find out anything, you'll be the first to know."

"All right. The Inspector seems to trust you."

"It's mutual."

He smiled and nodded. "He's an engaging man."

"And a fine cop, I imagine."

"Yes. He asked me to tell you that we have the lab report on Kloss's car."

"Did you find any fingerprints?"

"The victim's, of course."

"Where?"

He pulled a file from the backseat and glanced at it. "On the dash, in the boot, and on the lid of the boot."

"Not on the steering wheel?"

"No. But that's not surprising. When people drive, they slide their hands along the wheel. The prints get smudged."

"I see. Were there any others?"

He looked at the file. "Two that we have not yet identified." He looked up. "Again, not surprising. There were also prints from a man named Barry Donardy."

"How did you know they were his?"

"We printed everyone at the conference."

"Except me."

He grinned and said, "No exceptions. We got yours when you were at the stationhouse."

"Very professional. Where did you find Donardy's prints?"

He looked at the file again. "On the dash and on the radio. On one of the buttons, to be precise."

"What part of the dash?"

"Excuse me?"

"Where on the dash were his fingerprints? The point is, does the location of the prints indicate that Donardy had driven the car?"

"Very good, Mr. Brodsky. The answer is yes. But that's not surprising, either."

"No?"

"No. We know Donardy traveled with Kloss from the airport. He might well have assisted with the driving."

"Possible," I said. "Did you find any other prints?"

"No."

"Not even Paul Hobart's?"

"No. But I'm afraid that doesn't prove anything. There was no need for Hobart to be in Kloss's car to commit the crime."

"Perhaps," I said. "Except that the car was found at St. Cat's."

134

"We have reason to believe that the car wasn't parked there before the murder."

"Then I have uncovered some evidence. A few minutes ago Donardy told me that after dinner on Monday, Kloss used his car to meet Calvin Barnett."

His face showed no reaction; he merely said, "Have you spoken with Barnett?"

"Not yet. I'm supposed to meet him for lunch."

He glanced at his wristwatch. "It appears that you're late."

"Yes."

I got out of the car, and he said, "Mr. Brodsky, Hobart could easily have driven Kloss's car without leaving fingerprints. He could have worn gloves."

"Possibly. Of course, there is another explanation."

Barnett was sipping a glass of sherry in the dining room of the Randolf Hotel when I arrived; he did not comment on my tardiness, although I was thirty minutes late. We chatted awhile, and he was his usual charming self, smooth and self-confident. I tried to determine what it was that made me so mistrust him. Eileen, Paul, and Howard—all of whose opinions I respected—thought highly of him, personally as well as professionally. I could not put my finger on it, but there was something . . . well, not right about him. Perhaps it was the degree of his self-assuredness: He was the first person I had talked to who did not appear at all nervous about the investigation. No, that wasn't it. Terry Henkler was equally at ease. Maybe, as Eileen had suggested, I did want him to be guilty. But why? And how could he be? *I* was his alibi.

The conversation got interesting when I asked, "What kind of relationship did you have with Kloss?"

"He wasn't an easy man to like, but we got along

okay." He smiled and added, "I was the only one in the department who was willing to tolerate him. I think he considered me his only friend on campus."

"And you. Did you consider him to be a friend?"

He took a deep breath. "No. Not a friend. He wasn't someone I liked in a personal way. Not that I disliked him. But no, he wasn't what I'd call a friend."

"Of course, professionally it was a different matter."

"You mean our joint papers?"

"Yes," I said. "One in particular."

Something seemed to flicker in his eyes. Did it mean anything? Probably not. After all, I had made similar observations with other witnesses.

He said, "You want to know how that paper came about?"

"Certainly. It seems to be at the heart of the matter."

"That I doubt, but I'd be happy to tell you about it."

"Please do."

He shrugged. "Martin showed me a technique he'd been working on for dealing with subnormal operators. He spent most of his time working on subnormal operators after Scott Brown's result. Anyway, I thought about the technique and came up with a couple of ideas. Then we wrote it up. That's about it."

"You didn't know that it originated with Paul?"

"Certainly not," he said, rather vehemently. "I would never have put my name on it if I had even an inkling that it was Paul's work."

"Yeah, that's what I thought. What did you do when you found out?"

"It was at least five years before I heard rumors that Paul had done it first. I asked Martin about it, and he denied that it had come from Paul. I assumed it was gossip and never thought about it again until everything flared up on Monday."

"I was under the impression that their quarrel was pretty well known in the community."

"I don't think so. You may have thought so because you were close to Paul."

"Could be." I remembered that Eileen had been unaware of the dispute. "How did you feel about Paul's little drama on Monday?"

"I hadn't thought about that paper in ten years, but it didn't take long to realize what he was doing."

"I imagine it made you uncomfortable."

"No, not really. I knew it had nothing to do with me. But I was concerned."

"Concerned? About what?"

"The conference. I was afraid that their fight would destroy it."

I didn't believe he cared what happened to the conference, but all I said was, "So what did you do?"

"Martin was upset, so I tried to calm him down. After lunch I talked with him and tried to persuade him to forget about it. He finally said okay, and I said I'd talk with Paul."

"Which you did?"

"Yes. We went to dinner. Paul said he didn't want to disrupt the conference and would forget about it if Kloss did."

"Doesn't sound like you talked about it very much."

"No," Barnett said. "I was satisfied that everything would calm down."

"So what did you talk about?"

"Nothing special." He looked at me as if trying to figure out why I had asked the question, and then added, "We talked about cars."

"Cars?"

"I own a couple of old ones, and Paul seemed interested."

"You know something about classic cars?"

"A little," he said. "Why? D'you have one?"

"Maybe. It's a '52 Studebaker Champion."

"If it's in good enough shape, it should be worth something." He paused again, eyeing me. "You might ask Barry Donardy. He knows a lot more about it than I do."

"I will," I said. "Did you see Kloss after dinner?"

"No. There was no time. I hadn't had a chance to get any English money during the day, so I wanted to stop back at my hotel on the way to the poker game."

"You hadn't agreed to meet him at seven-thirty?"

"Certainly not. I was expecting to go straight to the game after dinner. Look, Dan, I could not have killed him even if I wanted to. I was playing poker when it happened."

"I know. You're not a serious suspect. I just want to tie up all the loose ends."

"Fair enough."

"Getting back to the paper, do you remember if it was written before or after Arthur Rothenberg's death?"

Again something seemed to flicker in his eyes, and again I sensed that he was trying to determine what I was thinking. He said, "I remember it very well. It was a week or so after his accident. I was in my office talking with Barry Donardy about Rothenberg. We were so shocked. Martin came in and showed me his—well, I guess, Paul's—work. Thinking about it was a kind of therapy. It took my mind off what had happened."

"Donardy wasn't involved?"

"No," he said. "Oh, I see what you mean. He was there when Martin showed me the technique."

"Yes."

138

"Well, he never said anything to me."

I was going to ask him more about Barry Donardy, but something clicked and my skeleton of a theory suddenly took shape. I said something to Barnett about getting Paul off, handed him a few quid to cover my lunch, and rushed to the police station.

$\int$ 14

"What a nitwit!"

I had been ushered directly into Detective Chief Inspector Bailey's office when I reached the police station; he greeted me with those words, displaying a degree of emotion that I had not previously seen.

"I presume that reference is not to me."

"No. Paul Hobart has been released on bail by an idiot magistrate." He sighed. "It's not your fault, Mr. Brodsky." He leaned forward and added. "To what do I owe this unexpected visit? I do hope another of your friends has not been arrested."

"No. Quite the contrary. In fact, what I have to tell you may ease your misgivings about Paul's release."

"That would be nice."

"To put it simply, I've solved the case."

Other than slightly raising his eyebrows, he didn't react; he merely said, "You realize that the evidence against Mr. Hobart is rather substantial. We know the motive, and we know he had a fight with Mr. Kloss; he has no alibi, and, of course, we have the car and the bloodstains."

"That can all be explained, Inspector," I said. "As to the fight, it was Kloss who threatened Paul, not the other way around. The lack of alibi and the bloodstains were both part of the frame. All the evidence against Paul can be explained by unveiling the real killer."

"You will enlighten me?"

"Certainly. It was Barry Donardy."

"You do have some facts to support your claim, I presume."

"Yes. I had one big advantage over you in the investigation: I knew Paul was innocent."

"That has yet to be established."

"Perhaps. But for the moment accept the hypothesis that Paul did *not* do it. Certain things then follow. For example, since Paul says that Kloss was never in his car, which we can believe if he's innocent, the only way traces of Kloss's blood could end up in the car would be if Paul was framed."

"That's true," he said. "*If* we make that assumption."

"I believed right from the beginning that the purloined paper was the key. I also believed that the public dispute between Paul and Kloss had set things in motion. What I tried to do was put together a theory that fit those assumptions as well as the established facts."

"From which you came up with Barry Donardy?"

"Yes. Since the murderer disabled Paul's car, it was likely that he was knowledgeable about cars. When I learned that Donardy was, everything fell into place."

"Okay. What's the motive?"

"There was a mathematician named Karel de Leeuw at Stanford University in California. Twenty years ago he was murdered by a student who blamed de Leeuw for preventing him from finishing his Ph.D."

"You think that Mr. Donardy killed Mr. Kloss for the same reason?"

"Essentially. When Donardy first started at the University of Texas, he worked with a man named Arthur Rothenberg. But Rothenberg died, and Donardy became Kloss's student."

"When was that?"

"Fifteen years ago," I said. "Rothenberg's death was convenient for Kloss. Without it, he could never have published Paul's work."

"I'm a bit confused, Mr. Brodsky."

"Rothenberg knew that Paul had done the research."

"I see. Are you implying that Mr. Donardy murdered Mr. Rothenberg as well?"

"No. His death was an accident. However, while I can't prove it, it's likely that Donardy knew that Kloss had stolen the work. What I believe happened was that Donardy tried to force Kloss to allow him to finish his Ph.D. by threatening to expose him."

"Mr. Brodsky, that would seem to be a motive for Mr. Kloss to kill Mr. Donardy."

"It might have been," I said. "However, Paul's melodrama Monday afternoon changed everything. It's my guess that Kloss laughed at him when Donardy tried blackmail."

"Mr. Hobart's actions removed the threat?"

"Pretty much. Everything was out in the open anyway."

"I'm afraid, Mr. Brodsky, that I don't see where this all leads to murder."

"First, Donardy didn't want to work with Kloss but felt that he had no choice. You have to understand, Inspector, as a student, Donardy was afraid to cross Kloss. He thought he'd done enough to earn a Ph.D., but Kloss wouldn't give his approval. Donardy wanted to find a new advisor."

"It's hard to believe that murder was his only alternative."

"It wasn't, but he may have thought it was. You see, if a student has a disagreement with a professor, the professor can have a lot of influence on the student's career." I shrugged and added, "I'm not certain of the motive. He may simply have hated Kloss for preventing him from finishing his Ph.D."

"Do you have any hard evidence, Mr. Brodsky?"

"Yes. First, several witnesses can verify that they argued about whether Kloss should approve Donardy's thesis. Secondly, they had dinner together that evening. Donardy claims that Kloss went to meet Cal Barnett afterward, but that's not very likely. Barnett was on his way to a poker game in my hotel."

"Appears rather thin to me."

"Your lab found Donardy's fingerprints in Kloss's car. Sergeant Smythe said that the location of the prints indicated that he had driven it. I also know that Donardy was aware that Paul and Barnett had dinner together that evening. He knew where they were going, and he knew they were going in separate cars. He had plenty of time to kill Kloss, drive to the restaurant, plant the bloodstains, and sabotage Paul's car. He probably followed Paul from the restaurant and made the anonymous call to the police when the car conked out."

"It is possible that you're correct, Mr. Brodsky. And we will follow up on what you've said. However, I'm not yet convinced and certainly not prepared to drop charges against Mr. Hobart."

"That's reasonable. But you will arrest Donardy?"

"Well, we'll question him."

"I suspect he'll break when you do. Will—"

The phone rang. Bailey picked up the receiver and said, "Yes? . . . Hello, Timothy. . . . Very good. I think that was wise. . . . We will, too. . . . Thank you." He hung up and said, "That was Liverpool. The children

143

were released in the custody of Mr. Williams. Let's hope they cause no more trouble."

"That's a safe bet now that Paul's been exonerated."

"Exonerated? Hardly, Mr. Brodsky. You present a sufficiently compelling case to justify further investigation. But—"

"I understand."

He sat back and sighed. "You're a persuasive man, Mr. Brodsky, and we will interrogate Mr. Donardy. Nonetheless, I'd be a lot happier if Mr. Hobart were still in custody. I do hope I'm not misjudging you."

I hoped so, too. As I explained my case to Bailey, some doubts about Donardy's guilt crept into my mind. Still, my theory seemed to fit the facts. And even if I was wrong, the police investigation would no longer be hampered by the assumption that Paul was guilty.

Having won Bailey's confidence, I decided to push my luck. "Inspector," I said, "perhaps you'd be willing to do me a favor."

"Yes?"

"I'd like to locate a woman who came to England about five years ago."

"Has she got something to do with the Kloss murder?"

"No. Her daughter hired me. She'd been given up for adoption when she was born. She's grown up and would like to meet her biological mother."

"I see. The woman's an American?"

"Yes."

"Do you have any reason to believe she's still here?"

"No. I'm hoping either to find her or to get a clue as to her current whereabouts."

"You realize that for her to be here that long she'd have to have permanent resident status?"

"Actually, I didn't know that."

"It's much like having a green card in the States."

"Where did you learn about green cards, Inspector?"

He shrugged. "American cinema."

I grinned and said, "If your immigration officials keep records, that might facilitate locating her."

"I'm sure they do. I'll check for you. What's her name?"

"May Connors. She was traveling with an Englishman named William Lancaster."

"You'll be at your hotel?"

"Probably. I'll try to find Paul. If not, leave a message and I'll call you."

"I'll get on it right away."

"Once again, Inspector, let me thank you for all your help."

Forty-five minutes later Paul and I were drinking beer in my room at the Moat House. He was pleased to be free, but he was considerably less confident than I that he was off the hook, and he found it hard to believe that Donardy was guilty. He was less pleased when I told him about Kathy and Amy. He wanted to go to Liverpool, but I convinced him that that was pointless since Howard was already driving them back to Oxford.

I described Bailey's reaction to his release, and Paul said, "I'm not surprised. The crown attorney was pretty upset, too."

"How did What's-his-name—your lawyer—do it?"

"Wellingham." A broad grin crossed his face. "He'd tutored the magistrate forty years ago here at Oxford. I think the magistrate was afraid of him."

"What was your bail?"

"It was high," he said. "Terry Henkler put up his house."

"I didn't know you and Terry were such good friends."

"Neither did I."

I was wondering why Henkler had been so generous when the phone rang; it was Inspector Bailey. He told me that Smythe and a constable had gone to St. Catherine's but were unable to locate Barry Donardy.

"You don't suppose he's run away?" I said.

"Not unless you let him know he's a suspect."

"I don't think I did, Inspector, certainly not intentionally. But I couldn't swear to it."

"No matter. We'll find him. We left two officers in his room."

"I'm sure you'll get him, Inspector."

"We will. You'll be interested to know that the immigration people returned my call."

"Did they know anything about May Connors?"

"Yes."

The information from immigration turned out to be exactly what I needed: Some four years earlier an American named May Connors had applied for permanent resident status. The application was approved because she had married an Englishman named William Lancaster. Bailey had perused the London telephone directory and found many William Lancasters, but none at the four-year-old address supplied by immigration.

I was sure that the hotel would have a London phone book and considered making telephone calls to each of the Lancasters listed but decided against it. After four years it was easily possible that none was the man I sought, and very likely that even were I to speak to the right one, he would not want to hear from anyone from the colonies looking for a former porn star.

I apprised Paul of the situation concerning May Connors and called Eileen to tell her that I would be in London for a day or two. She was certain that I was wrong about Donardy when I described the current status of the investigation to her, insisting that he was too much of a wimp to kill anyone. I packed a bag, Paul drove me to the train, and I slept for forty-five minutes during the short ride to Victoria Station.

$\int$ 15

By six o'clock that evening I was settled in a room at the Strand Palace, a large, centrally located hotel on the Strand (where else?) in London. I weighed several alternatives for proceeding with the search for May Connors but wasn't satisfied with any of them. The easiest thing to do would be to call every William Lancaster in the phone book, but, even assuming that he and May Connors were still together, in view of Big Bad Bob Clemenceau's message, I feared that they might run if they learned that an American was looking for them. I considered knocking on the door of each one, but that would be very time-consuming. My choices were limited since I did not have the connections that were available to me back home—indeed, I knew no one.

I was nevertheless feeling confident about the search while sitting in the hotel restaurant after having eaten a rather tasteless dinner. The optimism I felt probably stemmed from the success of the Kloss investigation—certainly the coffee I was sipping, which was not much better than the brew served at St. Cat's, could not have been the source of any good cheer. I wasn't one hundred percent sure of Donardy's guilt, but at least Paul would no longer be the sole suspect, and that was my primary concern. I knew most of the conferees, so I suppose the fact that a friend might have had a hand in Kloss's demise made me shy away from doing the kind of investigation that could have provided a definitive solution to the mystery. In any case, it was now in the hands of the local constabulary, and I fully expected that they would provide proof of Donardy's guilt—very likely in the form of a confession—by the time I returned to Oxford.

The conference would not return to normal, but it would resume, and I wanted to be there. That meant finding May Connors quickly. One idea did occur to me. I was embarrassed to inquire but nonetheless got up the nerve to ask a bellhop where I could find a pornographic movie. His smirk made me feel even more uncomfortable, but he did tell me that there were several in Soho.

England is fairly far north, so in July it doesn't get dark until almost ten o'clock. As a result, although it was close to eight, there was still plenty of daylight, and the walk through Covent Garden and along Charing Cross Road to Soho was a pleasant one.

Down a side street—it was little more than an alley— I saw a man behind a makeshift table constructed from a cardboard box dealing cards to two others. One was short and very slender; the second was taller but equally thin. The red-haired man behind the box was much larger and tougher looking than the other two. He threw three cards, two black aces and a red queen, face down, and the two men tried to pick out the queen. They were betting five and ten pounds at a time, and they were winning regularly. Even when they lost, the queen was always where I expected it to be.

They were playing three-card monte, a game not uncommon to the streets of San Francisco and New York. The two gamblers were surely shills—that was the only explanation for their success. One thing I had learned from watching in the States: The real players *never* win.

After a while the little fellow started talking to me. "I've got this guy's number now. Watch me. It's easy." He bet twenty pounds and picked out the queen. "Let's you and me take him for a big bet. We can go a hundred quid—fifty each. You've been watching him. You know we can take him."

"You're probably right, but I'm not a gambler."

"Ah, c'mon. It's easy."

"I know, but you go ahead."

He shrugged and approached another tourist who had been watching. This man was speaking German with the woman at his side. She was wearing a wedding ring, so I assumed they were married. They were in their twenties and might have been on their honeymoon.

The shill gave the young man the same routine he had given me and then bet twenty pounds and won again. He smiled at the German, who then placed a five-pound note on the box. The shill matched the bet and said, "Me and my buddy here will try you for ten." The dealer threw down the three cards, and the German and the shill agreed on which one was the queen; they certainly picked the card I would have chosen. The German turned it over; it was an ace.

"No, no," the shill said. "You picked the wrong card."

The German looked puzzled, and the dealer said, "Sorry, gents, but you can't win 'em all. Try again?"

The shill said, "Look, all we gotta do is be more careful. We'll get him this time." The German put twenty pounds down, and again the shill matched the bet. The routine was identical, including the shill's claim that the German had picked the wrong card.

150

The woman whispered something and tugged on her husband's arm. He pushed her away and stood there, gazing at the cards. The shill whispered something to him—I couldn't hear what it was—and the German pulled out a fifty-pound note. The shill matched it and said to the dealer, "We're goin' a hundred this time, you bastard, and you're gonna pay off or I'll break your neck." That threat seemed a bit ridiculous in view of the size discrepancy of the two men; the German didn't seem to notice.

The dealer showed the three cards, then threw them down. It appeared as if the queen had to be the middle card, and that was the one they chose. The shill offered to pick the card to play it safe, but the German shook his head and turned over an ace.

The woman pulled on her husband's arm, and, reluctantly, he walked off with her. The shill followed. The woman, in German, and the shill, in English, talked simultaneously to the young man. The one thing I could hear before they were out of earshot was the shill saying, "C'mon, I know we can get 'im."

The maxim about those who don't learn from history being doomed to repeat it came to mind: I could not believe it, but the young man came back with the shill. His wife remained down the block, staring after them; I could only guess what she was thinking.

The young man and the shill each put a fifty on the box, the dealer moved the cards around, and—surprise, surprise—the German turned over an ace. He was livid.

The dealer said, "I guess this ain't your day." He was not smiling, and the German got the message. He walked quietly down the street toward his wife; the dealer and the taller shill closed up shop and disappeared in the opposite direction.

The remaining shill turned to me. "Well, sir, there must be something I can do for you. Perhaps you'd like to see a blue movie? Or maybe a live show?"

It sounded like the kind of lead I was looking for. I said, "What kind of show is it?"

"Well, sir, it's like everything else. You get what you pay for." I didn't respond, and he continued, "We have some absolutely fabulous shows, if you can afford it, and we have some cheaper ones. Even the cheap ones are pretty good, but our better shows you'll never forget."

"What's your best show?"

"Our very best is really something, sir. There are three young ladies. Beautiful ladies. Around twenty years of age. They take you into a bedroom with a king-size bed. They slowly undress each other and start fooling around as if you're not there. After a bit they ask you to tell them if there's anything you'd like to see them do to each other. When they're good and hot, they tell you to take off your clothes and join them." He leaned close to me. "If you're at all like most of their customers, sir, you'll have already taken off your clothes."

"Sounds pretty nice, but how much will it cost?"

"A hundred pounds, sir. That's for all three girls."

"I don't know if I can afford that much."

"Well, sir, it's been a slow night. I could probably get them to do it for eighty."

"That's still kind of high."

"I'll tell you what. You can have the same thing with two girls for fifty pounds."

"Okay," I said. "Let's do it."

I followed him across the street, down an alley, and into an old building. We went up a flight of stairs in what appeared to be an apartment house. He said,

152

"Okay, sir, they're on the next floor. If you give me the fifty pounds, I'll take it up to the girls and arrange everything."

"I'd like to meet them first."

"The girls don't like to do it that way, sir. They're always afraid of coppers, if you know what I mean."

"I understand, but I'd still like to meet them first."

"I don't know, sir. I'll ask them." He went up the stairs and returned in a minute. "You're in luck, sir. The third girl's there, and they'll give you the three-girl show for fifty." He moved close and added, "I think she's kind o' horny, if you know what I mean."

"Let's go, then."

"Well, sir, they want to see the money first. You know how it is. They have to worry about the coppers. But they're gonna give you the time of your life."

"It sounds like a lot of fun," I said, "but I still want to meet them first."

"You're gonna ruin the whole thing, sir. Up in that room are three of the sexiest girls you're ever gonna see. Or not see, if you don't give me the money right away."

"Just like the other fellow couldn't lose in the card game?"

"Cards are a matter of luck, sir."

"I've seen that game played in New York and in San Francisco," I said. "The player never wins."

"Well, sir, you may be right. But that was different. He was a foreigner."

"I sound like an Englishman?"

"Well, no," he said. "But America isn't foreign. We're like cousins. D'ya think I'd cheat my cousin?"

"If there were any girls, you'd let me meet them."

"These girls are here to make a living," he said. "You can be sure they're there."

"I'm not giving you any money until I meet the girls."

"You don't understand, we don't work that way. This is my business. It's—"

"The card game wasn't your business?"

"Nah. I was just helpin' out some friends. This is different."

"So let me talk to the girls."

"I'm afraid, sir, we don't . . ." He stopped in mid-sentence and ran down the stairs.

I called after him, "Hey, wait a minute. At least let me buy you a beer for your trouble." He stopped at the landing below and looked up at me. I said, "You can't win 'em all."

He grinned. "I can always use a pint."

We found a table in a nearby pub, where I learned that his name was Eddie; he didn't tell me his surname. He had lived on the streets of London most of his life. He was a petty thief at ten and was picking pockets by the age of twelve. That career ended abruptly when his hand got caught in the wrong pocket and two fingers were broken. At seventeen he tried pimping but got beat up by a competitor. He then began shilling for Red and Bobby. He said he was twenty-four, but to me he looked ten years older.

An hour later I was still nursing my first beer when Eddie ordered his third. He asked me what I was doing in London.

"I'm looking for a woman."

He smiled. "I've already tried to help you with that."

"No, no. I'm looking for a specific woman. An American. She came here five years ago."

"What d'ya want her for?"

"Her daughter hasn't seen her since she was born and wants to find her."

154

He eyed me suspiciously. "You a copper?"

"Private investigator."

"Nah. You can't be. Who's shillin' who here?"

"It's the truth."

"Then what're you doin' in this part of town?"

"In the States she'd been a prostitute and made some pornographic films. She came here with an Englishman she'd met making one of those films. It'd be worth some money if you could help me find her."

"How much?"

"Twenty quid."

"It'd have to be more like a hundred."

"No way. Maybe thirty."

"Seventy-five."

"Forty."

"Sixty."

"Fifty."

"Deal."

He held out his hand, and I took it. "You get the fifty only if you get me a real lead."

He nodded. "What's 'er name?"

"May Connors. She acted under the name of Heavenly Box. She came to England with a man named William Lancaster. He used the name Billy Bang." I wrote my name and the phone number of the hotel on a napkin and handed it to him.

"What's this?"

"I'm staying at the Strand Palace. You can leave a message for me there."

He got up and said, "Well, I dunno. Come back tomorrow afternoon. If you don't see me on the streets, just ask for Eddie the Finger." He turned and left.

$\int$ 16

I returned to the hotel and crawled into bed at midnight. After the stress and exhaustion of the previous three days, the eleven-hour interlude that followed was peaceful and much needed. In the morning I made coffee in my room (with a potentially long day ahead, there was no way I would start it with the hotel brew), and I was back in Soho by one.

I inquired after Eddie the Finger in the pub he had taken me to. The bartender hadn't seen him but suggested I try a betting parlor behind a small grocery store. Eddie wasn't there, and none of the patrons had seen him, but one thought I might find him in a bookstore two blocks away.

Ye Olde Book Shoppe was a small establishment filled with shelves and tables of used books; there was barely room to walk. The bespectacled, elderly gentleman who greeted me was on a ladder putting books away when I opened the door, in the process ringing a bell that hung from it.

He looked down and said, "How may I be of assistance, sir?" His English was perfect, but there was a trace of a German accent.

"I'm looking for Eddie the Finger."

"You must be the American. Eddie said you might be by and asked me to tell you he'd be here at two o'clock." It was one-thirty.

He climbed down the ladder and turned to me. Holding out his hand, he said, "I'm Heinrich Levin." His sleeve slid back a few inches, revealing numbers tattooed to his wrist.

"Daniel Brodsky." I accepted his hand, but my eyes were on the tattoo.

Seeing my gaze, he said, "Dachau. It is the past."

"But not forgotten."

"No. Not forgotten. You are Jewish? Had you relatives who . . . ?"

"Part Jewish, but I wasn't born until after the war. My grandfather's brother was killed in Auschwitz, and an uncle of mine died in France, but I never knew them."

"It was a terrible time. I was eleven years old when they took my family. My father and mother were killed. My brother, too. I never knew what happened to my sister."

"I may not have experienced the horror directly, but I do know enough to hate."

"Hate is a terrible thing. It eats you up inside."

"Can you forgive?"

"Never. But what punishment can fit the crime?"

The question hung in the air for several seconds. I said, "None."

"But I am being rude. May I offer you coffee?"

"I'd love some."

He made room on a desk and removed some books from a chair, waving me to sit in it. "It will take but a minute." He disappeared behind a curtain and did indeed return in a minute, carrying a tray with cups, cream and sugar, a pot of coffee, and a plate filled with extraordinary-looking pastries.

Filling a cup with his brew, he said, "Cream and sugar?"

"Black."

He raised his eyebrows but simply passed me the cup. I could see why when the black liquid passed my lips: It tasted like mud. It had been sitting for several hours, very likely since breakfast, and probably hadn't been that good to begin with. I managed to say nothing. The pastries were another matter. I bit into a cream filled thing that was fabulous. I finished it in a couple of gulps.

He smiled. "My wife, she knows how to bake. No?"

I nodded. "Absolutely delicious."

"Have another."

I greedily consumed what can best be described as an éclair filled with chocolate mousse. If anything, it was even better than the first one. I thought, How well it would go with the Jamaica Blue Mountain, but said, "You could get rich selling these."

"Not quite rich," he said. "But my wife does sell them. To restaurants."

"That's—"

I was interrupted by the bell on the door; it was Eddie the Finger. Surveying the scene with a large grin on his face, he said, "I see you've been taking good care of my new friend, Hank." Before the shopkeeper could answer, Eddie said to me, "I've got what you want, Danny boy."

"That was fast."

"We aim to please."

"What did you find out?"

"I believe you said something about fifty quid."

"If you delivered."

"Don't worry about that," he said. "I know where you can find this William Lancaster."

"Where?"

"Where's the fifty quid?"

"As I recall our last meeting, you wanted me to pay for something you couldn't deliver."

"That was before we were friends. My friends can trust me—right, Hank?"

Levin said, "Well, yes, I suppose. But then, don't you think you should trust your new friend?"

Eddie looked at him, then at me, then at Levin again. He sighed. "I've found a man who knows Lancaster. He makes blue movies. This Lancaster once worked for him."

"Who's that?" I said.

"I don't think he wants me to tell you who he is. But I can take you to him."

"When?"

"Right now."

I stood and said, "Mr. Levin, I'd like to . . ."

"My friends call me Henry." He glanced at Eddie. "Most of my friends."

"Henry. Let me thank you for your hospitality. And please tell your wife that her pastries are the best."

"I'm glad you enjoyed them."

Eddie said, "Shall we go, mate?"

"Yes." I shook Levin's hand and said, "Once again, Henry, thank you. For your hospitality and, especially, for your wife's masterpieces."

"You are most welcome."

In the street I said, "Eddie, don't misunderstand me, but you and Henry—well, you're something of an odd couple."

"Yeah, that's right. We met in the clink. I'd been picked up by a copper."

"Henry was in jail? He doesn't seem like the criminal type."

159

"They brought him in the next day."

"For what?"

"Bombs."

"Henry can't be a terrorist?"

"No. No. He doesn't like 'em. He was with a crowd. They didn't want us to build the A-bombs."

"Now I see," I said. "You shared a cell?"

"For almost a week. Maggie—that's 'is wife—she'd bring cakes and books. We talked and ate the cakes. He got me to read one. It was written by an American. About a whale."

"*Moby Dick?*"

"You read it?" He sounded surprised.

"Yes."

"A wonderful book," he said. "I read it twice that week."

We had walked several blocks, and I followed him down an alley. He said, "We're to meet a man here. You can trust 'em, but they're the nervous type, if you know what I mean."

"I can probably handle it."

"Well, yeah, I know. But you gotta understand, they won't trust you. They'll drive you to see the man. But they're gonna want to blindfold you."

"You're kidding."

"No. The man doesn't trust you yet."

"Couldn't we have talked on the phone?"

"He wants to know who you are."

"You keep saying the man," I said. "Who is he?"

"I can't tell you. That was the condition of your seeing him."

"He trusts you?"

"Well, sure, Danny. Everybody trusts Eddie the Finger."

The idea of being blindfolded didn't excite me, but I liked Eddie, maybe because of his friend, Heinrich Levin. Well, what was the worst that could happen? They could rob me, I suppose, but I had less than a hundred pounds in cash. There was really no reason to expect any physical violence. After all, what possible motive could they have?

A black saloon pulled up within a few minutes. A large, not very pleasant-looking man got out; the driver didn't thrill me all that much, either.

"Hello, Eddie. This the Yank?"

"Yeah."

The man opened the rear door and said to me, "Get in."

I did. Eddie took the front seat, and the man sat next to me. He removed a red bandanna from his pocket and tied it around my head.

"Is this really necessary?" I said.

No response.

"Either of you ever been to the States?"

No response.

"I hope everybody's having a good time."

No response.

I gave up and we rode in silence. After fifteen minutes of driving through traffic, the car sped up; we were evidently on one of the motorways. Ten minutes later we slowed down, drove a few more blocks, and came to a stop. Someone got out of the car, and then I heard a noise that I interpreted as a garage door opening.

The car moved a few more feet and stopped. The man next to me removed the blindfold and said, "Out."

"You're a great conversationalist," I said.

Eddie and the driver went through a door, and the other man said, "Move." I followed the first two, and he walked behind me. We entered some kind of storeroom, waded past cardboard boxes piled high, went up some stairs, and ended up in a long hallway. The man behind me opened a door and said, "Eddie, wait here." Eddie and the driver went through the door, and the man said to me, "Down the hall, last door on the left." He then followed the other two, closing the door behind him.

A door to my left opened and a woman came out; her apparel consisted of a pair of high-heeled shoes. She smiled and winked at me. "You want some, honey?" She turned and slowly ambled down the hallway, disappearing through a door on the right.

I followed the instructions given to me and found myself in a large office. A middle-aged, portly man in a three-piece suit sat behind a desk, sucking on a pipe. He looked up and sat back when I came in.

"You must be the American."

"Yes. My name's . . ."

"I don't want to know your name. Sit."

I took a chair near the desk. He banged his pipe against his hand, shaking the ashes into a wastebasket, put the pipe down, and leaned forward. "You're looking for William Lancaster?"

"Yes. I—"

"What do you want him for?"

"I'm looking for a woman. She's an American and came here with—"

"And you think I know where they are?"

"Eddie the—"

"No names, please."

"I was told you could help."

"Why should I?"

"Why shouldn't you?"

"I don't know you, and I don't owe you."

"So what am I doing here?"

"If you could do something for me in return, perhaps I might . . ."

"What did you have in mind?"

"Lancaster has something that belongs to me. I want it back."

"Then you do know him."

He shrugged. "True."

"But you don't know where he is, or you wouldn't need me."

"Also true," he said. "It is possible, however, that I possess some knowledge that might be of assistance in your search."

"Just what is it you want me to get for—"

"You don't need to know that. He knows."

"Then what do you expect of me?"

"I want to know where he is."

"I can't promise that. It could conflict with the interests of my client."

"Client?"

"Yes. I was hired to find the woman."

"Who is this client?"

"An American. Nobody who could possibly have anything to do with you."

"I'd still like to know who it is."

"No names, remember. Your rules." He smiled but didn't speak. I said, "Look, if I can find him with information from you, then you could've found him yourself if you'd cared enough."

"You're right, I suppose. The only reason I'm bothering now is that I heard you were looking for him. I'll

163

tell you what. I'll give you what I know if you agree to tell Lancaster I want the object back."

"I have no problem with that," I said. "What do you know about him?"

"He used to work for me. Seven or eight years ago. Then he went off to America."

"That doesn't help a whole lot. I know he returned to England five years ago."

"I have also heard some rumors."

"Would you like to enlighten me?"

"My information was that he got married and bought a fishing boat in Cardiff."

I had no idea where Cardiff was but felt uncomfortable asking him. I said, "When was that?"

"Four, five years ago."

"Was that all you heard?"

"I'm afraid so, but Cardiff's not a very big city."

"Well, if your information is accurate, I may be able to find him." I stood and added, "Thank you."

His only response was a slight nod.

The ride back to Soho included the blindfold and the same stimulating conversation and was generally uneventful.

Walking back to Henry's place after being dropped off, I said, "You have some interesting friends, Eddie."

"They're not my friends. They was the right people."

I nodded and counted out ten five-pound notes. "You've certainly earned this."

"You're bloody right. Thanks, mate."

Henry was in the bookstore when we got there, and the place was no busier than it had been earlier that afternoon. I wondered how he stayed in business but thought better of asking.

164

He greeted us with a warm smile. "Everything went well, I trust?"

"Yes," I said. "Very well."

"Perhaps some coffee?"

"I'd love some," I said, "but I have to get to Cardiff tonight."

"It's a long way. A hundred fifty miles."

"Then I really must be going."

We shook hands, and I said, "You told me before that your wife sells her pastries. May I buy some?"

"Which would you like?"

"Any. All."

He smiled and went through the curtains and returned in a few minutes with a pink box in his arms; he handed it to me. "Be sure you keep them in the Frigidaire," he said.

"What do I owe you?"

He shook his head. "We only sell to restaurants."

$\int$ 17

I was still hoping to get back to the conference the next day, so I returned to the Strand Palace, packed my bags, and made arrangements to rent a car that could be returned in Oxford.

Two problems arose when I stopped at the front desk to check out. First, they insisted that I pay for two nights. Well, what can you do? At least it wouldn't come out of my pocket—it was a legitimate expense that would be charged to the Leopolds. The second was a message from Detective Chief Inspector Bailey asking me to call him. It sounded urgent. Nonetheless, I decided to let him wait until the morning.

Cardiff is a hundred fifty miles west of London, out the M4, one of the motorways. The driving speeds common to that part of the world made it possible for me to be sipping beer in a pub near the docks by eight o'clock.

Looking around the pub, filled mostly with sailors, I felt out of my depth. I didn't have the contacts I had back home, and, while the language may be the same, England is a foreign country. I'd been lucky so far, but when I found no William Lancasters or May Connors listed in the telephone book, I could think of nothing better than spreading the name William Lancaster around the pub.

Good fortune continued to shine: One sailor in a group crowded around a table that said a William Lancaster captained the *Heavenly Vessel,* which docked in Port Talbot, a town some twenty-five miles farther west on the Bristol Channel.

The telephone book in Port Talbot was no more useful than the one in Cardiff. It was after ten by then, so the quest for May Connors would have to wait until the next day. I rang the bell at a house with a sign that read, "Bed and Breakfast." The white-haired woman who greeted me grumbled something about it being "awfully late to be knocking people up," but yes, I could have a room. She was not familiar with the *Heavenly Vessel;* she was quick to point out that the fishing boats generally went to sea at dawn.

The next morning, with nothing under my belt but a cup of Jamaica Blue Mountain and four hours of sleep in a surprisingly comfortable bed, I was on the docks of Port Talbot at the ungodly hour of five o'clock. Locating the *Heavenly Vessel* turned out to be easy, requiring only a single question of the first man I saw.

A short, stocky, bearded man on her deck was doing something with what appeared to me to be a fishing net when I pulled up near the boat. He saw me and said, "'S there anythin' I can do for you, sir?"

"Yes. I'm looking for William Lancaster."

"'E's below. 'Oo should I say's callin'?"

"Dan Brodsky."

He turned, climbed through a door, and, I presume, went below. A few seconds later a tall, athletic-looking man with a ruddy complexion appeared. He said, "I'm Lancaster. You lookin' for me?"

"Yes. I hope so. I'm trying to locate an American woman named May Connors."

He froze and his face turned white. I said, "I assure you I'm the bearer of good tidings. If I find her, she will certainly be very pleased."

His expression did not change. He said, "What do you want her for?"

"She had a daughter eighteen years ago. Her daughter's anxious to meet her."

He gazed at me. Then his expression softened and the color slowly returned to his face. "Joanne." It was almost a whisper.

"Yes."

"She wants to find May?"

"Yes. Believe me, May will be very happy when she meets her."

He mumbled something that sounded like "Hmmf." He then turned and called out, "Arty." The first man's head appeared from below, and Lancaster said, "We won't be goin' out today. Could you tie things down?"

The other man looked puzzled but simply said, "Aye."

Lancaster jumped down from the deck. "May's my wife. We live in Maesteg. Have you a car?"

I pointed to the rental parked behind me. "Shall we go?"

I drove, following his directions. He said, "How did you find us?"

"I spoke to a man named Big Bad Bob Clemenceau in San Francisco. He—"

"Clemenceau?"

The tone in his voice reminded me about Clemenceau's message. "Yes. He asked me to tell you he's not mad anymore. I have no idea what he was talking about."

"'Twas nothin'. When May and I decided to quit, he threatened us. That's why we thought it would be safer to come back here. What'd he tell you?"

"Just that you'd gone back to England."

"Take a right here. That doesn't seem like enough to find us."

"It wasn't. I was lucky when I got to London. I met a man you'd worked for before you went to the States."

"Who was that?"

"He didn't tell me his name. But he also gave me a message . . ."

"Take a left. It's only a couple more miles. Yes?"

"He said something about some object he thinks you stole from him. He wants it back."

He laughed. "I know who he is. His name's Harry Linton. He knew where I was?"

"He'd heard that you were back. He told me you'd bought a fishing boat in Cardiff. It was easy after that."

"Make a right. It's the second house on the left."

"What is it he wants so much?"

"Nothing. You don't want to know. I'll send it to him if I can find it."

We pulled up in front of a charming, very English house surrounded by a white picket fence. We went inside and Lancaster called out, "May."

A female voice answered, "Billy, is there something . . . oh." She had come through a door and stopped when she saw me. I recognized her from the picture I had, though she was older and heavier. A two-year-old boy behind her said, "Daddy," but clung to his mother's skirts.

Lancaster said, "This man is from America. He . . . well, you tell her."

"My name is Dan Brodsky. Your daughter—Joanne—wants to meet you."

Her mouth opened and she inhaled quickly. Tears welled up in her eyes. "My baby?"

The boy at her side sensed the strong emotions and began to cry. She picked him up and hugged him and kissed him. Sobbing softly, he put his head on her shoulder. She said, "Joanne . . . what's she . . . well . . ."

"I'm sure you'll be very proud when you meet her. She's charming, well-spoken, and very nice. You'll like her."

"I've . . . I've wondered about her. I always . . ." The tears burgeoned forth again.

Lancaster moved to her side and put his arm around her and his hand on the boy's back. He said, "Well, this will take some getting used to. Would you like some tea?"

"He's an American, Billy. I'm sure he'd prefer coffee."

"Coffee would be fine."

I followed them into a small kitchen. Something that looked like oatmeal was boiling away on the stove. May said, "Oh, no" and quickly moved the pot to an unlit burner. She smiled at me. "I was cooking Kenny's breakfast. Sit down."

I took a seat at a small table under the one window in the room while Lancaster put young Kenny in a high chair. Kenny said, "Bekfist."

"It's coming, honey," May said. "How did you find me?"

"I met a friend of yours in L.A. She told me about Big Bad Bob—"

"You know about him?"

"Yes."

"So you know . . . about . . . what we did for him?"

"Yes."

"Does Joanne?"

"I don't know. But her parents . . . I mean . . ."

"Does Joanne think they're her parents?"

"Yes. They're a family."

"I'm glad."

"I had to tell the Leopolds about you. They're footing the bill. I really had no choice."

"I understand."

"I don't know if they said anything to Joanne," I said. "But I don't think you should worry about her reaction. She's a mature young woman, and I'm sure she'll understand."

"Does she know you've found me?"

"Not yet. I didn't know until an hour ago."

She put a bowl of oatmeal down across the table from her son. "You can have it soon, honey," she said. "It's too hot now."

"'Ot," the boy said.

She poured coffee for me. "How do you like it?"

"Black." She put the cup down in front of me. I took a sip; it was almost acceptable.

Lancaster said, "Mr. Brodsky. . . ."

"Dan."

"Dan. Call me Bill. What do we do now?"

"You do want to meet her?"

"Oh, yes," May said. "Certainly."

Bill smiled. "Me, too."

"I'll call them, and we'll make some arrangements."

"We have a phone."

I glanced at my watch. It was still only six A.M., which made it ten the previous evening in California.

A few minutes later a familiar female voice answered my ring and said, "Hello."

"Joanne?"

"Yes."

"This is Dan Brodsky. I've . . ."

"You've found her?"

"Yes."

"That's wonderful!"

"I'm at her home right now."

"I . . . What? . . . I . . ."

"Try to keep calm. I know you've waited eighteen years, but . . ."

"Yes, I will. Is she all right? I mean . . . Daddy told me about . . . what she did."

"Don't worry. Everything's fine. She's married to a man named William Lancaster. They live in a small town in western England and have a young son named Kenneth. They're both anxious to meet you."

She didn't say anything, and I could sense the tears running down her face.

Her father picked up the phone. "Dan, you've found her?"

"Yes."

"That's great. Did . . . Hold on—Joanne says there's a twelve-thirty plane tonight. She got a passport as soon as she heard you were going to England and has been studying the airline schedules ever . . . Yeah, all right."

"What?"

"Sorry. I was speaking with Joanne. She's already packing. She wants me to book the flight and call you back."

I gave him the phone number, and twenty minutes later he was saying, "We were able to get reservations.

The plane arrives at Heathrow at 4:25 tomorrow afternoon. That's your time."

"Are you coming, too?"

"No. Joanne wants to go alone. We might join her in a day or two."

"Sounds like a good idea."

"I've got to get her to the airport. But listen, Dan. This is really great."

The Lancasters were pleased, too. I described the conversation to them and agreed to meet Joanne at Heathrow with them.

May served me a beautiful breakfast consisting of fried eggs, sausage and bacon, potatoes, and fried tomatoes. The trimmings included toast, butter, several kinds of cheeses, a variety of jams, and fresh orange juice. I was quite hungry by then and managed to put away most of the large quantity of food that she laid before me.

We chatted for a couple of hours. They told me that they'd met making a film in San Francisco. They both had hated what they'd become and had come to England to escape from that world. They had saved enough money to make a down payment on the boat and had succeeded in making a life for themselves. The name of the boat was a reminder of where they had come from and of all they now had to live for.

We also talked about San Francisco and Berkeley and about the academic world. I was surprised to discover that they had been as upset as I when the Raiders left Oakland for the smoggy south.

We discussed the conference in Oxford, and, naturally, the murder of Martin Kloss. With all that I knew about their background, I did not feel uncomfortable telling them about Eileen. They said that I was crazy not to have married her when I had the chance, and that I should run away with her now.

When the old windup clock on the wall struck nine bells, I remembered the message from Detective Chief Inspector Bailey. I called the Oxford Police Department with some trepidation and was quickly put through to Bailey by the constable who answered.

"Mr. Brodsky," Bailey began. He sounded exasperated. "I do believe you mean well, but you have caused me more trouble. . . ."

"What's the problem, Inspector?"

"Don't you know?"

"No."

"Barry Donardy has been murdered."

"What!"

"That is correct, Mr. Brodsky. Mr. Donardy was killed by the same weapon that was used on Mr. Kloss."

"I'm afraid to ask, but do you have any suspects?"

"Yes. He's in custody again."

"Paul."

"Yes."

"Inspector, I know this won't mean much to you now, but I am certain that Paul Hobart is innocent."

"We believe otherwise."

"I don't suppose you'd like to tell me on what evidence you base that conclusion."

"Personally, I like you, Mr. Brodsky. I believe you're sincere, and I know you want to assist your friend. But under the circumstances, it would be highly inappropriate to discuss the evidence."

"I'm not sure I understand, Inspector. I've given you everything I've uncovered."

"No, you don't understand," he said. "If Mr. Hobart hadn't been released, Mr. Donardy would still be alive."

"You're assuming that Paul's guilty. I—"

"No, no, no!" I was a bit taken aback by the degree of his anger. "Even if Hobart is innocent, it's unlikely the murderer would have acted again had he still been in jail." He paused, calming himself down. "We do have some experience in this sort of investigation, Mr. Brodsky. Had Mr. Hobart remained in our custody, in our own plodding way we would have eventually discovered the truth. Whether or not he is innocent, the second murder would never have been committed. I am sorry to say this, but you must take some responsibility for Mr. Donardy's death."

His words hit me like the proverbial ton of bricks. He was right: Donardy would most likely still be alive had I simply done nothing. Without much conviction I said, "You're wrong, Inspector. I hope you won't be too upset if I continue investigating."

"Would you listen to me if I asked you not to?"

"No."

"I presume you'll be returning to Oxford."

"Yes. I'll be there in two or three hours. I'll come straight to the police station."

"There's nothing you can do here."

"I'd like to see Paul."

"Only his solicitor or family will be permitted to see him."

"I see."

"Good-bye, Mr. Brodsky." He hung up.

The Lancasters had heard my half of the conversation, and Bill said, "Is something wrong?"

"Yes." I explained briefly and then added, "I've got to get to Oxford as soon as possible."

"Does this mean you won't be able to meet Joanne with us?" May asked.

"Damn it, I'd forgotten about that." I looked at my watch. "I'll be there. One way or another, I'll be there."

∫ 18

Panic set in. It had one positive side effect: My foot was on the floor the entire trip, and I drove to Oxford in record time. I was barely aware that I was behind the wheel; my thoughts were on Paul and on Barry Donardy. I tried to convince myself that a madman was on the loose and that I could not be blamed, but Bailey was most likely correct when he said that the murderer would not have killed a second time had Paul remained in jail. It was possible that Donardy would have died anyway—the perpetrator may have had to act to protect himself. But in that case, Paul would now be off the hook instead of in deeper trouble than ever.

It was still before noon when I knocked on the door of the brick building that was the home of Sir Reginald Wellingham, Queen's Counsel, in Oxford. A middle-aged man answered and said, "May I help you, sir?"

"I'd like to speak with Sir Reginald Wellingham."

"Who should I say is calling, sir?"

"Daniel Brodsky."

"Please come in." He ushered me into a room that appeared to me to be a traditional English parlor, at least if the movies I'd seen were accurate. "Please wait here." He returned shortly and said, "Sir Reginald will see you in the library."

I followed him into a large room with sufficient

books to justify his description. A portly, distinguished-looking man in his seventies was seated in a leather chair with an open book in his lap. He gave me a friendly smile and said, "I suppose there's no need to ask the purpose of your visit."

"No."

"Sit down. Would you like some tea? Perhaps something a bit stronger?"

"Coffee would be fine."

"Barclay, coffee for the gentleman and brandy for me."

"Very good, sir."

"It would appear," Wellingham began after Barclay had made his exit, "that we have done our client a disservice."

"You mean by getting him bailed out?"

"Exactly."

Barclay returned with Wellingham's brandy and my coffee. I don't know about the brandy, but the coffee was not very good. I did have the sense not to suggest using the Jamaica Blue Mountain, probably because my supply was dwindling rapidly.

Barclay departed to do whatever it is that butlers do when they're not serving their masters, and I said, "Have you seen Paul since he was arrested again? The police won't let me see him."

"They're not very happy with me, either."

"What do they have against you?"

"I put some pressure on the magistrate to set bail. Detective Chief Inspector Bailey considers me responsible for the second murder."

"He said the same thing to me."

"I suppose that makes us, as you Americans would put it, partners in crime."

I smiled and felt considerable relief. I had not been at all sure how Wellingham would react to me, and I was pleased that he was not antagonistic and was probably prepared to work with me.

"I'd like to talk with Paul," I said, "and I imagine they can't prevent you from seeing him."

"No. I did speak with him yesterday. He's in good spirits."

"He puts on a good front, but I'm sure he's frightened."

"Under the circumstances, could he be otherwise?"

"No," I said. "He's a good friend." It was barely a whisper.

"So I understand."

I took a deep breath and exhaled. "What do you know about the second murder?"

"Not much, I'm afraid. Neither do the police."

"Why did they arrest Paul? I mean, did they have any evidence against him, or was it simply that the same gun was used?"

"Only the revolver," he said. "And Paul didn't have an alibi. I'm afraid that the evidence for the first murder combined with the weapon is sufficient for the police to keep him incarcerated."

"You believe him to be guilty?"

"That's not my concern. My only interest is seeing that he is provided with adequate counsel."

"Mr. W. . . . Sir. . . . I guess I don't know the proper way to address you."

He laughed. "Being knighted is a British affectation. If we're to work together, the use of our Christian names would not be inappropriate. Please call me Reginald."

I felt uncomfortable addressing him that way, but I

said, "Reginald, Paul's more than a good friend. He's a man I've admired for many years. I know him very well. He did not commit either murder. I'm as confident of his innocence as I am of my own."

He sipped his brandy and put the glass down. "As I said, Daniel, it does not matter to me. But I believe you."

"Good. I'd appreciate it if you'd fill me in on whatever information you do have. I knew nothing about the second murder until a few hours ago when I spoke to Bailey on the phone."

"What did he tell you?"

"Nothing except that Donardy was killed, the same weapon was used, and Paul had been arrested again."

"That's all?"

"Yes."

"I assumed you knew everything. A great deal has happened. Donardy's body was discovered Tuesday evening in the basement of one of the dormitories at St. Catherine's. There was a suicide note in his pocket confessing to the first crime, and the weapon was in his hand."

"But the suicide was faked?"

"Yes. A parafin test indicated that it was unlikely that he had fired the revolver. There was also a contusion on his head. It might have been caused by falling after shooting himself, but they also thought that to be unlikely."

"Was there medical evidence?"

"Yes. The bullet passed through his brain, making it most likely that death was instantaneous, and they were certain the contusion occurred before death."

"So the assumption is that he was hit on the head

and then shot, the gun being put in his hand afterward."

"Yes."

"What about the suicide note?" I said. "How was that faked?"

"That's a bit of a mystery. It appears to have been written in Donardy's own hand."

"Strange. Maybe the killer forced him to write it."

He shrugged. "That's what the police think. But why would a man make it easier for the killer to murder him? No, I'm not satisfied with that explanation."

"What exactly did the note say?"

"I haven't seen it."

"There's something else that's strange," I said. "Why did the killer keep the gun after the first murder? Had it been found by the police or—"

"That's an interesting question. Of course, hiding a revolver isn't that difficult."

"Even so, it was a risk. He could not have been sure the police wouldn't search everybody's room, car, anything."

"You're assuming the killer to be one of the conferees?"

"Certainly," I said. "Now more than ever. Both Kloss and Donardy were in Oxford for the conference. It has to be one of—"

"All right, let us accept that assumption. There are some local mathematicians, I presume."

"Yes."

"If one of them was the culprit, he would have no difficulty hiding the revolver."

"Possibly, but there's still some risk."

"Yes, Daniel, I think you're right. The murderer had some reason for keeping the weapon."

"Let's look at it this way. Suppose you were driven to kill someone. What would you do?"

"I don't really know," he said. "It's not the kind of thing I've spent too much time thinking about."

I smiled. "No. But I can tell you this. I'd be terrified. I'd get rid of the gun as soon as possible. Unless I had some specific use for it."

"You think the killer was already planning to kill Donardy?"

"Maybe. More likely, he had Donardy's faked suicide as a backup. He frames Paul. He fears that the frame is unraveling, so he kills Donardy. With Paul out of jail, if the suicide is not convincing, the frame against Paul gets tightened."

"You could be correct, Daniel, but think of what an amoral mind you're talking about. Can you imagine being that cold-blooded and calculating? The man commits a murder. When he does it, he frames another man and plans the death of a third. This is a much more devious, evil man than one who kills out of passion or self-interest."

"Yes."

"It doesn't make sense," he said, "if we believe that Paul's actions Monday morning led to the first murder."

"Unless . . ."

"Unless what?"

I shook my head. "I don't know. A strange possibility. Suppose Kloss wasn't the first murder?"

"What? I don't understand."

"If the murderer had killed before, he could have been cool-headed enough to put together the entire plot on the spot."

"I don't think so," he said. "The first crime was well

181

planned. The second was not. Is there any reason to believe there had been an earlier murder?"

"I don't know. Maybe." I glanced at my watch. It was two o'clock, which made it early Friday morning in Texas. "I've got an idea that requires immediate action."

"Would you like to tell me what it is?"

"I would, but there's no time. It'd be good if you can arrange for me to see Paul tomorrow morning."

"I'll try, but . . ."

"Please trust me," I said, standing. "I've got to run."

My first stop was the Randolf Hotel. Eileen was in her room; I was relieved to catch her alone. Tears welled up in my eyes when she opened the door and smiled. It had been a long, emotional, week. I felt guilt about Barry Donardy's death and panic about Paul's troubles. I was confused and overwhelmed, a little boy lost. Seeing her was like that little boy finding his mother, and like that little boy, I needed her to take me in her arms and hold me close. She did, the embrace allowing me to hide my fears for a fleeting moment.

"Are you all right?" She spoke softly, close to my ear.

I gazed into those beautiful eyes. "Come back to Berkeley with me. Let's get married."

"I'm already married."

"I don't think I'm joking, Eileen. I love you."

"Oh, Danny. There was a time when I'd've done anything for you. But you're six years too late."

I sat on the bed and sighed. "I know."

"What brings all this on? You look terrible."

I shook my head. "I'm scared. It may be my fault that Donardy's dead and Paul's in trouble."

182

She sat next to me and held my hand in hers. "That's ridiculous. There's a crazy killer around. You're not responsible."

"Yeah, I guess."

She kissed my cheek. "I have more faith in you than you do. You'll figure it out."

"I hope so."

"You will."

I managed a smile and said, "Let me ask you something. When your father died, you said there was some kind of investigation."

"Yes, but it can't have anything to do with this."

"I'm not so sure. The insurance company did the investigating?"

"Mostly, yes."

"Do you remember anything about it?"

"Not really. Only that the police looked into it under pressure from the insurance company. They didn't question the accident."

"Okay. I want you to do two things. First, call your mother right away. Tell her that it's urgent that I speak to the man who investigated your father's accident."

"Why?"

"It's just a guess, but it's important."

"All right. What's the other thing?"

"Find Howard. He told me about a Swedish or Danish student who had been in Austin . . . maybe you remember him. He'd been in some sort of accident."

She frowned. "I think so, but I'm not sure. Why don't you talk to Howard?"

"If I see him, I will. But I've got to be at Heathrow in two hours."

"You're leaving?"

"No. It's a long story. I'll be back in time to have dinner with you."

"Good. What do you want me to tell Howard?"

"Ask him to track down that student. I want to talk to him, too."

"What's this all about?"

"A crazy idea I had. I'll tell you about it later. By the way, why aren't you at the conference?"

"Don't you know? Obviously not. We decided to call it off."

"The whole thing?"

"Yes. After the second murder nobody felt comfortable continuing."

"Yeah, I suppose. Have many people left?"

"Not yet. Our reservations were changed, and it's not that easy . . . I don't know. Very few of us have left."

"Probably too shocked." I kissed her and said, "I'll see you at seven."

The Moat House had held my room for me (why not, I was paying for it), and I dropped my luggage off and took a quick shower. Howard was not in his room, but the girls were in theirs; I could hear their chatter in the hallway.

Kathy opened the door when I knocked and gave me a big hug. "Uncle Danny, I'm so glad you're here."

"How're you holding up?"

"I'm okay. It's Daddy I'm worried about."

"You needn't be. He'll be fine."

I said hello to Amy and asked Kathy about Steve. Evidently she and Steve were getting along quite well, as were Amy and Colin.

"Now, then, ladies," I said, "what happened in Liverpool?"

"We were in a pub," Kathy said. "Someone said something to Steve because he was an American. Colin tried to help, and this awful man punched Colin. Steve jumped in, and it became a big brawl and everybody got arrested. But it wasn't our fault. It was this mean man."

"That's right," Amy said, rather emphatically. She smiled. "But everything's okay now. They dropped all charges and let us go the next day. My dad came to Liverpool—"

"He was late," Kathy said, evidently still annoyed. "We had to wait over an hour."

Amy stuck out her tongue at Kathy. "He called and we got the message. And he did drive us back to Oxford."

"We didn't expect you to be out until after one," I said, trying to explain Howard's tardiness.

"It was later than that," Amy said, "but he called to let us know he might be late."

I wondered what took him so long—he certainly left Oxford in plenty of time to be there. He probably got lost. I said, "Speaking of your dad, where is he?"

"At St. Cat's. He's meeting with some mathematicians."

"I'll find him there," I said. "But tell me. What were you doing in Liverpool in the first place?" I almost added, If someone had been watching Barry Donardy, he might not be dead now. Fortunately, before saying anything, I realized that I would only be trying to pass off some of the guilt I felt.

Kathy's face lit up when I asked the question. "We had this great idea. Do you remember how difficult it was to get on the plane?"

"No. What d'you mean?"

"The security checks. Looking through our baggage and everything."

"Right. What does that have to do with anything?"

"We figured the killer would have been searched, too. So he couldn't bring the gun with him."

"Yeah, so?"

"So where did he get the gun from? I mean, did he just go into a store and buy one, or what?"

"Not in England," I said, "but how does that get you to Liverpool?"

"Well, Colin said he knew someone there who might know how to get a gun. I mean, we thought maybe we could find out if an American got one somewhere."

"Did you find out anything?"

She looked down. "No. We got arrested before we had a chance."

"It was a good idea, Kathy. Maybe one I can make use of. But I do hope you'll leave the detecting to me from now on."

"Don't worry, we will."

"Good." I stood and said, "I have some chores to do. I assume you can take care of yourselves?"

"We'll be fine. Please don't worry about us, Uncle Danny. You have to solve the mystery and get Daddy out of jail."

"I will." I tried to express a degree of confidence that I did not feel, but I didn't do a very good job of it.

I stopped at the front desk of the hotel and, with some effort, managed to convince them to refrigerate the pastries Heinrich Levin had given me (at least those I hadn't eaten).

I drove to St. Catherine's College hoping to find Howard. He wasn't there, and none of the three people I asked had seen him. It was after four, so I headed for Heathrow, hoping that Eileen would find Howard and give him my message.

I arrived at the airport late, but the plane was apparently even later. I found Bill and May Lancaster in a crowded area that was cordoned off from customs by a Plexiglas partition.

"We were afraid you wouldn't make it," Bill said when he saw me.

"Got hung up a bit. The plane's late?"

"It just landed," May said. "As soon as she gets out of customs. . . ." She trailed off, and I could see that she was overwhelmed, awaiting the arrival of the daughter she had never met. Bill had his arm around her shoulders; young Kenny was asleep in a stroller.

Joanne appeared shortly through sliding doors of the partition; she caught sight of me and waved.

As I held up my hand in acknowledgment, May leaned close to me and said, "That's her?"

"Yes."

She closed her eyes and inhaled deeply as Joanne approached us. I intercepted Joanne a few steps from the Lancasters and took her suitcase; the tightness with which she gripped it revealed the anxiety she felt about meeing the mother she had never seen.

I whispered to Joanne, "Relax. You'll like her," and in a louder voice, I said, "Joanne, this is May and Bill Lancaster. May this . . ."

May reached out and took Joanne's hands. "Let me look at you." They stood there, saying nothing, betraying no emotions.

The two women remained speechless. Bill said, "Let's find a place to talk."

Nothing else was said until we were sitting in a booth in an airport restaurant and had placed our orders.

The uncomfortable silence returned. I finally said, "This is silly. There's nothing to be embarrassed about. Joanne, this is May. That's her name, and I'm sure she'd like you to use it. We all know that she and Bill did some things they're not proud of. But they've made a good life for themselves and put the past behind them. They also happen to be very nice people."

May reached out for Joanne's hand again. She was smiling as a tear trickled down her cheek. She said, "Joanne, I'm so sorry. I was a frightened kid. But maybe it was for the best. I know the Leopolds love you, and you've had a good home to live in. Maybe you can't think of me as your mother, but I do want us to be friends."

"So do I." The tears filled Joanne's eyes; indeed, I was close to crying myself.

May said, "Please tell me about . . . well, about everything."

The awkward tension was gone. Joanne proceeded to describe her life: school, college plans, career choices, boyfriends, her parents. Bill and May talked about fishing and living in England. Kenny awoke and settled in Joanne's lap. I sat there quietly and listened, smiling to myself.

I had another important job to complete. I said, "Well, it doesn't look like you need me anymore, and I do have to get back to Oxford."

Joanne smiled at me, and Bill said, "Dan, I don't know how we can thank you. If there's anything I can do for you—anything at all—please ask."

"Maybe there is something," I said. "Did you find that object we talked about?"

"No. I haven't looked yet. But . . ."

"Try to find it. If you can, return it and ask Harry Linton to find out something for me."

"Sure. What?"

"I believe that some time in the last two or three weeks an American picked up a nine-millimeter revolver somewhere in England. It's unlikely he did it through legitimate channels. I want to know if I'm right, and if so, who the American is."

He raised his eyebrows but simply said, "Sure, if you want."

"The man I'm seeking wouldn't have given his real name, so what I really need is someone who can recognize him."

Joanne and May thanked me again, and I left very pleased with myself; in fact, I felt quite the hero.

Reality set in as I drove back to Oxford and thought about Paul and about Barry Donardy. The fears returned, and I had to fight to control the panic that was beginning to overwhelm me.

$\int$ 19

It was Friday evening and time was running out. Most of the conferees were leaving on Sunday, and there would be little chance of solving the murder after their departure. That time limitation was the primary cause of the panic that was threatening to become hysteria. The police had a strong case against Paul, and they were not about to accept his innocence based on my say-so. It was up to me to discover the identity of the murderer, but all that I had accomplished so far was inciting the culprit into killing a second time. I had to do something, and fast. But what? There wasn't enough time. I had to act, but time was running out. There wasn't enough time, there wasn't enough time. . . ."

Slow is fast. It's a Brodsky maxim for doing mathematics: If you want to solve a problem, you will find the solution most quickly if you proceed slowly and carefully—my computer friends tell me that it also applies to writing programs. Driving back to Oxford, I realized that controlling the panic that was controlling me was my first priority, and the best way to do that was to spend some quiet time with Eileen.

"Eileen, Eileen, Eileen." She had been waiting for me in her room, and she was holding me in her arms.

She leaned back, put her hands on my shoulders,

looked at me with the smile that had stolen my heart, and kissed my nose. "I guess we're not going to dinner."

I smiled weakly. "There's always room service."

She sat on the bed and patted the covers next to her. "Sit."

We talked a little and cuddled a lot.

Eileen told me that she had called her mother and spoken with Howard. Her mother would try to find the insurance investigator, and Howard would try to contact the Scandinavian student, whose name, he had said, was Hans Nystrom.

It was nine o'clock, early enough to make some phone calls or maybe to catch some people at St. Catherine's. I tried Sir Reginald first. He was at home and told me that if I met him at the police station at nine the next morning, he would get me in to see Paul. Howard was not in his room, nor were the girls, so I ambled over to the college.

I took a long route, giving me the opportunity to consider what I knew—and didn't know. The second murder strengthened my belief that the killer had been in Texas when Kloss and Barnett published Paul's work. That eliminated one hundred ninety suspects but still left more than I wanted to deal with.

In my mind, the suspect list could be cut further. I of course had been certain of Paul's innocence from the beginning, and I had never entertained the possibility of Eileen's guilt. Howard had lied to me about his whereabouts on the evening of the murder, but, while I did not have the close relationship with him that I had with Paul, he was a good friend, and it was difficult for me to believe that he would have framed

Paul. Nonetheless, I would have to confront him with his prevarication.

Cal Barnett would have been high on the list were it not for his airtight alibi. On the other hand, the murder had been well conceived and well executed by a devious mind. If Barnett were the culprit, he may have been able to fabricate such an alibi. One certainly would have been part of his plan since he could not be certain that the frame he was tying around Paul's neck was adequate. However, if Barnett were the murderer, how did he do it, and how could I break his alibi? Trying to prove one of the other suspects guilty—for example, Ross White or Terry Henkler, neither of whom had alibis—appeared to be a more promising road, given the time constraints.

I had known Henkler for ten years and had always liked him. Our only contact had been professional, and he was not really a friend, but he was not my image of a killer. But then, what does a murderer look like? And why would he put up his house to bail out Paul? Paul's short-lived freedom had been awfully convenient for the murderer.

I hardly knew Ross White, and there was the mysterious note from Kloss that I had found in his room. Both Eileen and Howard had thought that he was something of a cold fish, but did that mean he was a cold-blooded killer?

There was another suspect whom I had not yet interviewed: Ann Laskey. I barely knew her and had no reason whatsoever to believe that she was guilty. However, although she was now at Oregon State, she had studied in Austin until Rothenberg's death.

An idea occurred to me as I neared St. Catherine's: search the rooms of Kloss and Donardy, both of whom had been staying at the college. Indeed, why hadn't I thought of it before? Perhaps my personal involvement with the case had clouded my thinking. It didn't matter—I was now prepared to pursue the kind of investigation required to unmask the killer.

The police had undoubtedly already been through both rooms, but since they were trying to build a case against Paul, it was possible they had not removed some piece of evidence that I would consider important.

It was almost ten o'clock when I wandered into the lounge at St. Cat's. The bar was open, but there were only a handful of conferees present, none of whom I wanted to interview. I was not at all confident of my ability to break into Kloss's room, so I telephoned Terry Henkler at home. He was in charge of local arrangements, and I hoped that he would be able to get me in. He resisted, not surprisingly since it was undoubtedly illegal, but after some pushing, he agreed to track down a custodian who could open the doors. He also told me that Ann Laskey was staying at the Ladbroke Linton Lodge, a hotel not too far from the Moat House. I called, but she wasn't there.

Henkler showed up forty-five minutes later accompanied by a bleary-eyed gentleman with drooping shoulders. I concluded that the half-asleep look was an act when I learned that it had cost sixty pounds to get him out of bed. "Overtime," he explained. He opened Donardy's door and then let us into Kloss's room, saying, "Be bloody sure ya' lock up when yer done or it's me 'ead." Henkler assured him that we would, and the man left, his shoulders still drooped.

"Do you really expect to find any clues here?" Henkler said.

"Probably not, but you never know."

"I still think the police would've removed anything useful."

"That's what you said on the phone. But I'm hoping they overlooked something."

He shrugged. "How can I help?"

"I should probably do it myself. I know what to look for and how to do it." That was a total lie—I knew no more than anyone else on the what and how of searching. I simply didn't want Henkler to be aware of any evidence that I might uncover.

"Sure, you're the professional," he said. "But I would like to do something. I don't want to see Paul convicted."

"Why?"

"What?" He had a puzzled expression on his face.

"Don't misunderstand me, Terry, but you don't know Paul that well. Yet you put up your house to get him out of jail. Why?"

He shook his head. "I don't think he's guilty."

"That doesn't answer the question. And what makes you think he's innocent?"

"*You* do, don't you?"

"Sure, but he's a friend of mine and a man I admire and respect."

"Do you have to be a close friend to admire and respect him?"

"No," I said. "I suppose not."

"Paul's a world-class mathematician. Some of his work demonstrates a degree of insight I can't fathom. I simply cannot believe he's a murderer."

His statement made sense. I met Paul as a student in a graduate course he was teaching at a time when I did not know what it meant to be a mathematician. My respect for him was based largely on a personal rela-

194

tionship, and it was several years before I understood the depth of perception required to produce much of his work. It was possible that Henkler's admiration for Paul's mathematics made him unable to believe that Paul was guilty; it was also possible that Henkler was a murderer.

I said, "I better get to it."

"If there's anything I can do to. . . ."

"As a matter of fact, there is. I'd like to speak with Ann Laskey. She wasn't in her hotel before, but maybe you'll be able to find her and ask her to meet me here."

"I'll try," he said. "I'll wait for you downstairs in the lounge."

Kloss's room was similar to White's, but his habits were not. Dirty clothes were strewn about; the clean ones remained in his suitcase; the closet and drawers were empty. I looked under the bed but found only more dirty clothing. There was no way of knowing what, if anything, the police might have removed, but it appeared as if they had left the room otherwise undisturbed.

His briefcase contained a number of files including one labeled COTCA and another labeled SUBNORMAL OPERATORS. The first contained nothing that could in any way further the investigation, but the second, which was particularly thick, was another matter. I looked through it mostly out of curiosity because I knew that Kloss had spent most of his career studying subnormal operators, but also to check out the mathematical questions he had been concerned with when he died. I found a preprint of one of his papers with a University of Texas cover on it. It felt fifty pages thick, which was strange because the journal version, which had recently appeared and which I had seen, was only seven pages long. I examined it carefully and found a manila envelope hidden among several sheets of paper stapled together.

The envelope contained a number of postcards and letters, several of which were revealing, one of which was quite disturbing. The latter was from Paul; it said that he would not meet with Kloss at COTCA and ended with, "Nothing you can say will interest me. I'll get you in Oxford." The significance of those sentences was clear to me: Paul was referring to his departure from Kloss's talk. I did not for a second consider the possibility that the letter was evidence of Paul's guilt; nonetheless, I was glad the police had not found it.

Many of the letters and all the postcards were requests for reprints or preprints. (A *reprint* is a copy of a journal article; a *preprint* is a copy of the typed version before it has appeared. Reprints are typeset and fully edited and are generally easier to read, but they're also less timely. Such requests are common.) Two of them were from Eileen, and there was one each from Howard, Ross White, Terry Henkler, and Ann Laskey, among others.

The letters from Eileen were friendly, consistent with the attitude toward Kloss that she had expressed several days earlier. The request from Ross White included the statement, "I have not been able to determine who did it. Have you learned anything more? Do you have a guess? Write to me if you do."

Henkler's letter said that he would be happy to read the paper—it sounded as if Kloss had asked him to look at something he had done and to compare it with some of Henkler's own work.

Howard and Ann Laskey had sent postcards requesting copies of papers, but neither contained anything personal.

There were two letters from Cal Barnett. One was more of a note than a letter. It read, "Barry's been talking to me about getting out of here. Isn't there anything we can do to help him finish?"

The letter, dated about a week after the note and two weeks before the conference, had been mailed in London. I wasn't surprised: Barnett had told me that he'd been traveling in England for a couple of weeks before COTCA. The part of the letter that struck me, though I had no idea if it had any significance, was, "I think you're making a mistake. Why open up a can of worms? Don't do it, if nothing else for old time's sake." My intuition was that it was related to the note about Donardy, not that I had any concrete evidence to that effect.

The remaining letters and cards were not even remotely related to the murders, and I found nothing else of interest, so I carefully locked the door and went up one flight to Barry Donardy's room.

Ross White's room had been immaculate when I searched it, and Kloss's was a mess—Donardy's room was somewhere in between. I didn't see anything as interesting as Kloss's correspondence, but I did find some mathematical notes. After ten minutes of examination I realized that I was looking at a sketch of the proof of the theorem that he thought would give him his Ph.D. I spent another twenty minutes reading through the notes and realized that it would take several hours of concentrated effort to determine whether it was correct. I wasn't at all sure that the correctness of the proof was important, but I had a feeling it might

197

be. I didn't have the time to check the details, but there were two hundred mathematicians close at hand who could.

I put Donardy's notes into Kloss's manila envelope and hid the envelope under my shirt—I was not prepared to let anyone know I had found anything. I locked the door and returned to the lounge.

Terry Henkler was sitting on a couch talking with a woman whom I recognized to be Ann Laskey. She was a short and slightly pudgy brunette with a very pretty face.

Neither seemed to notice me until I said, "Hi, Ann. Thanks for coming out so late."

"No problem. Terry said it was important."

Henkler said, "Did you find anything?"

"No. It was a waste of time."

"That's a shame. You were gone so long I thought you might have turned up something."

"No. I'm just thorough. I don't mean to be rude, Terry, but it'd probably be better if I talked to Ann alone."

"Sure. It's past my bedtime anyway." He bade us good night, and I sat on the couch.

She said, "I enjoyed your lecture."

"Thanks, but that doesn't seem very important anymore."

"No. What is it that you wanted to talk to me about?"

"I'm not sure, exactly. You were in Austin fifteen years ago."

"What does that have to do with anything?" She looked puzzled.

"Everything, I think. That was the time when Kloss stole Paul Hobart's work."

"I still don't understand."

"Paul apparently set things in motion when he walked out of Kloss's talk, and everything that's happened seems to be related to that paper."

"Okay, I'm willing to accept that," she said. "But I don't see how I can help."

"I want to hear anything you can tell me about the people who were there then, anything you can tell me about the paper, whatever you know about Kloss and Donardy and their relationship to other people. That sort of thing."

She had little to add to what I had already learned about the operator theory group led by Arthur Rothenberg, and she said that she hardly knew Kloss and Donardy. That surprised me since both she and Donardy had been students of Rothenberg at the same time. She insisted that the only time she saw him was in seminars and at Rothenberg's luncheons. As for Kloss, she said that she had avoided him because she had heard that he could create problems for students.

Her comments about the purloined paper were more interesting. "I don't know much," she said. "I'm sure I was back in Oregon before I heard rumors that Kloss had stolen the work from Hobart. I do remember that I thought they were probably true."

"Why?"

"Because of everything I knew about Kloss. He was arrogant and egotistical and didn't care about anyone besides himself. He seemed to have this strong need to prove that he was smarter than anyone else. So his stealing Hobart's results was consistent with what I knew about him."

It struck me that she seemed to have strong feelings and know a lot about someone she had always avoided.

Of course, I knew that much about Kloss, and I'd had very little personal contact with him over the years.

"Can you remember anything unusual after Rothenberg's accident? Was anyone acting strangely?"

"We were all upset. Even Kloss appeared upset, so I'm sure we were all acting strangely."

"There was nothing in particular that you noticed?"

"No. Not that I recall," she said. "But then I left Austin shortly after Arthur's death. Right after the funeral."

"You left in the middle of the semester?"

"I needed to get away for a couple of weeks. I was in my third year, so everything I was doing centered around Arthur. There was nothing that prevented me from taking off."

"But you ended up leaving permanently."

"Yes. It's kind of ironic the way death can bring people closer together. As soon as I got home, I went to see an old college sweetheart. He consoled me—all the way to the wedding chapel. I returned to Austin for Arthur's memorial, packed up my stuff afterward, and haven't been back since."

"You finished your degree in Eugene?"

"That's right. I'd known John Ling as an undergraduate. I talked with him when I got home, mostly to invite him to my wedding. He said he could get me a TA if I wanted to study at Oregon. He may not be Arthur Rothenberg, but he was a good advisor. I've never regretted the decision."

"I've seen some of his work," I said. "Never met him, though."

She stared off into space. A tear ran down her cheek. "I loved Arthur." She wiped her face and looked at me. "You know, he was a good mathematician but not in a class with, say, Paul Hobart. What made him so special was the man he was. He was like a father to me. He . . ."

"I understand. I met him briefly once," I said. "I wish I'd had the chance to know him better."

We lapsed into silence. After several minutes I said, "It has been fifteen years, Ann."

"I know," she said. "All this talk has brought back a lot of memories. Is there anything else you'd like to know?"

"Only if you know anything more about the writing of that paper."

"The first I knew about it was when John Ling asked me to read a preprint the following year. Come to think of it, John was the one who told me Kloss had stolen it from Hobart. He said he didn't think Kloss and Barnett were good enough to have done the work themselves."

"He was right. Anything else you can tell me about it?"

She shook her head. "I don't think so. No."

"Well, Ann, thanks again for taking the time." I stood up to leave. "I can't say that you've shed any light on the matter, but you never know."

"Dan, why are you investigating this mess, anyway?"

"Paul's a good friend."

"Don't you think the police can handle it?"

"They think he's guilty."

"All right, but you're a mathematician, not a private investigator."

"Wrong."

"What?" She had a very strange look on her face.

"I *am* a private investigator. That's how I put bread on the table."

"Don't you have a job at Berkeley?"

"No. I hang around the department and sometimes teach a course."

"How do you find time to do research?"

"In practice I'm a part-time investigator, which is probably why I'm always broke."

"I can't believe you'd rather be a private investigator than a mathematician."

"I wouldn't. I haven't been able to find a decent job."

She sat up. "Really? Think you'd be interested in coming to Oregon State?"

"Maybe. You looking for an analyst?"

"Yes. We have an opening, and we've been negotiating with Morris Zinkowski. But it looks like he won't be coming."

"Does he want to leave M.I.T.?"

"That's what he said. He and I have done a couple of things together, and he said he was thinking of getting out of Boston."

"But he decided against it?"

"Apparently." She smiled and added, "I'll tell you, Corvallis is a nice place."

"I've been there." She was right: Corvallis was a beautiful town.

"Interested?"

"I think so. What kind of position are we talking about?"

"We were prepared to offer Morris a professorship. We might be able to make you the same offer. More likely associate."

"With tenure?"

"With your publication record? Sure."

"Then I'm interested. Very interested."

"I'll check as soon as I get back. I'll be in touch with you within two weeks."

202

$\int$ 20

It was 1:30 A.M. when I got into the rental car and drove to the Moat House. I had no intention of sleeping there—I had promised Eileen that I would eventually come back to the Randolf—but it was time to confront Howard about what he'd been doing at the time of the murder and, presumably, to eliminate him as a suspect. He was most likely asleep, but that was his problem: He should not have lied to me.

I knocked on his door ten minutes later. I heard rustling sounds inside—apparently I had awakened him—and knocked again. There were more noises, as if, in the dark, he had fallen out of bed. There was a muffled "Hold on," and in a few seconds the door opened. Howard was wearing a bathrobe and scratching his head. "Oh, Dan." He appeared surprised. "I thought you were Amy."

"Did I wake you up?"

"Afraid so."

"May I come in?"

"Um . . . Yeah, sure."

I followed him inside. He sat on the bed; I took a chair next to a table by the window.

"I hope you won't be too long," he said. "I need my beauty sleep."

"I shouldn't be. I have only one question: Why did

you lie to me when you said you were with the girls Monday night?"

He looked at me and said, "I thought we went over this already."

"We did. But I want the truth this time."

"Do you suspect me?"

"No. Of course not. But you did lie to me, and I want an explanation."

He stared at me. "There's nothing to explain," he said. "I was shocked about the murder and got flustered. I . . . um . . . figured I needed an alibi."

"Why should you need an alibi?"

"I don't. But anyone could be accused. Look at the trouble Paul's in."

"Howard, you're a lousy liar, so cut the bullshit."

He stood up and reached into a drawer in the night table as if he were looking for something. He turned back to me and said, "All right. I was with a woman. For a variety of obvious reasons, I didn't want anybody to know about it."

"It probably has no bearing on the case, so I won't say anything unless it's necessary, but you better tell me who she is."

"I can't unless she says okay. I will tell you that she was a student of mine."

"Helen Orosco?"

"How did y . . . Oh, shit."

"I guessed," I said. "I notice when one of your students becomes a Benjamin Pierce Fellow at Harvard."

"I'd prefer it if you don't talk to her."

"I may have to. But what's the big deal? You know about me and Eileen. It's not that different."

"It is to me. I'm married."

"So's Eileen."

"But, Dan, you're not."

"Howard, Anita won't learn anything from me. Neither will Amy. I'll let you know if I talk to Helen. But don't worry. It won't make any difference."

He smiled. "You mean I don't have to worry about you trying to blackmail me for a job?"

"I hadn't thought of that. Maybe you should worry."

"Fortunately, the dean won't let us hire any analysts."

"Yeah, I know. It's all computers these days." Then, with an admittedly childish grin on my face, I added, "I may actually have a chance at a job. Ann Laskey wants me to come to Corvallis."

"Really? You? With a job? It's hard to believe."

"It's not definite," I said.

"You should accept if you get an offer. Settle down, become a real person. Take it from me—the academic life is the good life."

"Ah, the man who has it all: great job, beautiful wife, wonderful kids, sexy mistress."

"Dan, that doesn't even deserve a smile."

I smiled anyway. "Getting back to the point at hand, I will probably want to talk to Helen."

"Could you at least wait until I talk to her?"

"It's all right, Howard." It was a woman's voice from behind me. I turned and saw a young woman draped in a towel emerging from the bathroom.

I said, "Dr. Orosco, I presume."

She nodded, "You wanted to ask me something?"

"Yes. Monday night. Where were you?"

"The night of the murder?"

"That's right."

"Howard needs an alibi?"

"Not really," I said. "But he did fib just a bit about his whereabouts."

"He was with me. In my hotel room."

"What time did he get there?"

She looked at Howard and then back at me. "About nine."

I would have felt a lot better if she'd said eight. I glanced at Howard. He couldn't be guilty. Even if he had sufficient motive to kill Kloss, he would never have framed Paul. I was certain of that.

Helen said, "Is there anything else you want to know?"

"No. You answered all my questions with your entrance."

"Dan," Howard said, "I'm sorry I lied to you. It . . ."

"Yeah, yeah. Don't worry about it. I'm glad we cleared it up. One last thing before I bid you adieu. Have you gotten in touch with Hans Nystrom?"

"No, not yet. I've left messages for him. But what do you want to talk to him for?"

"Just a theory I'm working on," I said. "By the way, how are the girls?"

He shook his head in disgust. "Before, when I said I thought you were Amy, I was *hoping* you were her. I haven't seen them since before dinner."

"What are they doing?"

"Running around with the boys they picked up. They think they're gonna solve the murder."

I was still a bit uneasy about Howard when Eileen opened her door and put her arms around me at three o'clock. She had waited up for me. After a sweet kiss she said, "I can see you're doing much better. Have you gotten anywhere?"

"It's possible. I found a bunch of letters in Kloss's room."

"Didn't the police search the place?"

"I would imagine so." I led her to the bed and we lay down on it. "Whew. I'm tired."

"I'm sure you are. What about the letters?"

"They were hidden in a folder of mathematical stuff."

"Why would he hide them? Was there anything in them that—"

"Nothing that unusual. Nothing worth hiding. I think he was just paranoid."

"Is it possible that someone else was there first and removed an important letter?"

"I doubt it," I said. "If the police had found them first, they would have kept them all. There was a letter from Paul that could be interpreted as incriminating. The police would certainly have taken it. So would the murderer. He'd have made sure the police got their hands on it."

"He?"

"The generic 'he'—sexist 'he' if you like. But nothing implied."

"Does that mean I'm a suspect?"

"No," I said. "There are three people who are definitely not suspects, and you're one of them."

"Thank God! For a second there, I thought I was guilty."

"Don't worry, you're not."

"Who are the other two innocents?"

"Me and Paul."

"I wouldn't be so sure about you," she said. I forgave her when she kissed me. "What was in the letter from Paul?"

"There was a kind of threat."

She pulled back and gazed at me. "Paul can't be guilty?"

"No. I'm sure that all he meant was the stunt he pulled during Kloss's talk."

"I hope you're right."

"I am."

She hugged me and said, "What are you gonna do with the letter?"

"Nothing."

"You won't turn it over to the police?"

"Definitely not. It would only strengthen their case."

"Isn't it illegal for you to keep it from them?"

"I'm sure it is," I said.

"You're so sweet." She kissed me again and said, "Were any of the other letters relevant?"

"I don't know. I think so, but I can't figure out how. You can read them if you want."

"I will," she said. "In the morning."

"Have you heard from your mom?"

"Yes. You'll be able to call the insurance investigator at home tomorrow morning between eight and ten Texas time. I've got the phone number."

"Very good. That could. . ."

"Dan, you don't really think Dad was murd . . . I can hardly say the word. Killed by someone."

"Would it matter after all these years?"

"It probably shouldn't," she said, "but, yes, it would."

"Well, I won't know anything until I talk to the investigator."

"Can my father . . . have anything to do with Kloss and Donardy?"

"It's possible. I had this feeling that something was missing. I couldn't quite get my hands on the motive, and I had an idea. Let's leave it at that until I check it out."

"I hope you're wrong. I know it's stupid after fifteen years, but it would hurt a lot to find out that he was . . ."

I hugged her and said, "In the last week I've heard the most wonderful things about your father. I wish I'd had the chance to know him. But whether or not someone took his life, he's gone and we can't bring him back. He was a special man. Remember him for that."

She sobbed quietly in my arms.

It was morning. We were still dressed, lying atop the bed. Eileen's travel alarm said seven fifteen. I'd had less than five hours' sleep, but some part of me knew that I had to get up to meet Wellingham at the police station. I lay there while and then eased myself out of bed and into the shower. I tried not to awaken Eileen, but two minutes later she was helping me wash. She took me in her arms and said, "I'm still in love with you, Dan Brodsky. You should have married me when you had the chance."

"I know," I said. "Maybe it's not too late."

Forty-five minutes later, under the covers and still in her arms, I said, "There are a couple of things I'd like you to do for me today."

"Anything."

"How about divorcing Bob?"

"I don't think I can get that done today."

"How about when you get back to Austin?"

"We'll talk about it when I'm in Austin," she said. "What do you want me to do?"

"First, there are two rolls of film in my briefcase. I'll leave them with you. Find a place that will develop them in a couple of hours. Have three prints made of each shoot. Pay whatever it takes."

"What else?"

"When I was in Barry Donardy's room last night, I found some notes. It appears to be a proof of a theorem he'd been trying to prove for some time. I'll leave the notes with you. See if you can figure them out and determine if his proof's correct."

"Can that have anything to do with the murders?"

"I don't know. But plagiarism seems to play a large role in all that's happened, and Donardy was one of the victims. I want to know if it looks like his own work."

She shrugged. "All right. Anything else?"

"Yeah. Call room service and have breakfast and coffee sent up. Ask them to hurry."

We both got out of bed, I to dress, she to make the phone call.

I called the Lancasters in Maesteg. Bill answered. He told me that they'd all been getting along well, that Joanne's parents were flying in that evening, and that everybody was happy. I then asked about the mysterious object he'd stolen from Harry Linton.

He said, "I found it last night. I called Linton and promised to return it straight away. He asked me to thank you and said he'd try to get the information you wanted."

"Very good. Listen, Bill, I'd like you to do a big favor for me. It's very important."

"Yeah, sure. What is it?"

"Call Linton again right away and tell him that if an American did pick up a gun in the last couple of weeks, I need to know today. Tell him you'll bring him some photographs of some people, and I'll want to know if any of them bought the gun."

"What photographs?"

"You'll have to stop here in Oxford on your way to

London to pick them up. Do you think you'll be able to. . . ."

"Sure," he said. "I've got to go to London for the Leopolds. Oxford's hardly out of the way."

"That'll be great. When you get here, come to the Randolf Hotel and ask for Eileen St. Cloud. She'll have the pictures for you."

"Will we get a chance to see you?"

"I don't think so," I said. "I'd love to say hello, but I have too much to do."

"I hope you'll be able to come back this way before you return to America."

"I'll try."

"I'll leave for Oxford straight away."

"Thanks. That'll be great. If Linton finds the man I'm looking for, it'll be a tremendous help."

"Glad to do it."

I said good-bye and turned to Eileen. "You heard?"

"Yes."

I reached into my briefcase and handed her the film and Donardy's notes. "When you get the photos back, write numbers on the faces. That way, if we're lucky and they can find someone who sold a gun to one of them, they'll be able to tell us which one."

"Without naming him."

"Right."

Room service showed up at ten to nine. I spent two minutes wolfing down some food and coffee and then ran to the police station.

∫ 21

I met Wellingham at nine, and we were brought to an interrogation room where Paul was waiting. I hadn't seen Paul in three days, and he looked terrible: There were rings under bloodshot eyes, his clothes were rumpled, and his shoulders sagged. He appeared defeated and worn out. I assured him that I was making progress, and Wellingham exuded confidence. Paul asked about Kathy, and I told him that she was holding up as well as could be expected, that he shouldn't worry. I don't think he believed a word I said—I'm not sure there was any reason to.

I suggested to Wellingham that he let me speak privately with Paul, explaining that Paul would be more at ease since he and I had known each other so long. Wellingham was skeptical but agreed. His skepticism was justified: My real purpose was to ask Paul about the letter he had written to Kloss without letting Wellingham know about it. I was not terribly familiar with English law, but my hunch was that he would be compelled to turn it over to the police.

After Wellingham left, I showed Paul the letter and said, "What did you mean by that?"

He glanced at it and smiled. "Where did you find this?"

"In Kloss's room. Hidden in a file."

"Hidden?"

"Yes. Don't know why."

He looked at the letter again and shook his head. "It doesn't mean anything. Kloss had written to me saying that he wanted to talk during the conference and suggested we go to dinner on Sunday evening."

"So you said no and told him to go to hell?"

"Essentially."

"What did you mean by, 'I'll get you in Oxford'?"

He shrugged. "Nothing. I just wanted to scare him."

"You weren't already planning to walk out during his lecture?"

"No." He smiled. "That idea came later. Once I made the threat, I decided to do something. Walking out of his talk was all I could think of."

"That was enough," I said. "What can you tell me about the second murder?"

"Not very much. Everything I know about it I learned from Wellingham. Haven't you talked with the police yet?"

"No. Our relationship deteriorated with Donardy's demise."

"Why? I thought you were getting along well with Bailey."

"I was. But he thinks I'm partially responsible for the second crime."

"That doesn't make sense."

"He thinks Donardy wouldn't've been killed if you were still in jail. I'm not sure he's entirely wrong."

"I am."

"I don't know," I said. "I don't think the killer would've acted a second time if you hadn't been bailed out."

"That's absurd. The first murder was carefully planned and executed—the second one was bungled."

"Why do you say that? It tightened the frame around your neck."

"That was pure luck. He tried to make it look like suicide. I doubt if he knew I was out. Even if he did, how could he be sure I wouldn't have an alibi? In fact, if Kathy hadn't been arrested or if you hadn't gone to London, I would've had an airtight alibi."

"Why didn't you have an alibi?" I said. "I mean, where were you?"

"I was in my room, waiting for Howard to bring the girls back. The killer couldn't have known that."

"You know, I think you're right. The first time, he made sure that you'd be alone with a dead car."

"Does that tell us anything?"

"I think so, Paul. At least three things. First, it tells us that the murderer is fallible. He slipped up badly the second time."

"Unfortunately, his slip turned to his advantage. What else does it tell us?"

"That Kloss's murder was at least partially planned before the conference. You and I organized the poker game at last year's COTCA, and everyone expected a game this year. The killer probably knew that."

"You mean he intended to use it as part of his plan even before coming to Oxford?"

"Yes, I think so. Which brings us to the third point: The killer had decided to frame you long before you walked out of Kloss's talk."

"If you're right, Dan," he said, "I've been giving him a lot of assistance."

"But not enough. Not enough. We'll get him. You can bet on it."

"I am. I'm betting my whole life."

I grinned and shook my head. "Always a joke."

"Anything to pass the time. What makes you so confident all of a sudden?"

"I've been working on a theory, and things are beginning to fall into place. There's a lot of checking to do, but I think . . ."

"Do you know who did it?"

"Not yet," I said. "But I'm close. I think I'll know before the day is out."

"Want to give me a hint?"

"It's—"

The door opened and Sergeant Smythe came in. He said, "Mr. Brodsky, Inspector Bailey would like to speak with you. Now."

I followed Smythe to Bailey's office. When we entered, Wellingham was sitting in a chair opposite Bailey's desk; the inspector was behind it, writing. He put his pen down, removed his glasses, dropped them on the desk, and sat back with a deep sigh. He said, very deliberately, "Mr. Brodsky. Mr. Brodsky. What am I going to do with you?"

"What have I done now, Inspector?"

"I think we both know."

"Maybe you should give me a hint."

"Well, let me see. There's breaking and entering. There's petty theft, interfering wtih an official investigation, withholding evidence. . . ."

Wellingham leaned toward me and, in his deep, resonant voice, speaking slowly and with perfect diction, said, "Your primary offense, I'm afraid, is being a pain in the ass."

"It might help if someone told me what I'm supposed to have done." I must admit that I was beginning to have an idea.

Bailey leaned forward and said, "You broke into

Martin Kloss's room, you stole some letters, and you concealed them from us."

I should have been upset. They could throw me in jail, making it impossible for me to complete the investigation before the murderer left Oxford. Even worse, the letter from Paul was in my pocket, and there didn't seem to be any way of avoiding turning it over to Bailey, strengthening their case. But I was feeling confident and said, "Is it legal for you to bug the interrogation room?"

"There are no bugs, Mr. Brodsky."

"Then how did you know about the letters?"

"We found them in Mr. Kloss's room on Tuesday, when we searched it. We left the room as we had found it, hoping to catch a murderer. Instead, we caught you."

"That's a nifty explanation, Inspector. But why would you have left the letters if you'd found them? And what murderer were you trying to catch? I knew Paul was innocent, but you. . . ."

"Daniel," Wellingham said, rather sternly, "there is no need to make accusations. I do not believe Inspector Bailey intends to press charges. However, you will have to relinquish the letters."

I pulled up a chair in front of Bailey's desk and sat down. "A few days ago, Inspector, there was a spirit of cooperation between us. It seems to me that you now want that cooperation to go in only one direction."

Bailey shot forward in his seat. "Goddamnit, Brodsky, you'll turn over those letters bloody quick or I will press charges."

"I don't think so, Inspector. Not as long as you have that bug in the interrogation room."

Wellingham broke in, holding up his hands, speaking calmly. "Gentlemen. Gentlemen. This will get us nowhere. I'm sure we can reach an understanding."

"Inspector," I said, "I'm not trying to hassle you, and I'll be happy to give you the letters. All I want is the answers to a couple of questions."

"Such as?"

"Mostly about the second murder."

He eyed me and apparently decided that compromise was the path of least resistance. He said, "All right, Mr. Brodsky. First, the letters."

I handed him the one from Paul. "I don't have the others with me."

"Where are they?"

"I'd prefer not to involve a third party."

"Mr. Brodsky, I will not sit here and fence with you. I want those letters."

"I'm not fencing with you. I assure you, they're safe, and I'll deliver them to you this afternoon. I simply don't want an innocent party accused of aiding and abetting or anything." It was true that I didn't want him to know that Eileen had the remaining letters, but my primary motive was to prevent him from finding Donardy's notes before she had the opportunity to study them carefully.

He stared at me, saying nothing. Wellingham looked at me and then at Bailey. "I will take personal responsibility for the delivery of any and all of the victim's correspondence that may be in Mr. Brodsky's possession."

Bailey looked disgusted but said, "All right. What do you want to know?"

"About Donardy's murder. But first, I'm curious about something. Why didn't you remove Kloss's belongings from his room?" I didn't mention Donardy's because I wasn't sure they knew I had been there, too.

"We're trying to get in touch with his family. For now, we'll leave his room intact." He didn't mention Donardy either—I wondered if he was afraid to give me any ideas.

"What about Donardy's murder?"

He opened a drawer and removed a file. Reading from it, he said, "We received a telephone call from a custodian at St. Catherine's College on Tuesday at 6:22 P.M. He said that he'd found a body in the basement of the dormitories. We dispatched two men to the scene." He looked up at me and added, "Sergeant Smythe was one of them."

Smythe, who, as usual, had been silent, said, "It was Barry Donardy. I recognized him straight away. There was a revolver in his hand. He'd been shot in the temple."

"There was also a suicide note?" I asked.

"Yes. An attempt had been made to make it appear that the victim had taken his own life."

"But he hadn't."

"No. The Home Office—that's in London—was called and a pathologist was dispatched. He performed an autopsy at . . ." He stopped and looked at Bailey, who in turn looked at the file.

"It was begun at nine-fifteen."

"From the autopsy you could determine it was not a suicide?" I said.

"That's correct," Smythe said. "The weapon had been fired at least three feet from the victim. There were other factors as well."

"Were you able to determine the time of death?"

Bailey glanced at the file. "Between two and six P.M."

Smythe continued. "Paul Hobart was unable to supply an alibi when we questioned him."

"I was with him until sometime after three."

"Yes, we know that. He was seen entering his room at the Moat House at three-thirty. However, he was unable to account for his movements between that time and six o'clock."

"He told me he was in his room," I said.

"Well, yes, that's what he told us, but . . ."

"So what you mean, Sergeant, is that he has no witnesses to verify that he was in his room at that time."

Bailey smiled. "Mr. Brodsky, we do not make a distinction."

"A jury might," Wellingham put in.

"I don't expect it ever to go to a jury," I said.

"Do you know something that we don't?" Bailey asked. "I do hope you're not holding anything else back from us."

"No. All I've got is some theories. However, I do expect to have some facts soon."

"When you've got some facts. . . ." He trailed off.

"May I see the suicide note?"

Bailey reached into the file and handed me a four-by-six sheet of memo paper. It was handwritten; it read: "I've eliminated Kloss and I'm finished." It was signed, "Barry."

"I understand that you were able to establish that it was written by Donardy himself," I said.

"That's correct," Smythe said. "We found several samples of his writing in his room at St. Cat's. An expert verified that he had written the note."

I was glad they had not removed all of Donardy's papers. I said, "How do you suppose the note got written?"

"We believe that Hobart fo—"

"Excuse me, Sergeant, but how about 'the killer' or 'the murderer'?"

He smiled and nodded. "We believe the perpetrator forced Donardy to write the note at gunpoint."

"If somebody was threatening to kill you, Sergeant, would you have written the note that would make it possible for him to get away with it?"

"We wondered about that, too," Bailey said. "Several witnesses have informed us that Mr. Donardy had a rather weak personality."

I nodded. "I have to admit he was a wimp."

"Is there anything else you'd like to know, Mr. Brodsky?"

"One last question. Have you established a firmer time of death for the first murder?"

Bailey reached into his desk and pulled out another file. He leafed through it and said, "We believe about nine P.M."

"What I want to know is what the pathologist said."

He looked in the file again. "It could have been as early as six P.M. But remember, we know when the body was dumped from Mr. Hobart's vehicle."

"You mean," I said, "that you know at what time an anonymous witness called to tell you that he'd seen the body dumped."

"Perhaps. But it is consistent with the facts."

"As you know them."

"As we know them. Do these questions have something to do with your *theory*?"

"Possibly," I said.

"You will inform us if you uncover any evidence."

"You'll be the first to know."

"And you will hand over the remaining letters."

"Within the hour."

220

$\int$ 22

I went to Eileen's room at the Randolf directly from the police station. I had to retrieve Kloss's letters and, more importantly, wanted to see how she was doing with Donardy's notes.

Her response to my question about the notes was, "He might've had it, but I'll need a couple more hours."

"What about the photos?"

"They're on the nightstand. Lancaster hasn't gotten here yet."

I looked through them, and there was a picture of each suspect. I was lucky to have the one of Ann Laskey—she had been behind Nick Zorn when I took a shot of him. A small number was written below each face.

"Did you make a list of the pairings of names and numbers?"

"Of course," she said. "It's on the nightstand, too."

I saw the list and put it in my pocket. "Got it."

"I tried to pick out the clearest pictures."

"These are fine. The faces are easily identifiable."

"Danny, did you learn anything this morning?"

"Yes. Things are definitely beginning to make sense."

"Do you want to tell me what you're thinking?"

"Yeah, I do. But there's no time now." I removed the

letters from my briefcase, which was on the table that Eileen was working on, and put them in my pocket. "Hang around here if you can. I'll keep in touch."

"Don't worry. I'll be working on Barry's notes."

I stopped back at the police station and, not wanting to waste time talking with Bailey or Smythe, left the letters with the constable manning the window in the entranceway. He assured me that Detective Chief Inspector Bailey would get them.

There was a lot to do, and I was still concerned about the time—more accurately, the lack thereof. I was especially anxious to speak with the insurance investigator in Texas, but that could not be done for another two hours. Another lack—sleep—was threatening to become more serious than the inadequate time, so I decided that those two hours could be put to best use with a nap, which I took atop Eileen's bed.

She woke me with a gentle kiss, her beautiful smile, and a cup of surprisingly good coffee—she had sent out for it.

"You slept soundly," she said. "Bill Lancaster was here. I gave him the photos, and he said that this Harry Lipton—"

"Linton."

"Yeah, whatever. Will be happy to do what you wanted, whatever that is."

"That," I said, "will tell us who killed Kloss and Donardy. If he can get the information."

"A big if?"

"Unfortunately, yes. Did you think to tell Lancaster to have Linton try both here and at my hotel if they get anywhere?"

"As a matter of fact, I did."

"Good. How did you do with Donardy's notes?"

"The proof's correct," she said.

I sat up. "It is?"

"Yes."

"How good's the result?"

"It's nice. Not a bad proof."

"But not outstanding."

"No. He'd already had the result for a smaller class of operators."

"Yeah, I know," I said. "He'd been trying to generalize it for a while." I sipped the coffee and added, "You're not surprised that Donardy got it?"

"Certainly not. If you'd been working on it, you'd've never got hung up on the special case."

"So by itself, it's not good enough for a thesis?"

"No, not close," she said. "But combined with other results. . . ."

"I get the idea."

"Is this good or bad? I mean for your investigation."

"Well, it destroys one theory I'd been working on. It was based on the assumption that Donardy was a wimp and a blackmailer, but it depended on his being unable to prove the theorem by himself."

"Does this mean you're in trouble again?"

"No," I said. "All it means is that I've got only one theory left. But then, one's all I need."

"You should call Texas."

"Yes."

It took some effort to get the call through, but in a few minutes I was speaking with a Michael Kornblum, a free-lance insurance investigator with a New York accent.

"I gather," he said, "that you're interested in an investigation from fifteen years ago."

"That's right. The man's name was Arthur Rothenberg."

"Yes. His wife called me. Since she asked me to give you the information, I don't have a problem discussing it with you. But I would like to know why you're interested after all these years."

"It may be related to two murders that were committed here last week."

"Where's that?"

"Mrs. Rothenberg didn't tell you?"

"No."

"Oxford. England."

"Oh." He sounded surprised. "Do you mind giving me some details?"

"I don't, but I'm under some time pressure. If you like, I'll be happy to call you next week and fill you in."

"Please do that," he said. "What would you like to know?"

"Primarily, was your investigation routine, or was there foul play involved?"

"It was murder."

"You're sure of that?"

"I was. Yes."

"What made you so sure?"

"The brakes had been tampered with. The killer tried to make it look like an accident, but I was sure."

"How could you tell it wasn't an accident?" Eileen gasped audibly; I reached out and squeezed her hand.

"The brake line had been loosened so the fluid leaked out."

"That couldn't have happened by accident?"

"Under some circumstances, maybe. But the car had not been in the shop for several months, and the family told me that he never worked on it himself. They assured me that there was one garage that handled all the maintenance."

"It's still not clear to me why that means it couldn't have been an accident."

"If it had happened shortly after the shop had worked on the car, that might be possible. You know, if a mechanic hadn't tightened things up properly."

"Why couldn't it've happened after a long time?"

"Because bolts in a car tend to freeze up, not to get loose."

"I presume you know the car hadn't been serviced . . ."

"Yes," he said. "I checked with the garage. According to their records, it had been almost three months since they'd serviced the car. Their records showed that the car had been driven over two thousand miles since it'd been there. There's no way the line could've come loose by itself."

"You were able to verify the dates?"

"Yes. The car had been serviced on December fifteenth. The accident occurred on March twenty-ninth. No, wait. The twenty-ninth was the day he returned from a trip . . . to . . . Los Angeles. The accident was on . . . the . . . thirty-first. Sorry, I'm reading from the file."

"Are you sure of those dates?"

"Yes. Is there something wrong with them?"

"Not wrong," I said. "Just not what I expected. But I've got someone here I can check with."

"Does that give you what you want?"

"I'm not sure yet. Let me ask a couple more questions."

"Shoot."

"Why did the insurance company pay off, and why was the investigation dropped?"

"I was certain that the beneficiary—the man's wife—was not the perpetrator. Neither were either of his children. So the company had to pay off anyway."

"Wasn't there a double-indemnity clause?"

"Umm . . . I'm looking in the file. . . . Yes, there was. But that wouldn't change anything. Murder is considered an accident, from an insurance point of view."

"I see. Why was the investigation dropped?"

"Well, the insurance company had no interest, and the police didn't accept my theory."

"Is it possible they were right?"

"No. I mean, sure, anything's possible. But they should have checked into it. I think they were embarrassed because I had checked on the maintenance history. They screwed up and wouldn't admit it."

"Okay," I said. "Thanks. You've been very helpful."

"You'll call me next week?"

"I will."

I hung up, and Eileen said, "He was mur. . . ." There were tears in her eyes.

I put my arms around her. "Yes. I'm sorry. Whoever got away with that crime committed two more. I'll get the bastard. That's a promise."

She looked up at me. "That won't bring him back, will it?"

"No."

I held her close and caressed her. We were interrupted by the telephone, and I picked up the receiver. "Hello."

"Brodsky?"

"Yes."

"This is Smythe. Bailey wants to see you. Right away. I wouldn't take very long getting here if I were you."

226

"His office?"

"Yes." He hung up.

I assumed that Bailey could wait an extra five minutes, and I wanted to ask Eileen a question: "The insurance investigator said one thing I don't understand. Didn't you tell me that your father's accident occurred three weeks after he returned from the UCLA conference?"

"I don't remember saying that, but it sounds about right. Why?"

"The investigator said that the accident took place on March thirty-first, but that he returned from L.A. on the twenty-ninth."

"Yes, that's right. I remember. Dad stayed on the West Coast for a couple of weeks after the conference. He went backpacking."

"Backpacking?"

"Yes."

"By himself?"

"Yes. Somewhere in the Sierras, I think. I dunno."

"It doesn't matter. It explains the dates."

Bailey was alone in his office, sitting at his desk.

"Mr. Brodsky," he began, his tone indicating that he was even more exasperated than before, "I've always liked Americans. They may abuse the language, but I've always gotten on well with them."

"I get the distinct impression," I said, trying to smile, "that your attitude toward the colonies is changing rapidly, and that you hold me responsible for the . . . shall we say . . . difficulties of the past week."

"That about sums it up."

"It can't be something I've done since I was last here. I've been in a hotel room the whole time."

"I thought we agreed that you would keep the children out of trouble."

"Oh, god." I pulled up a chair and plunked myself in it. "What have they done now?"

"I'm afraid they've gotten themselves arrested again."

"Where?"

"Right here in Oxford. At a pub. Another fight."

I leaned forward. "They're okay?"

"They're not seriously injured, if that's what you mean."

"Thank god for small favors." I leaned back and added, "Inspector, I don't know what to say. I—"

"It's not your fault, Mr. Brodsky. I know that. But this week has created some difficulties for me. I shouldn't be here. I should be with my wife in Scotland."

"You were planning a vacation?"

"Yes."

"To tell you the truth, this wasn't the week I'd planned, either."

"I'm sure it wasn't." He looked at the ceiling and sighed. "I realize you're not to blame. You're not responsible for a murderer running rampant or for a couple of crazy kids."

"Can you tell me what happened?"

"We're not entirely sure. We've got two different stories. You can talk to the children yourself. As best we can tell, they went into a pub and got into a fight with a patron. The man claims they started it; the children say he started it. I will say this. The man was drunk. He's been arrested as well."

"What will it take to get this mess cleared up?"

"I think we've already done that," he said. "The

drunk will be kept overnight until he sleeps it off. The pub owner said that there was some damage. Several bottles and a bar stool were broken. But he agreed to let the two boys work it off. He'll have them wash dishes, I believe. He wants them there at six this evening."

"Well, thank you, Inspector. I know it's been difficult for you."

"The last time I said something to you about international relations. I'm beginning to think that we may have chosen the wrong allies."

"At least you haven't lost your sense of humor."

"I'm not entirely sure that was a joke." Nonetheless, he was smiling. "Would you like to see them now?"

"Yes."

"They're in an interrogation room downstairs." He pressed a button and said into the intercom, "Sergeant Smythe, Mr. Brodsky is ready to see the young Americans." He said to me, "Tell them about the arrangements. I'll be disappointed if they're not at the pub on time tonight."

"They will be if I have to drag them there by the ear. I'll make sure the girls remain in the hotel."

"That should keep them out of trouble."

"At least until tomorrow."

"Uncle Danny. I'm so glad you're here."

"I'll leave you alone with the prisoners," Smythe said, closing the door behind him.

Kathy hugged me, and I said, "What have you done now?"

"It wasn't our fault. It wasn't."

"All right. Sit down. Take it easy." Amy, looking sullen, was already sitting; Steve was holding a handkerchief to a bloody nose with one hand while the other was being bandaged by a woman dressed in white (I assumed she was a nurse); a teenager who must have been Colin had a black eye. I said, "Now, tell me what happened."

Kathy looked at the woman and whispered to me, "I think we should wait until she leaves."

I grinned. "Whatever you say." I was reasonably certain that Bailey would be listening through the bug that wasn't there, but I could not imagine anything they would say that I would not want him to hear. I looked at the four of them and said, "At least nobody was seriously injured."

"Nah," Colin said. "Only me eye and Stevie's nose. We don't count 'is 'and since 'e 'urt it on the man's bloody jaw."

"You must be Colin."

"You got that right, mate. You's the Dan Brodsky little Katie talks about?"

"I guess I am."

"Yer a private eye, eh?"

"That's what they tell me," I said. "If I'm not mistaken, the last time you had a bloody nose and Steve a black eye."

"There's nothing broken," the nurse said to Steve. "You'll be all right in a day or two." She stood and said, "Has the bleeding stopped?"

Steve pulled the handkerchief down, and she examined his nose. "You'll live," she said.

She turned to Colin and looked at his eye. "You can see all right?"

"'Pears so. Don't you worry yer pretty little head 'bout me."

The nurse shook her head but left without otherwise responding.

"What am I going to do with you?" I said.

"Oh, Uncle Danny, we were only trying to help."

"I'm afraid it was my doin', mate," Colin put in. "You see, this gentleman was be'avin' less than gentlemanly. 'e made some downright impolite remarks about the little ladies. We couldn't 'ave that, could we?"

"He's right, Professor Brodsky," Steve said. "The man made insulting remarks about Kathy and Amy."

"So you punched him in the nose?"

"Not exactly. Colin asked him to keep his dirty thoughts to himself. Something like that."

"It wasn't Colin's fault, Uncle Danny. The man became more abusive. He was *mean*."

Amy said, "The man threw the first punch. He hit Colin in the eye."

"That's when you stepped in, Steve?"

"Well . . . er . . . I couldn't just sit there and do nothin'."

"Steve was great!" Kathy said. "He stayed calm and asked the guy to stop. The guy hit Steve in the nose. So Steve decked him. With one punch. It was great."

"I can see that." I said to Steve, "I guess you're proud of yourself."

He was smiling but said, "Well, no. I mean, I know it was wrong and all. And my hand hurts."

"You'll get over it." I didn't know whether to laugh or cry. I must admit that it sounded as though they had handled themselves pretty well. Of course, I had no intention of telling them that. I said, "You will have to pay for your crimes."

"Oh, Uncle Danny. What are they going to do to us?"

"Nothing serious. Steve and Colin will spend the evening washing dishes, and you and Amy are confined to quarters."

"You mean we have to stay in our room?"

"In the hotel, anyway. And if you get into trouble again . . ."

"We won't. We won't. I promise."

"Me, too," Amy said. "I promise, too."

"Gentlemen, if the two of you are not in that pub by six o'clock sharp, I will personally break every bone in your bodies, one by one."

"You can count on it, mate."

"We'll be there," Steve said. "Are we free to go?"

"No. You're grounded, too. I'll drive you all back to our hotel, and at exactly five forty-five, you and Colin will take a taxi to the pub."

"A cab?" Steve said. "Umm . . ."

"Don't worry about the fare. I'll pay for it."

"Can we get out of here now, Uncle Danny?"

"Not quite yet, young lady. What did you mean when you said you were only trying to help?"

"Oh, yeah. We *were* trying to help. You see, we knew the real killer had to be one of the Texans."

"Right," Amy said. "There were only three Texans left. One was a woman. Eileen St. Somebody-or-other. We figured the perpetrator had to be a man."

"So what did you do?"

"You told us to follow someone when we first offered to help," Kathy said.

"I remember."

"So that's what we did. There were two of them. A Ross White and a Calvin Barnett. You know who they are?"

"Yes."

"Well, we followed them," Amy said. "Colin and I stayed with Barnett, and Steve and Kathy took White."

"How did you all end up in the same pub?"

"They met there," Steve said. "I think they were having lunch."

"Really? Did you hear anything of what they had to say to each other?"

"Nah, 'fraid not, mate," Colin said. "We didn' wanna be too conspicuous, if you know what I mean."

"So instead you got into a fight?"

"Well . . ."

Kathy took the heat off Colin by saying, "Does that help, Uncle Danny? Their being together?"

"You never know," I said. "It's possible."

"So what we did wasn't completely bad?"

She had a pleading look in her eyes, and I relented. "No. Not completely. It was a good idea. And it does sound like the fight wasn't your fault. But no more trouble. Agreed?"

"Agreed. But isn't there something we can do to help?"

"Only if you can do it from the hotel, and only with specific instructions from me, and only if you do it with adult supervision."

"Okay." She was looking at her feet. She was also smiling.

I stopped at the Randolf to pick up Eileen St. Somebody-or-other and the duplicate photos. I drove the five of them to the Moat House and gave the kids specific instructions to be carried out under Eileen's supervision: Talk with every hotel employee they could find and ask each one if he had seen anyone breaking into a car on the evening of the murder. I went to St. Catherine's.

∫ 23

It was five P.M. Saturday—the last evening before most of the conferees would be departing—and many had gathered in the dining hall at St. Catherine's. I wanted to ask questions of several of them, mostly to fill in details and to verify some guesses. One was Ross White, and he found me.

"Hey, Dan," he said, flagging me from across the room when I walked into the lounge with the bar. Coming toward me, he asked, "Have you heard what happened to Paul Hobart's daughter?"

"I've got a pretty good idea. How did you know about it?" I hadn't forgotten that he had been in the pub when the kids were arrested, but I wanted to hear his description of the incident. He started to say something, but I interrupted. "Why don't we go into the next room? It's a little quieter there."

He followed me into a large, dimly lit room. When the conference had been functioning, it was brightly lit, and coffee and tea were served there after lunch. It was furnished with long tables and chairs, a small version of the dining room.

We took seats, and White said, "To answer your question, I was in a pub having lunch. I heard a ruckus, and when I turned around, the boy she was with was punching someone. Looked like a drunk. A constable must have been close by because he was there right away. He arrested four kids and the drunk."

"I'm curious about a couple of things, Ross."

"Yes?"

"First, how did you know who she was and who she was with?"

"Well, I saw her around the conference. Somebody told me she was Hobart's daughter."

"And the boy. How did you know they were together?"

He stared at me for a few seconds. "I saw them together last night and again this morning. To tell you the truth, I think they were following me." He stared at me again and said, "Did you put them up to it?"

"No. Certainly not. Why would I?"

"You think I killed Kloss and Donardy."

"Not true. If they followed you, they took it upon themselves to do so."

"Why don't I believe you?"

I smiled and shrugged. "Ross, I'm telling you the truth. Kathy has succeeded only in getting me in trouble with the police. Call Detective Chief Inspector Bailey. He'll tell you that I'm not on his good-guy list, largely because of Kathy Hobart. To be honest, you are a suspect, but not very high on my list."

"Why?"

"Why are you a suspect or why aren't you high on my list?"

"Why a suspect."

"You were in Texas fifteen years ago, and you're still there," I said. "All the Texans are suspects."

"I'm not in Austin anymore."

"I know, but Rice is close enough. And the main thing is you were in Austin when Kloss and Barnett

235

stole Paul's work. Doesn't matter, Ross—you're not a serious suspect."

"If you want my opinion, it was Kloss that did the stealing. He used Cal to cover his theft."

"That's probably what happened," I said. "I merely meant they published the work jointly."

"I'm glad you think that, because I don't think Cal makes a very good suspect."

"I don't know why you think he's innocent, but he does have an airtight alibi."

"He was playing poker."

"Right," I said. "I see you've been keeping up with the case."

"I'm sure everyone has. We're all involved, one way or another."

"How do you mean?"

"Most of us knew Kloss and Donardy, and the murders took place at our conference. How could we not be involved?"

"Of course. I guess I'm too close to it."

"You said you were curious about a few things, Dan. What else?"

"Why did you choose that particular pub?"

"If what you're getting at is why was I eating lunch in the same place that Kathy Hobart got arrested, I think she was following me, even if you didn't put her up to it."

"I didn't. I'm just in the habit of asking questions."

"Well, I didn't choose the pub. Cal did. We met there for lunch. To anticipate your next question, I suggested we go to lunch. I wanted to ask him about a recent paper of his."

"Innocent enough," I said.

"You really are suspicious about everything."

"I have to be if I'm to expose the real killer."

"You still think Hobart didn't do it?"

"Yes. No doubt in my mind. You think he's guilty?"

"I didn't at first," he said, "but it was quite a coincidence that Donardy was killed during the few hours he was out of jail."

"Nonetheless, he's innocent."

"I hope you're right," he said. "I don't know Paul that well, but I've always like him."

"I do know him that well, and he is innocent."

"I'll take your word for it. I doubt there's anything useful I can tell you."

"You never know," I said. "What do you remember about the now infamous paper?"

"I read it, of course. It . . ."

"How about its origins?"

"You can't think I was involved with—"

"No. Of course not. Nobody would steal anything that good and let someone else get the credit. All I meant was that you were in Austin when the paper was written. When did you first hear about it? What did you—"

"I remember exactly. It was maybe a week after I got back from a conference."

"At UCLA?"

"Yes. Were you there?"

"Yeah. I was still a student. That was my first conference. It was also the place that Kloss met Paul and learned his technique."

"Of course. That's it."

"Sorry?"

"I was talking to myself," White said. "Arthur took Paul out to dinner after Paul's talk. He invited Kloss to join them. I remember because I was jealous." He smiled. "I was a kid and could sometimes be a real jerk."

"Weren't we all. You were saying something about hearing about the results shortly after the conference?"

"It made quite a stir in Austin. The proof was so elegant and answered so many questions. That's why I remember it so well. That and the fact that it was Kloss that got it."

"How's that?"

"I told you the last time we talked that I didn't like him. I resented his getting such a good result."

"How soon after the conference?"

"At most two weeks."

"It couldn't have been longer?"

He thought for a few seconds and said, "I doubt it."

"Do you know if Arthur Rothenberg was in town?"

"Probably. It was the middle of the semes. . . . No wait. He stayed in L.A. for a couple of weeks. I remember him missing the seminar."

"Who first showed you the results?"

"Howard Williams. We were both post docs. We spent an afternoon talking about it. Several days, really. Until Arthur died."

"Did you discuss it with him?"

"No. I assumed we'd talk about it in the seminar, but it was their result and their job—privilege—to show it to him."

"Who else did you discuss it with?"

"Cal, of course. I wouldn't have talked with Kloss. I'm sure Terry—Terry Henkler—and I talked about it. I may be the one that showed it to him."

"What was Terry's reaction?"

"He was impressed, naturally," he said. "He and I looked at it and saw how many interesting corollaries there were. In fact, there was one we found that I showed to Cal. Don't get me wrong. It was their work. They just hadn't noticed one of the corollaries." He paused and added, "At the time, I thought it was their work."

"What kind of discussion did you have with Cal?"

"I showed him the corollary. I guess I congratulated him. It isn't every day you get a result like that. It was funny."

"How do you mean?"

"He was fairly modest about it. Out of character."

"Anything else you remember?"

"Can't think of anything," he said. "Does any of this help?"

"It fills in some details. That always helps."

We returned to the lounge. Passing the bar, I overheard Cal Barnett saying, "God, this stuff's awful."

I said, "Then why do you drink it?"

He turned quickly. When he saw me, he smiled and said, "Hi, Dan. How's tricks?"

"As well as can be expected. Why *do* you drink the stuff?"

"I like coffee."

"I haven't touched the poison since Monday. I make my own."

"Yeah, I heard you were a coffee gourmet. What's your secret?"

"I buy good beans and make it properly."

"You'll have to show me sometime."

"I will."

White said, "Dan, let me say good night. I have to pack up, and I'm supposed to meet Terry for dinner in an hour."

"Sure. Good night." I said to Barnett, "Say, do you

have a few minutes? I'd like to ask you a few more questions."

"Don't you ever stop?" He looked at his watch. "I'm afraid I don't have the time. I've got an early plane to catch tomorrow morning. I still have to pack, and I'd like to get some dinner. Why don't you call me when you get home?"

"It won't take that long," I said. "I'll tell you what. Three hours should be enough time to eat and to pack up. If you come to my hotel at nine, I'll make you the finest cup of coffee you've ever had. I'll even throw in some of the best pastries you've ever tasted."

He thought about it for a few seconds. "I guess I can't refuse an offer like that."

"Good. See you at nine."

He said, "I'll be there," and left.

There were two other witnesses—suspects—I wanted to interview for a second time: Terry Henkler and Ann Laskey. I found them talking in one of the lounges. I would have preferred to speak with each one separately, but there was the time factor, and they were already together.

They greeted me in a friendly manner, and I said, "Can you stand a few more questions?"

Henkler said, "Sure, why not? What's on your mind?"

"I want to fill in or verify some details. Mostly about the paper that Barnett and Kloss wrote."

"You mean the one that was based on Paul's insights?"

"That's the one. When did you first hear about it?"

"That's easy," he said. "Ross White called me and invited me over for dinner. He wanted to show me this great result. We spent most of the evening looking at it.

It had a lot of implications. We even found one that Cal and Kloss had missed."

"So Ross was the one who told you Barnett and Kloss had discovered it?"

"Yes."

"Who else did you discuss it with?"

"I remember talking about it with Cal," he said. "He seemed embarrassed. I don't think he was used to getting so much attention around the department."

"Anyone else?"

"Howard Williams. He already knew about it. I showed it to Ann, too."

"Did you?" she said. "I thought I first saw it when John Ling asked me to read a preprint."

"I'm sure I showed it to you. It was during a luncheon when Arthur was out of town."

"If you did," she said, "I don't remember. Of course, I was still a student and wouldn't have understood its significance."

"It doesn't matter," I said. "Terry, you mentioned that Rothenberg was out of town. Can you remember when he got back? What was the relative timing of his return and his death?"

"He'd gone to Los Angeles for a conference. He stayed a couple of extra weeks." He looked away and then back at me. "I never saw him after he got home. He was in Austin for two or three days when the accident . . ." He stopped and closed his eyes.

"Is that consistent with your recollections, Ann?"

"It's not inconsistent, anyway. I don't remember the dates that well."

"Can you—"

"Sorry to interrupt." It was Ross White.

"Hi, Ross." Henkler turned to me. "I hope that answers your questions, Dan. We would like to go to dinner."

"That's all right. You've been very helpful. Where're you headed?"

"A place called La Salle à Manger," Terry said. "The food's quite good. You're welcome to join us."

"Thanks, but I don't think so. I've got too much to do."

I drove to the Moat House, getting there at seven-thirty; Eileen and the girls were in my room.

Because of the presence of Kathy and Amy, Eileen did not give me the hug I needed. She said, "Did you accomplish anything? We did."

"You may report."

"Yessir. First, we haven't heard anything from Lancaster or Lipton."

"Linton."

"He's the one."

"You may continue."

"Yessir. I put Steve and Colin in a cab myself, and I'm sure they got to the pub on time. Sounds like a song, doesn't it?"

"Terrific. What did you learn?"

"Yessir."

"Enough, Eileen. Tell me what you found out."

"We spoke to everyone we could who was working at the hotel Monday night. We found the witness you wanted."

"You're kidding! Who was it?"

"A clerk."

"No," I said. "What I mean is, who did he identify?"

"She. We don't know. Not yet. We didn't have the photographs when we talked to her."

"How did that happen?"

"We had spoken to a lot of people and then took a dinner break. We left the photos here. We found her right after we ate."

"Why didn't you get them then?"

"She was on her way home. She said she had a date, but she promised to stop back later. She did leave a phone number where we could reach her."

"You'll have to call her. I want the timing to work right."

"The timing of what?"

"Let's not worry about that right now," I said. "She did say she could identify the person she saw?"

"Yes. But I still don't see what difference it would make if someone was playing with Paul's car at the hotel two hours after the murder."

"Don't worry about that, either. Trust me, it's important."

She shrugged and said, "Did you learn anything?"

"Yes. I also did something stupid."

"What was that?"

"I need to have all the key people here tonight. I invited Cal Barnett, who said he'd come. Then I was talking to Ross White, Terry Henkler, and Ann Laskey but didn't think to ask them."

"Is there anything you can do?"

"Yes, fortunately. They're having dinner together. They gave me the name of the restaurant."

"So you can call them."

"I could, but I won't. I want you to go and pick them up. First, call the woman you spoke—"

"The witness we found?"

"Yes. Tell her it's extremely important that she meet you in the lobby at exactly nine o'clock. No, not in the lobby. Somewhere where you won't be seen. She knows the hotel and can choose a place to meet. When you pick up Henkler, White, and Laskey, drop them off in Howard's room by ten to nine."

"Then I meet the witness and have her identify the photo?"

"Yes. Then go back to Howard's room and call me. I'll be here." I gave her the keys to the car I had rented. "You better leave now. I want them on time."

"Okay. I wish I understood what was going on."

"You will soon enough. Oh, one last thing. After you call me, call the Oxford police and ask for Detective Chief Inspector Bailey. If he's not there, tell them to find him. They'll do it when you tell them that I'll have a murderer for him when he gets here."

"You know who did it?"

"I think so. I'm within epsilon of putting it all together."

"That's—"

Kathy broke in. "What does that mean? Within epson?"

"*Epsilon.* It's a mathematical expression. It means very close."

"Oh."

"Will you tell us who did it?" Eileen asked.

"Not now. There's no time to explain. Now get going."

"But—"

"On your way."

After Eileen left, I said to Amy, "Do you know where your father is?"

"He's in his room waiting for you. He said he had something important to tell you."

"Good. I'll go over there now."

244

"Aren't you going to tell us who did it?" Kathy said.

"Not now. It's too complicated."

"Oh." She frowned but then smiled and said, "Okay. What do we do?"

"First, go down to the restaurant and get some food. Anything that looks edible. Bring it to Howard's room. I've hardly eaten all day, and I'm starved."

"Then what?"

"Then you go to your room and stay put."

"But we want to be here."

"You're grounded, remember?"

"But . . . but you said anywhere in the hotel."

"That was before. Now I'm telling you to stay in your room." She was crestfallen. "Kathy, listen to me. This is not a game. I don't want you and Amy to get hurt. You'll have to trust me on this."

She put a brave smile on her face. "Okay, Uncle Danny. Whatever you say."

I gave her a hug and said, "I'm very proud of you. And your dad will be, too, when I tell him how great you've been." I looked at my watch; it was almost eight o'clock. "Now get to it. We don't have much time."

"I finally got in touch with Hans Nystrom," Howard said.

"Excellent."

"He's waiting for your call." He handed me a piece of paper. "That's the phone number."

"Thanks, I'll call him right away."

"How's the investigation coming? There's not much time left."

"I'm painfully aware of the time," I said. "But I'm close to fitting all the pieces together."

"Anything I can do?"

"As a matter of fact, there is. Can you remember when you first heard about the paper that Kloss and Barnett wrote?"

"*The* paper?" he said.

"Yes."

"I'd gone into Cal's office to ask him a question. Barry Donardy was there. In fact, it was Donardy that asked Cal to show it to me. I don't think he was ready to tell people about it, but Donardy knew about it and asked him to show me. Cal was a little reluctant to talk about it at first."

"Who did you show it to?"

"I don't remember specifically, but I certainly discussed it with Terry Henkler and Ross White. We were kind of excited about it."

"Did you ever talk about it with Arthur Rothenberg?" I said.

"Umm. . . . I don't think so. He may have been out of town."

"It couldn't have been after his accident?"

"No. I'm sure of that."

There was a knock on the door. Howard admitted the girls; Kathy was carrying a much-needed tray of food. I sent them to their room and, between bites, gave Howard instructions to come to my room later with the other guests.

I was back in my room at 8:35, having retrieved Mrs. Levin's pastries from the hotel kitchen. I managed several bites of the food Kathy had brought while dialing Hans Nystrom. His English was very good, but his memory wasn't. After considerable prodding, I learned that my supposition about him had been remarkably accurate.

At 8:48 I had assuaged my hunger, at least enough

to function, and tried to call several people. I found Nick Zorn on the third attempt, and he remembered looking at his watch at a key moment, verifying my own faulty memory.

It was 8:57. I filled my teapot with water and plugged it in.

The stage was set.

∫ 24

There was a knock on the door at 9:07. It was Cal
Barnett. I greeted him with a friendly smile. "C'mon
in. The water's boiling away." He followed me into the
room, and I added, "I'll show you the proper way to
make a cup of coffee."

"This I've gotta see."

"Sit down." I unplugged the pot. "You don't want to
use boiling water, so you let it cool for a minute or
two." I pulled out the last of my coffee beans and
dumped them into the coffee mill. Over the noise of
the grinder I said, "Freshness is essential, so you have
to grind the beans yourself. The bean quality's important, too. This is Jamaica Blue Mountain, the finest coffee available anywhere." I turned off the mill. "But you
can do okay with a less expensive—"

"How expensive is it?"

"Usually close to twenty bucks a pound."

He raised his eyebrows. "Wow."

"Like I said, there is very good, less-expensive coffee. I don't usually drink this myself." I folded a filter,
put it in the cone, and measured in the grounds.
"Whatever you do, *never* percolate your coffee." The
sweet aroma of the freshly ground beans filled the air.

"Smells good," he said. "Why not?"

I poured the water through the coffee, using a circular motion. "A percolator boils the coffee as it brews it. There's no better way to ruin coffee than to boil it."

"Never knew that."

"You may have without realizing it," I said. "During the heyday of the percolator, coffee consumption in the U.S. reached an all-time low. It increased again when people started using electric drip machines."

"You think it's because they made better coffee?"

"Exactly." I poured more water. "It's my theory that people drank less because unconsciously they recognized that it wasn't as good."

"You're making a lot of coffee."

"There are more guests coming," I said. "It'll be ready in another minute."

"I have to admit I'm looking forward to this."

"How do you like it?"

"A little milk if you have some."

"I do," I said. "I had dinner here and saved some just for this occasion." Using the cup from my dinner tray and the mug I always have with me, I poured coffee for both of us, adding a little milk to Barnett's. "Here, try that." I put the plate of pastries in front of him. "You'll find these go very well with the coffee."

"Is this a special occasion?"

"Yes. How's the coffee?"

The telephone rang. It was Eileen. She said, "Everything's set. Are you ready?"

"Yes."

"I should make the call now and then bring them up?"

"Yes." I hung up.

Barnett took a sip, looked at the cup, and said, "Quite strong, but *very* good. What makes this a special occasion?"

I drank some of that exquisite brew and said, "I expect to bring a murderer to justice."

He looked surprised. "I thought you wanted to ask me a few more questions."

"I did. But I now have all the answers I need."

"Do you want to tell me who did it?"

There was a knock on the door, and Eileen, Howard, Ross White, Terry Henkler, and Ann Laskey entered together.

"I see you all met up," I said. "Very convenient. The coffee's ready, and if it sits any longer it'll deteriorate." I pulled out some foam cups from a drawer. "Sorry, but you'll have to use these. They're all I've got." I put the cups on the table. "Help yourselves. You'll have to fight over the pastries, but I'm afraid I've been rather greedy with the rest."

Eileen handed me a manila folder. "The photos are inside," she whispered. "She identified the one on top. You'll be surprised at who it is."

"I doubt it."

I wasn't.

I waited for everybody to get settled. They each tried the coffee and were complimentary, but, then, the situation did not lend itself to criticism.

"I was just telling Cal," I began, "that I know the identity of the murderer."

An eerie silence enveloped the room. Barnett said, "Well, as they say, who dunnit?"

"In due time. In due time." I drank some coffee and looked around the room—all eyes were upon me. "It's funny. I had it solved right from the beginning, but I didn't have enough confidence in my intuition. There were a couple of facts I couldn't reconcile and some motivations that didn't make sense. If I had pursued that line from the beginning, life would've been a lot simpler."

Henkler said, "Now you've got everything figured out?"

"Yes. I was able to reconcile the facts, at least in my mind, this afternoon, though it was only a short while ago that I was able to verify that I was right. And it wasn't until this evening that I could make sense out of the motivations."

"I wish you'd get to the point," Barnett said. "It's getting late, and I've got an early plane to catch."

"I'm afraid this is my show, and we'll do it my way."

"I don't think so." He stood up. "I'm leaving."

I stared at him and said, "This is more important than your beauty sleep."

He returned my stare, looked around the room, and sat down. He shook his head. "All right. But don't take too long, will you?"

"Let me tell you a little story," I said. "Fifteen years ago there was a young, unknown mathematician. He happened to be very good but no one knew it yet, least of all him. One day he discovers a remarkable proof of a spectacular theorem, and then he meets a famous mathematician. Anxious to impress the famous man, our hero describes his proof. Were this a fairy tale, he would have received instant fame and fortune and lived happily ever after. Unfortunately . . ."

"Dan, I'm enjoying your homespun story telling," White said, "but we all know who the players are, so how about telling it straight and getting to the point?"

"Okay. I—"

The phone rang. I picked it up and said, "Hello."

"Is this Brodsky?"

"Yes."

251

"Do you recognize my voice?"

"Yes." It was Harry Linton.

"I found the man you're looking for."

"Was he able to identify anyone in the photos I sent you?"

"Yes. It was—"

"Number four."

"You already knew."

"I needed confirmation," I said. "Will the man testify in court?"

"I don't think so. Consider the business he's in."

"Suppose we could arrange some sort of immunity? His testimony will help put away a man who has murdered three people."

"With immunity, maybe. But don't count on it. I will ask him."

"Thanks. You've been a tremendous help."

"Thank *you*," he said. "I was very pleased to have my property returned."

"Glad I could help."

"It was also good to see our mutual friend again. We had a pleasant dinner together."

"Good. Thanks again." I hung up and returned to my audience. "That," I said, "was the final piece of evidence. Not that I needed it."

"Did you say *three* murders?" Henkler asked.

"Yes. Three."

"You will explain?"

"Certainly. And I will speed up the narration of our little tale." I finished my coffee. "Paul described his work to Arthur Rothenberg and Martin Kloss. It never occurred to him that anyone would try to steal it, so he was in no hurry to get a paper out. In fact, he liked the idea of having a mathematician of Rothenberg's stature

252

spread the news. In any case, six weeks later Kloss and Cal submitted Paul's results to a journal. One irony that some of you may not be aware of is that Paul was asked to referee the paper."

"You're kidding," Laskey said.

"No."

"What'd he do?"

"He simply declined. Of course, he was furious."

White said, "Sounds like a motive for murder to me."

"I'm not so sure about that," I said. "But if it was, Kloss would have been dead fifteen years ago. No, Paul is not the murderer."

"Then who is?" Barnett said.

"I'm getting there. The key is to understand how the purloined paper got written. That was where I had difficulty with some of the motivations. This afternoon I learned that Arthur Rothenberg went backpacking after the UCLA conference, and he died two days after returning to Austin. The point is, he never had a chance to describe Paul's results to anyone. That was one thing that had bothered me."

Howard, who had been silent until then, said in a husky voice, "Was Arthur the third victim?"

"I'll get to that," I said. "When Kloss got back to Austin, he explained Paul's work to Cal. Now, this may not be too important, but in my mind it clarifies some of what happened. Kloss was gay. Based on some things I've heard, I suspect that Cal was one of his, shall we say, paramours."

"That's crazy," Barnett said. "Where d'you hear that?"

"It's supposition, really. But I don't know why you're so upset. Most homosexuals, certainly in academic circles, have come out of the closet. There's nothing to be ashamed of."

"I'm not ashamed. I'm not gay, either."

"It doesn't really matter," I said. "At some point, Cal and Kloss were discussing the results in one of their offices. There may not have been any intention of stealing the work, at least not then. They were probably looking at it simply because it was interesting."

"Then how did the paper come about?" Henkler said.

"Barry Donardy came in and overheard their conversation. He got the impression that it was their work. They may not have done that on purpose. We'll probably never know. At some time later, Cal and Howard were talking, and Donardy ran into them. Donardy told Howard that Cal and Kloss had an interesting result and asked Cal to describe it. Cal was reluctant because he knew it was Paul's and he could've corrected—"

"Wait one second," Barnett said. "I never knew it was Paul's work. I never would have . . . This is ridiculous." He got up. "I won't stand for this. I'm leaving."

"You're not going anywhere." My tone left no room for argument.

He looked around; everyone was staring at him.

"Sit down, Cal. You'll listen with everyone else." He looked at the six of us; reluctantly, he obeyed my command. I said to him, "There were two reasons for asking everyone to join us here. First, these are the people who knew and loved Arthur Rothenberg, so they deserved to be a party to your capture. Secondly, I'm not terribly brave, and I was afraid of you. You'd already killed three times. I had no doubt that you'd try to kill me, too. I figured it'd be a lot safer if you were outnumbered six to one."

He looked around, looking for something, anything, that would get him out of there. "You'd give your right arm for that gun, wouldn't you?" I smiled. "Trying to set up the suicide was a mistake. Not only did you bungle the job, you left behind what might have been your one means of escape."

He was beginning to squirm. I must confess that there was a third reason—in reality, the primary reason—for setting up this little get-together: I wanted to see him squirm. I wanted him to feel trapped, caged, to feel the despair that Paul had felt. I wanted him to hear the details of the case against him, to know that there was no escape.

The phone rang again. This time it was Sergeant Smythe. He told me he was in the hotel lobby as requested, and I asked him to wait there for my call. He objected until I guaranteed to deliver the killer along with an open-and-shut case.

"Even the gun wouldn't help now," I said after putting the receiver back in its cradle. "That was the police." I did my best, albeit rotten, Humphrey Bogart imitation: "They got the place surrounded, sweetheart."

"You can't prove anything."

"I think I can. All of it. Shall I continue?"

"Please do," Howard said, "I'm enjoying this."

The intent eyes of the others demonstrated that their feelings, like Howard's, were not too different from mine: We hated this man for what he had done, for what he had taken from us. The tears rolling down Eileen's cheeks pointed to her greater loss.

"You were explaining how the paper got written," Terry said.

"Yes. When Barnett didn't tell Howard that it was Paul's work, the news made its way around the department in Austin. Barnett was in the limelight, and he liked it. Kloss was not a popular man, so Barnett was the one to get the accolades. I don't know why Kloss never said anything. I suppose he assumed it would end when Rothenberg returned from the West Coast. We'll never know."

Through her tears, Eileen cried, "You mean he killed my father so he could get credit for a lousy theorem?"

I wanted to take her in my arms and hold her and comfort her. I merely said, "That's about it."

"You'll never prove any of this," Barnett said.

"I will. Which is fortunate for you. Otherwise, you'd never leave this room alive."

He stood up. "I—"

"Shut up and sit down! If you don't, we'll tie you to the chair and gag you."

He glanced around the room and suddenly ran toward the door. Ross, who was closest, stuck out his foot and tripped him. He tried to get up, but Eileen picked up a plate from the dinner tray and broke it over his head. He was groggy but conscious, and Ross and I picked him up by his arms and slammed him into a chair, in the process banging his head against the wall behind it. We tied him to it with a sheet from the bed.

We sat down, and I continued. "As I was saying before you so rudely interrupted me. . . ."

Barnett glared at me and said, "You're having a good time, aren't you?"

"As a matter of fact, I am. There's ample evidence that you sabotaged Rothenberg's car."

"What evidence?" he said sullenly.

"First, there's an insurance investigator in Austin who can testify that Arthur Rothenberg's brakes had been tampered with. I know that you're a car buff and easily capable of disabling the brakes. Additionally, there's a man who saw you tamper with the car."

"Who?" He sounded surprised.

"Hans Nystrom." His expression changed when he recognized the name. "I see you remember him." To the others I said, "I don't know how many of you knew him, but he was a student at Texas. He hadn't thought anything of Barnett's working on the car, but he made the mistake of telling Barnett that he'd seen him. So another accident was arranged. Nystrom wasn't killed, only permanently injured. He returned to Denmark, but he's prepared to testify if the Austin district attorney decides to prosecute." I turned back to Barnett. "You'd have been a lot better off if you hadn't bothered with him. He wasn't a threat."

"That may explain what happened fifteen years ago," Ross said, "but what about Kloss's murder? How did he do it? He was in the poker game, wasn't he? And what was his motive?"

"As to motive, shortly before the conference, Kloss wrote a letter to Paul asking for a meeting at COTCA. Paul pretty much told him to go to hell, and we all know what happened during Kloss's lecture. It's my surmise that Kloss planned to apologize to Paul for the theft, and he obviously would've implicated Barnett in the process. I'm not sure of Kloss's motives, but I am reasonably certain that was his intention. Moreover, he told Barnett he would do so. That I know from a letter I saw that Barnett wrote to Kloss."

"That's why Barnett killed Kloss?" Ann Laskey was speaking.

"Yes."

"What about the poker game?"

"I'm almost there. Barnett came to England two weeks before the conference, during which time he purchased the murder weapon. The seller remembers him. Paul's demonstration at Kloss's talk fell right into Barnett's plans. He invited Paul to dinner and cut the fuel line while Paul was waiting inside the restaurant. After dinner he met Kloss and killed him and then came to the poker game. Meanwhile, Paul got stuck after driving a couple of miles. That left Paul without an alibi."

I paused, having reached the key point. "The police received an anonymous call at 9:17 telling them that a man was seen dumping a body. As a result, all Barnett needed was an alibi at the time of that phone call. He was quite clever about that. He played very poorly, betting heavily, and losing heavily, right from the beginning. What I missed, and what I remembered after seeing Donardy's ostensible suicide note, was that he took a ten-minute break a little after nine. I wasn't sure of the time, but Nick Zorn happened to look at his watch when Barnett took his break."

Terry said, "Ten minutes wouldn't give him enough time to dump the body."

"No, but it was enough to telephone the police. Barnett dumped the body when he killed Kloss. He used the break only to make the phone call."

"What about the bloodstains?" Ross said. "Paul hadn't gotten to the game when Barnett made the phone call."

"That was easy. After Paul showed up, Barnett started losing again, and he quit early."

"We have a witness who says Cal was inside Paul's car around eleven-thirty," Eileen said, now understanding the significance of Barnett's actions. "Several of us spent the afternoon talking to hotel employees. We found one who saw him breaking in with a hanger. Cal told her that he'd locked his keys in the car, and she didn't think anything of it. But she remembered."

"That's right," I said. "I always take pictures of people at conferences, and she identified Barnett from one of them."

"Those pictures were in the folder Eileen gave you when we got here?" Ross said.

"Yes. I didn't need that identification, though. I was certain it was Barnett when I read Donardy's so-called suicide note."

"What'd that tell you?" Howard said.

"I knew that Donardy had asked Barnett to be his advisor. Barry told me that Barnett had said maybe, but that Barnett also said that if Barry could get a certain result he'd been working on, it would be enough for a thesis."

"What'd that have to do with the suicide?"

"Donardy had proved a theorem about subnormal operators satisfying Kloss's condition. He wanted to get rid of the extra hypothesis. He told me he'd succeeded, and Eileen read through his notes and verified that he was correct."

"So?"

"The so-called suicide note read: 'I've eliminated Kloss and I'm finished.' It was signed 'Barry.' He meant that he had gotten rid of.Kloss's condition and was finally finished with all requirements for the degree."

"Of course," Howard said, snapping his fingers. "Donardy sent the note to Cal to say—"

"You got it. In fact, Barry told me he'd sent Barnett a note to that effect. That was the most important clue for me. As soon as I read the note, I knew Barnett was the killer."

"Why'd he kill Barry?" Eileen said.

"I'm not completely clear on that. I think he made the same mistake with me he'd made with Hans Nystrom. Nystrom wasn't a threat, but Barnett thought he was. It's a lot like when you're throwing a surprise party. You know you're doing it, so you think the victim is suspicious. I asked Barnett about cars, since sabotaging Paul's car was the key to the frame."

"What do cars have to do with being suspicious?" Terry asked.

"That's when Barnett began to worry about me. He told me that Barry knew about cars to throw suspicion at Barry. I wasn't close to figuring it all out, but Barnett was afraid I was. I was probably his first target. Fortunately for me, I had gone to London, so he killed Barry because the note made him a convenient fall guy."

We were talking as if Barnett were not there, but we all watched him as we spoke. He sat still, almost frozen, his face colorless, his eyes darting around the room. He was trapped and helpless. Totally helpless.

"That seems to wrap it up," Terry said. "Didn't you say something about the police being here?"

"They're waiting downstairs. I can call them, or we can try him first. Right here and now."

"Sounds like a good idea to me," Howard said. "Maybe we should just string him up."

"You can't do this," Barnett shouted. "It's . . . You can't. . . ."

"As a matter of fact, we obviously can," I said. "And there's not a whole lot you can do to stop us. Luckily for you, we're a lot more civilized than you are."

I called the front desk and asked them to send Smythe up; he came to my room with two constables. He took Barnett into custody and asked me for the evidence. Since Bailey would also want to hear the case against Barnett, the six of us went with him and the constables to the police station, where we were met by the D.C.I. We carefully laid out the case against Barnett, and by three A.M. Paul was free.

At 3:20 Paul was hugging Kathy.

At 3:42 I was hugging Eileen. "It's over," I sighed. "At last."

"You're all right, Dan Brodsky."

∫ epilogue

Cal Barnett was convicted of both murders. The man who sold him the revolver did not testify, but Detective Chief Inspector Bailey and Sergeant Smythe had found additional evidence after searching Barnett's hotel room and car and were able to tie the weapon to him; the crown attorney's case left no doubt in the minds of the jurors. It is being appealed, but he'll probably spend the rest of his life in a British prison.

I returned to London for the trial. Although she didn't testify, Eileen joined me. Her excuse was that Barnett had murdered her father—I'd like to think that there was another reason.

The Austin district attorney's office is planning to prosecute Barnett for the murder of Arthur Rothenberg and for the attempted murder of Hans Nystrom. I don't know how they'll work out the extradition or where he'll serve his time—indeed, if I'm not mistaken, he could get the death penalty in Texas—but it's safe to say we've heard from him for the last time.

The morning after Barnett's arrest, those conferees who had not yet departed decided to dedicate the next COTCA to Barry Donardy and to Martin Kloss. Eileen told me that she would write a paper in Donardy's name; it would contain his proof of the theorem that would have finally given him his Ph.D.

Howard Williams is back in Santa Barbara. His marriage is intact, and, as far as I know, so is his affair with Helen Orosco. Howard tells me that Amy corresponds regularly with her English friend, Colin. (I never did learn his last name.)

Kathy Hobart is thinking about college. She had vowed that she would not go to Berkeley under any circumstances, but an ongoing relationship with Steve Vadney has evidently changed her mind.

Paul Hobart was, of course, grateful for my assistance with his travails in Oxford, but what are friends for? (I learned the answer to that question the next time we played poker.)

Several months after COTCA, Paul stunned the mathematical world by solving a problem that had been open for a century.

As for me, Ann Laskey wrote and said that Morris Zinkowski had, after all, accepted the position at Oregon State; they would not need me.

Two weeks after returning from Oxford, Eileen and I had a long telephone conversation. She said she still loved me but wasn't ready to divorce Bob. He was safe and secure, and I was, well, me. She wasn't prepared to end our relationship, either, and promised to attend the next COTCA. I would be there, too.